PRAISE FOR

Every Tongue Got to Confess

"An extraordinary treasure."

—*Boston Globe*

"A real song of the South."

—*Elle* magazine

"Splendidly vivid and true. . . . A sharp immediacy and a fine supply of down-to-earth humor. In stories that are variously jokey, angry, bawdy, [and] wildly fanciful . . . the speakers present a world in which anything is possible and human nature is crystal clear."

—*New York Times*

"A vivid portrait of the turn-of-the-century South."

—*Washington Post*

"Quite funny, and profoundly emblematic."

—*San Francisco Chronicle*

"Vibrant, evocative, heartwarming, and sometimes hilarious."

—*Philadelphia Inquirer*

"Fascinating, funny . . . priceless."

—*Cleveland Plain Dealer*

"Invaluable tales of mischief and wisdom, spirit and hope. Mordantly clever and quintessentially human stories about God and the creation of the black race, the devil, the battle between the sexes, and slaves who outsmart their masters."

—*Booklist*

"[An] entertaining collection. . . . A rich harvest of native storytelling."

—*Kirkus Reviews*

"Stories rich in insight [and] humor."

—*Rocky Mountain News*

"[A] delightful collection of authentic African-American folklore."

—*Library Journal*

"Entertaining and thought-provoking."

—*Vibe*

About the Author

ZORA NEALE HURSTON was born in Notasulga, Alabama, in 1891. She is the author of eight books—four novels, three books of folklore, and an autobiography— as well as some fifty shorter works. She died in 1960.

ALSO BY ZORA NEALE HURSTON

Jonah's Gourd Vine

Mules and Men

Their Eyes Were Watching God

Tell My Horse

Moses, Man of the Mountain

Dust Tracks on a Road

Seraph on the Suwanee

Mule Bone
(with Langston Hughes)

ZORA NEALE HURSTON

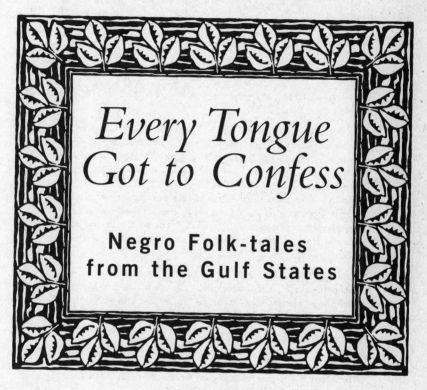

Every Tongue Got to Confess

Negro Folk-tales from the Gulf States

Foreword by
JOHN EDGAR WIDEMAN

Edited and with an Introduction by
CARLA KAPLAN

Perennial
An Imprint of HarperCollinsPublishers

First Perennial edition published 2002.

Designed by Elliott Beard

The Library of Congress has catalogued the hardcover edition as follows:
Hurston, Zora Neale.
    Every tongue got to confess : Negro folk-tales from the Gulf states / by Zora Neale Hurston ; foreword by John Edgar Wideman; edited and with an introduction by Carla Kaplan.— 1st ed.
        p.   cm.
    Includes bibliographical references and index.
    ISBN 0-06-018893-6
    1. African Americans—Folklore. I. Kaplan, Carla. II. Title.
GR111.A47 H83 2001
398.2'089'96073—dc21   2001024521

ISBN 0-06-093454-9 (pbk.)

08 09 ❖/RRD H 10 9 8

Acknowledgments

The estate of Zora Neale Hurston is deeply grateful for the contributions of John Edgar Wideman and Dr. Carla Kaplan to this publishing event.

We also thank our editor Julia Serebrinsky, our publisher Cathy Hemming, our agent Victoria Sanders, and our attorney Robert Youdelman who all work daily to support the literary legacy of Zora Neale Hurston.

Lastly, we thank those whose efforts past and present have been a part of Zora Neale Hurston's resurgence. Among them are: Robert Hemenway, Alice Walker, the folks at the MLA, Virginia Stanley, Jennifer Hart, Diane Burrowes and Susan Weinberg at HarperCollins Publishers, special friends of the estate Imani Wilson and Kristy Anderson, and all the teachers and librarians everywhere who introduce new readers to Zora every day.

Contents

Foreword

With the example of her vibrant, poetic style Zora Neale Hurston reminded me, instructed me that the language of fiction must never become inert, that the writer at his or her desk, page by page, line by line, word by word should animate the text, attempt to make it speak as the best storytellers speak. In her fiction, and collections of African-American narratives, Hurston provides models of good old-time tale-telling sessions. With the resources of written language, she seeks to recover, uncover, discover the techniques oral bards employed to enchant and teach their audiences. Like African-American instrumental jazz, Hurston's writing imitates the human voice. At the bottom in the gut of jazz if you listen closely you can hear—no matter how complexly, obliquely, mysteriously stylized—somebody talking, crying, growling, singing, farting, praying, stomping, voicing in all those modes through which our bodies communicate some tale about how it feels to be here on earth or leaving, or about the sweet pain of hanging on between the coming and going.

In the spring of 1968 a group of African-American students arrived at my University of Pennsylvania Department of English office and asked if I would offer a class in Black Literature. I responded in a predictable fashion, given my education, social conditioning, and status as the only tenure-track assistant professor of color in the entire College of Arts and Sciences. No, thank you, I said, citing various reasons for declining—my already crowded academic schedule, my need to keep time free for fiction writing, family obligations, and the clincher— African-American literature was not my "field." The exchange lasted only five or ten minutes and I remember being vaguely satisfied with myself for smoothly, quickly marshaling reasonable arguments for refusing the students' request, but before the office door closed behind them, I also sensed something awful had occurred. Something much more significant than wriggling out fairly gracefully from one more demand on my already stressed time, something slightly incriminating, perhaps even shameful.

I'd watched the students' eyes watching me during my brisk, precise dismissal of their proposal. I'd seen the cloud, the almost instantaneous dulling and turning away and shrinking inward of the students' eyes speaking a painful truth: I had not simply said no to a course, I'd said no to them, to who they were, who I was in my little cubicle in Bennett Hall, to the beleaguered island of us, our collective endeavor to make sense of the treacherous currents that had brought us to an Ivy League university and also threatened daily to wipe out the small footholds and handholds we fashioned to survive there.

To cut one part of a long story short, by the next day I'd changed my mind, and I did teach a Black Literature course the following semester.

No white people in my office on that spring day in 1968. On the other hand, visualizing the presence of some sweaty, ham-fisted, Caucasian version of John Henry, the steel-driving man, hammering iron wedges between the students and me, incarcerating us behind bars as invisible as he was, clarifies the encounter. Why weren't novels and poems by Americans of African descent being taught at the university? Why were so few of us attending and almost none of us teaching there? What rationales and agendas were served by dispensing knowledge through arbitrary, territorial "fields"? Why had the training I'd received in the so-called "best" schools alienated me from my particular cultural roots and brainwashed me into believing in some objective, universal, standard brand of culture and art—essentialist, hierarchical classifications of knowledge—that doomed people like me to marginality on the campus and worse, consigned the vast majority of us who never reach college to a stigmatized, surplus underclass.

Yes, unpacking the issues above would surely be a long story, one I've undertaken to tell in thirty years of fiction and essay. So, back to the shorter story. The class I initiated partly, I admit, to assuage my guilt, to pay dues, to erase the cloud of disappointment I've never forgotten in the students' eyes. It pains me all these years later, since the conditions brewing the cloud's ugly presence remain in place, and the scene may be replicating itself, different office, different university and victims today. But the class, let's stick to my first African-American Literature class that turned out to be a gift from the students to me rather than my offering to them, the class that leads back to Zora Neale Hurston and this folklore collection.

At the end of the first trial run of the class an appreciative student handed me *The Bluest Eye* and said, Thank you for the course, Professor Wideman. Isabel Stewart, since she was a sweet, polite, subtle young woman and didn't wish to undercut an expression of gratitude by mixing it with other, more complicated motives, didn't add, You really must teach this wonderful novel, especially since you saw fit to include only one work by a female writer in your syllabus.

The one work was *Their Eyes Were Watching God*. I had discovered it when I began teaching myself what my formal education had neglected. At the time African-American writing was dominated by males and framed intellectually by a reductive, apologetic, separate-but-equal mentality whose major critical project seemed to be asserting the point: we too have written and do write and some of our stuff deserves inclusion in the mainstream.

By coincidence the two female writers who in separate ways—one by her presence, the other by her absence—were part of my first course would help transform African-American literary studies. Toni Morrison—as writer-editor and Nobel laureate—became point person of a band of awesomely talented women who would precipitate a flip-flop in African-American letters so that women today, for better or worse, dominate the field as much as men did thirty years ago. Zora Neale Hurston's representation of the folk voice in her anthropological work, autobiography and fiction expanded the idea of what counts as literature, reframing the relationship between spoken and written verbal art, high versus low culture, affirming folk voices, female voices. Hurston foregrounds creolized language and culture in her fiction and nonfiction, dramatizing vernacular ways of speaking that are so independent, dynamic, self-assertive and expressive they cross over, challenge and transform mainstream dialects. Creole languages refuse to remain standing, hat in hand at the back door as segregated, second-class, passive aspirants for marginal inclusion within the framework of somebody else's literary aesthetic.

Though Africanized vernaculars of the rural American South are not separate languages like the Creole of Haiti or Martinique, they are distinctively different speech varieties marked by systematic linguistic structures common to Creoles. The *difference* of these Africanized vernaculars is complicated by what could be called their "unwritability," their active resistance to being captured in print.

> I began to write, that is: to die a little. As soon as my Es-
> ternome began to supply me the words, I felt death. Each
> of his sentences (salvaged in my memory, inscribed in the
> notebook) distanced him from me. With the notebooks

piling up, I felt they were burying him once again. Each written sentence coated a little of him, his Creole tongue, his words, his intonation, his eyes, his airs with formaldehyde . . . The written words, my poor French words, dissipated the echo of his words forever and imposed betrayal upon my memory . . . I was emptying my memory into immobile notebooks without having brought back the quivering of the living life. [Chamoiseau: *Texaco* (321–2)]

All spoken language of course resists exact phonetic inscription. But Creole's stubborn survivalist orality, its self-preserving instinct to never stand still, to stay a step ahead, a step away, the political challenge inherent in its form and function, increases the difficulty of rendering it on the page.

The difference of vernacular speech has been represented at one extreme by blackface minstrelsy and Hollywood's perpetuation of that fiction in the porn of race showcasing for the viewer's gaze deviant clowns and outlaws whose comic, obscene, violent speech (often the embodied fantasies of white scriptwriters) stands as a barely intelligible mangling of the master tongue. At the opposite end of the spectrum of imitation is a self-aware, vital, independent, creative community that speaks in Hurston's stories and the African-American narratives she gathered for this collection: "I seen it so dry the fish came swimming up the road in dust."

How speech is represented in writing raises more than questions of aesthetics. An ongoing struggle for authority and domination is present in any speech situation interfacing former slaves with former masters, minority with majority culture, spoken with written. Such interfaces bristle with extralinguistic tensions that condition and usually diminish mutual intelligibility. Put in another way, any written form of creolized language exposes the site, evidence and necessity of struggle, mirrors America's deeply seated refusal to acknowledge its Creole identity.

Traceable in court transcriptions of African testimony (see the Salem witch trials) and eighteenth-century comic drama, then refined and conventionalized by a Plantation school of highly popular nineteenth-century white writers (Sidney Lanier, Joel Chandler Harris, George Washington Cable), the so-called "eye dialects'" organized graphic signs such as italics, apostrophes, underlining, quotation marks, misspellings *tuh*, *gwine*, *dere*, *dem* along with tortured syntax, malapropisms, elisions, comic orthography, signifying, Joycean portmanteau words to *show* the sound of Black vernacular. Whatever else the mediating visualized scrim of eye dialect accomplished by its alleged rendering of Africanized speech, inevitably, given the means employed, it also suggested ignorant, illiterate southern darkies, a consequence bemoaned by African-American novelist Charles Waddell Chestnut. Ironically, because he used a conventional version of eye dialect (very similar to the look Hurston chooses for the voices of these Gulf narratives), his book *The Marrow of Tradition* was rejected out of hand by African-American students in my first Black Literature class. They found Chestnut's picturing of Black speech both embarrassing and taxing to decipher. Whether or not readers can see through the veil of eye dialects' incriminating constructions and ignore or resist the prejudice they embody remains an open question. Even here in these narratives.

So what does all the above tell us about reading this collection?

"Oral literature" is an oxymoron. Creole speech is approximated, at best, by any form of written transcription. In this context it is useful to read these folk-tales from the Gulf States as you would foreign poetry translated into English, grateful for a window into another culture, yet always keeping in mind that what you're consuming is vastly distanced from the original. Translation destroys and displaces as much as it restores and renders available. In the case of these oral narratives, some major missing dimensions are the immediacy and sensuousness of face-to-face encounter, the spontaneous improvisation of call and response, choral repetition and echo, the voice played as a musical instrument, the kinesics of the speaker.

Translations ask us to forget as well as imagine an original. The nature of this forgetting varies depending on the theory of translation. The inevitable awkwardness of a literal rendering, emphasizing ideas and meaning, asks the reader to forget the evocative sonorities of rhythm and rhyme or rather recall their presence in the original as a kind of ennobling excuse for what often appears on the page as a fairly bare-bones, skimpy transmission of thought. Freer translations posit themselves as admirable objects of consideration within the literary tradition of the language into which they have been kidnapped, and to that extent ask readers to forget the original, except for acknowledging the original's status as a distant relative or celebrated ancestor.

So as your eyes read these folk narratives remember and forget selectively, judiciously, in order to enhance your enjoyment, your understanding of the particular species of verbal art they manifest. Imagine the situations in which these speech acts occur, the participants' multicolored voices and faces, the eloquence of nonverbal special effects employed to elaborate and transmit the text. Recall a front stoop, juke joint, funeral, wedding, barbershop, kitchen: the music, noise, communal energy and release. Forget for a while our learned habit of privileging the written over the oral, the mainstream language's hegemony over its competitors when we think "literature." Listen as well as read. Dream. Participate the way you do when you allow a song to transport you, all kinds of songs from hip-hop rap to Bach to Monk, each bearing its different history of sounds and silences.

What's offered in this volume is finally a way of viewing the world, a version of reality constructed by language that validates a worldview, and vice versa, a view that legitimizes a language. Hurston is not curating a museum of odd, humorous negroisms. She's updating by looking backward, forward, all around, the continuous presence in America of an Africanized language that's still spoken, still going strong today. A language articulating an Africanized vision of reality: unsentimental, humorous, pantheistic, robustly visceral, syncretic, blending tradition and innovation, rooted in the body's immediate experience of pleasure and pain yet also cognizant of a long view, the slow, possibly just arc of time, the tribal as well as individual destiny.

Because Hurston is a product of that world, its language describes her and *is* her. As folklore collector she's not merely an outsider looking in, taking data away. She's both writer and subject, an insider, a cultural informant engaging in self-interrogation.

The doubleness of Hurston's stance as self-conscious subject of her writing requires the reader also to realign herself or himself. Any writer who chooses to break away, to cross over and occupy liminal turf between radically different linguistic modes, between two antagonistic ways of perceiving and naming the world, takes a great risk of betraying the integrity of his first cultural community and language. Breaking away can lead to assuming the role of guide and reporter (panderer) objectifying, introducing the exotic, erotic other to a reader's gaze. When she positions herself firmly, insistently within the language of her Africanized culture and her goal is self-knowledge, self-gratification as she recalls, reconstitutes, the pleasures of speaking and acting within the culture, Hurston accomplishes crossover with minimal damage to integrity. Her crossings are expressed through language and customs she shares with the people she interviews and invents. Hurston displays otherness to a perceptive reader not by packaging and delivering it as a commodity C.O.D. to the reader, but by remembering who she was, who she is, by listening, respecting, by staring clear-eyed at her self, her many selves past, future and present in the primal language, the language of feeling they speak.

A model for this self-conscious, self-appraising work mani-
fests itself in the critique of language contained in these Gulf
narratives. First, the folk-tales inhabit a pantheistic world where
everything talks—peas grunt when bursting through the hard
soil in which they're planted; corn gossips in a cemetery;
mules, alligators, horses, dogs, flies, cows, converse or sing. Language resides in the boundless sea of Great Time. One summer
words frozen during a particularly severe winter thaw and sud-
denly the air is filled, like the air of Prospero's enchanted island, with ghostly voices.

Language is treacherous, the tales school us. Interpretation,
translation of words, leads to dangerous misapprehensions or
not-so-funny comic predicaments, such as one slave bragging
to another that he got away with looking at Ole Missus' drawers and the second slave receiving a painful thumping when he
tries to look at Ole Missus' drawers when they're not hanging
on the clothesline but wrapping her behind. The tales warn us
that anyone speaking must be eternally vigilant and circum-
spect. For one thing, tattlers' ears are everywhere and always
open. Even a prayer is liable to interception and subversion.

> Once there was a Negro. Every day he went under the
> hill to pray. So one day a white man went to see what he
> was doing. He was praying for God to kill all the white
> people; so the white man threw a brick on his head. The
> Negro said, "Lord can't you tell a white man from a
> Negro?"

A master's penchant for extravagant metaphorical overkill in
his speech is satirized by a slave who transposes the master's
style into an equally fanciful rhyming vernacular version and
fires it back at him, "You better git outa yo' flowery beds uh
ease, an put on yo' flying trapeze, cause yo' red ball uh simmons
done carried yo' flame uh flapperation tuh yo' high tall mountain."

"What you say, Jack?"

The problematic relationship between oral and written is documented playfully in a tale quoting an illiterate father who chides his educated daughter because she can't write down in the letter he's dictating a mule-calling sound he clucks.

> Is you got dat down yit?
>> Naw sir, I aint' got it yit?
>> How come you ain't got it?
>> Cause I can't spell (clucking sound).
>> You mean tuh tell me you been off tuh school seven
> years and can't spell (clucking sound)? Well, I could al-
> most spell dat myself.

Thus these narratives from the southern states instruct us that talk functions in African-American communities as it does in Zora Neale Hurston's fiction and life—as a means of having fun, getting serious, establishing credibility and consensus, securing identity, negotiating survival, keeping hope alive, suffering and celebrating the power language bestows.

—JOHN EDGAR WIDEMAN

Introduction

"I want to collect like a new broom."
—ZORA NEALE HURSTON[1]

"I am using the vacuum method, grabbing
everything I see."
—ZORA NEALE HURSTON[2]

Zora Neale Hurston is now famous—iconic even—as the author of the justly celebrated black female *bildungsroman*, *Their Eyes Were Watching God* (1937). But her first love was African-American folklore, and without an understanding of what she saw in it—a people's artistry and sensibility, their humor, their grievances, their worldview, "the first thing that man makes out of the natural laws that he finds around him"—her fiction, with its unexpected segues into folklore, magical realism, and myth, loses some of its force.

In February of 1927, after two years spent helping launch New York's celebrated Harlem Renaissance and studying anthropology as Barnard's only black scholar, Hurston headed to Jacksonville, Florida, to initiate an in-depth study of the rural, southern, African-American folklore she loved. She had a small ($1,400) grant from Carter Woodson's Association for the

Study of Negro Life and History, and the intellectual support of Columbia University's renowned anthropologist Franz Boas. Over the next two years she traveled to Florida, Alabama, Georgia, New Orleans, and the Bahamas, collecting material she would draw on for the rest of her life, recycling it often and in various forms into her work, and attempting, in spite of constant resistance, to bring authentic black folklore to mainstream, popular audiences.

While she had to learn to build bridges between a heritage among free-flowing storytellers exchanging dramatic "lies" (folk-tales), and an academic training that emphasized objective "facts" and cautioned against "the habit of talking all over your face," Hurston ultimately amassed huge amounts of invaluable material.[3] "I am getting some gorgeous material down here, verse and prose, <u>magnificent</u>," she wrote to Langston Hughes.[4] She collected so much material from just the American South that she had the basis for seven volumes of American folklore: "My plans: 1 volume of stories. 1 children's games. 1 Drama and the Negro[.] 1 'Mules & Men[,]' a volume of work songs with guitar arrangement[.] 1 on Religion. 1 on words & meanings. 1 volume of love letters with an introduction on Negro lore."[5] Had she published these seven volumes she could certainly have laid claim to being *the* leading folklorist of her generation. But doing so might also have derailed a career as a major American novelist. Of the seven books she eventually did publish, four were novels, one was an autobiography, and only two were folklore. The folklore books, *Mules and Men*, a collection of American folk-tales and Hoodoo material from New Orleans, and *Tell My Horse*, a study of Haitian and Jamaican voodoo, were published in 1935 and 1938, respectively. *Mules and Men* drew heavily on her fieldwork from the twenties. But vast amounts of material collected at that time seem to have disappeared.

According to her biographer, "the material [Hurston collected] was so extensive that Thompson [Hurston's secretary] often typed half the night."[6] Some of this material (games, songs, and an essay on religion) eventually found its way into *Mules and Men* and some reappears in Hurston's contribution to the Federal Writers Project's book-length study "The Florida Negro." But together they account for less than a third of the "gorgeous" stories Hurston originally vacuumed up.[7] Some of this missing material may still be found. After all, the full text of these stories Hurston considered "the life and color of my people" settled anonymously into a basement storage room at Columbia University for thirty years. It spent another twenty years at the Smithsonian, unrecognized as the vital core of Hurston's missing fieldwork, let alone as the "boiled-down juice of human living" she intended it to be.[8] This missing text is published here, in full, for the first time.

Hurston wanted to present authentic African-American folklore, not something doctored to suit either dominant aesthetics or stereotyped notions of black culture. "White people could not be trusted to collect the lore of others," she confided to Professor Alain Locke, one of the "midwives" (her term) of the Harlem Renaissance; they "take all the life and soul out of everything," she wrote her patron, Charlotte Osgood Mason.[9] In her view, "the god-maker, the creator of everything that lasts" was "his majesty, the man in the gutter."[10] The stakes of such collecting were high. Oral folklore was both crucial to cultural anthropology's legitimacy and a valuable tradition on its own terms, especially if those terms could be shook free of external pressures. Hurston feared that "the greatest cultural wealth of the continent was disappearing without the world ever realizing that it had ever been."[11] "It is fortunate that it is being collected now," she wrote Franz Boas; "the negro is [having his] . . . Negroness . . . rubbed off by close contact with white culture."[12]

Years later, Hurston reflected on the cultural meaning of black folklore:

In folklore, as in everything else that people create, the world is a great, big, old serving-platter, and all the local places are like eating-plates. Whatever is on the plate must come out of the platter, but each plate has a flavor of its own because the people take the universal stuff and season it to suit themselves on the plate. And this local flavor is what is known as originality.... One fact stands out as one examines the Negro folk-tales which have come to Florida from various sources. There is no such thing as a Negro tale which lacks point. Each tale brims over with humor. The Negro is determined to laugh even if he has to laugh at his own expense. By the same token, he spares nobody else. His world is dissolved in laughter. His "boss-man," his woman, his preacher, his jailer, his God, and himself, all must be baptized in the stream of laughter.[13]

I thought about the tales I had heard as a child. How even the Bible was made over to suit our imagination. How the devil always outsmarted God and how that over-noble hero Jack or John—not *John Henry*, who occupies the same place in Negro folklore that Casey Jones does in white lore and if anything is more recent—outsmarted the devil. Brer Fox, Brer Deer, Brer 'Gator, Brer Dawg, Brer Rabbit, Ole Massa and his wife were walking the earth like natural men way back in the days when God himself was on the ground and men could talk with him. Way back there before God weighed up the dirt to make the mountains.[14]

Negro folklore is not a thing of the past. It is still in the making. Its great variety shows the adaptability of the black man: nothing is too old or too new, domestic or foreign, high or low for his use. God and the devil are paired, and are treated no more reverently than Rockefeller and Ford. Both of these men are prominent in folklore, Ford being particularly strong, and they talk and act like good-natured stevedores or mill-hands. Ole Massa is sometimes a smart man and often a fool. The automobile is ranked alongside of the oxcart. The angels and the apostles walk and talk like section hands. And through it all walks Jack, the greatest culture hero of the South; Jack beats them all—even the Devil, who is often smarter than God.[15]

Hurston sought the most out-of-the-way locations for collecting. "Folklore is not as easy to collect as it sounds," she wrote. "The best source is where there are the least outside influences and these people being usually under-privileged are the shyest. They are most reluctant at times to reveal that which the soul lives by."[16]

Evidently, she cut an unusual figure: a single black woman, driving her own car, toting a gun, sometimes passing for a bootlegger, offering prize money for the best stories and "lies."[17] It's easy to romanticize Hurston with Model T and pistol, searching out his shy "majesty" and "woofing" in "Jooks" along the way. But the truth is that she worked hard under harsh conditions: traveling in blistering heat, sleeping in her car when "colored" hotel rooms couldn't be had, defending herself against jealous women, putting up with bedbugs, lack of sanitation, and poor food in some of the turpentine camps, sawmills, and phosphate mines she visited.

Hurston's situation was unusual. She was from the Alabama and Florida regions where she traveled, but her New York education and Columbia University pedigree made her seem an outsider. She was committed to the systematic study of folklore as an academic enterprise, but before any American university had yet to create such a department or program. Hurston's Harlem Renaissance art circles were steeped in notions of race "propaganda"—contesting white racism by showing black culture at its best (i.e., most middle-class). But the bawdy stories

Hurston collected from sawmills, small towns, dance halls, and turpentine camps were hardly what the "Talented Tenth" had in mind. Combined with a form of feminism that rattled some of her male colleagues, Hurston's unwavering commitment to a relatively unfamiliar folklore aesthetic may help account for the sharply negative reviews she received from peers like Richard Wright, who accused her of pandering to white audiences, or Alain Locke, who eventually charged her with "oversimplification."[18]

Most unusual in Hurston's situation was her funding. At the end of 1927, she signed a contract with a wealthy, white New York patron: Charlotte Osgood Mason, an eccentric, demanding woman who had supported Langston Hughes, Aaron Douglas, Alain Locke, and others, but who also thought nothing of directing their creativity as a self-appointed empress of art. Encouraged by Locke, Mason promised to support Hurston's folklore-collecting to the tune of $200 a month. For her part, Hurston saw Mason as someone who understood the importance of recording "the Negro farthest down" and she insisted that she and Mason shared a "psychic bond."[19] But their arrangement proved profoundly constricting. In the view of Hurston's biographer, Mason was both "soul mate" and "meddling patron."[20] Whereas Boas's cultural relativism sought to overturn the premises upon which "other" cultures were devalued, Mason was every bit the primitivist, convinced that African-Americans were emotionally and aesthetically superior to whites, but inferior in other ways. Louise Thompson, among others, viewed Mason's largesse as a way of "indulging her fantasies of Negroes."[21] The terms of the Hurston/Mason contract obliged Hurston to act as Mason's "agent" by collecting, *for Mason*, "all information possible, both written and oral, concerning the music, poetry, folk-lore, literature, hoodoo, conjure, manifestations of art and kindred subjects relating to and existing among the North American Negroes." Hurston's charge was "to return and lay before [Mason] all of said information, data, transcripts of music, etc., which she shall have obtained."[22] Hurston was not even allowed "to make known to any other person, except one designated in writing by said first party any of said data or information."[23] This meant that while Hurston had *her* idea of African-American folklore, she had to answer to two outside powers with different ideas, one of whom sought control over every word she wrote.

Indeed, while Mason reportedly kept her copy of the manuscript Hurston called *Negro Folk-tales from the Gulf States* in her safe-deposit box, Hurston surreptitiously circulated other copies (possibly different ones) to Langston Hughes, Dorothy West, Helene Johnson, and Franz Boas.[24] Mason did eventually "press" publication of the stories, but only in her own edited version. "She says the dirty words must be toned down. Of course I knew that. But first I wanted to collect them as they are," Hurston told Hughes.[25] At the same time as she was juggling Mason's expurgations, Hurston was also trying to meet Boas's exacting standards for precise transcription:

> About the material I have been collecting. It is decided that the stories shall be one volume. . . . I have tried to be as exact as possible. Keep to the exact dialect as closely as I could, having the story teller to tell it to me word for word as I write it. This after it has been told to me off hand until I know it myself. But the writing down from the lips is to insure the correct dialect and wording so that I shall not let myself creep in unconsciously. . . . Now in the stories, I have omitted all Pat and Mike stories. It is obvious that these are not negroid, but very casual borrowings. The same goes for the Jewish and Italian stories.[26]

Boas encouraged scientific, uncensored publication, yet, ironically, he also wanted Hurston to contextualize the stories and provide a sense of " the intimate setting in the social life of the Negro," as he put it in his preface to *Mules and Men*, where he praised Hurston for providing the reader with "the charm of a loveable personality."

Apparently, what *Hurston* wanted was a volume of folklore that would stand on its own, without interference, interpretation, anthropological voice-over, or her own personal "charm." "I am leaving the story material almost untouched. I have only tampered with it where the storyteller was not clear. I know it is going to read different, but that is the glory of the thing, don't you think?" she wrote Langston Hughes.[27]

We cannot know exactly what stopped publication of the stories in 1929 when Mason first "pressed" ahead. Maybe she intervened. Maybe Boas did. Maybe publishers were the problem. According to Hemenway, Hurston's publishers "demanded something more than the mere transcription of collected tales."[28] Whatever the reason, the volume Hurston hoped for was scrapped. This is its first publication.

This manuscript turned up at the Smithsonian in the papers of William Duncan Strong, an American anthropologist known to have been a friend of Franz Boas's. There are a number of ways that Hurston and Strong might have crossed paths. In 1925 and 1926, while Hurston was studying with Boas, Strong worked as a research assistant in the Anthropology Department at Columbia. He left in 1926 to finish a Ph.D. at the University of California and then went to Chicago, Labrador, and the University of Nebraska. In the mid-1930s, he worked in Honduras, a country in which Hurston developed strong interests in the mid-1940s. In the late 1930s, Strong returned to Columbia University where he taught until 1962. Strong also served as the president of the American Ethnological Society, of which Hurston was a proud member. There is no mention of Strong in Hurston's known correspondence and he is unfamiliar to Hurston's biographer. Professor Akua Duku Anokye, who helped authenticate the manuscript in 1991, speculates that *Negro Folk-tales from the Gulf States* may have found its way into Strong's papers by accident. Suppose that Boas "kept it with other Department files which were later stored in the basement for lack of space. Later still the Strong papers were stored there and all the stored papers transferred to the National Anthropological Archives in Washington."[29]

Unfortunately, nothing found with the manuscript indicates exactly which version of the "stories" this was or through whose hands it had passed. Hurston does not tell us how she wanted it seen or where it fell in her publication plans for *Mules and Men*. Readers, especially those already familiar with *Mules and Men,* will now be able to compare the two volumes and, in light of her letters, determine which book *they* think Hurston would have preferred.[30]

Had there been less accident and outside interference in Hurston's life, this volume might have appeared seventy years earlier. How this would have changed Hurston's career can only be a matter of conjecture. How seventy years with it might have changed *our* views of African-American artistry is also worth contemplation.

—CARLA KAPLAN

NOTES

[1] Zora Neale Hurston to Langston Hughes, April 12, 1928. *Zora Neale Hurston: A Life in Letters*, Carla Kaplan, ed. (New York: Doubleday, 2002). All letters cited in this introduction are from this volume.

[2] Zora Neale Hurston to Alain Locke, October 15, 1928.

[3] Zora Neale Hurston, *Dust Tracks on a Road* (New York: HarperCollins, 1991), p. 123.

[4] Zora Neale Hurston to Langston Hughes, March 17, 1927.

[5] Zora Neale Hurston to Langston Hughes, August 6, 1928.

[6] Robert Hemenway, *Zora Neale Hurston: A Literary Biography* (Urbana: University of Illinois Press, 1977), p. 132.

[7] Almost every tale published in *Mules and Men* was intended, originally, for publication in *Negro Folk-tales from the Gulf States*. Of the 122 sources listed in *Negro Folk-tales from the Gulf States*, at least 17 are also listed as sources for *Mules and Men*. Hurston appears, as well, to have recycled some

of that material and some of those sources in the mid-1930s, when she collected folklore with Alan Lomax and Mary Elizabeth Barnicle.

[8]Zora Neale Hurston to Langston Hughes, April 30, 1929; Zora Neale Hurston, "Folklore and Music," Cheryl Wall, ed., *Zora Neale Hurston: Folklore, Memoirs, and Other Writings* (New York: Library of America), p. 875. A slightly different version of "Folklore and Music" can be found, under the title "Go Gator and Muddy the Water," in Pamela Bordelon, ed., *Go Gator and Muddy the Water: Writings by Zora Neale Hurston from the Federal Writers Project* (New York: Norton, 1999).

[9]Zora Neale Hurston to Charlotte Osgood Mason, August 14, 1931.

[10]Zora Neale Hurston to Langston Hughes, September 20, 1928.

[11]Zora Neale Hurston to Thomas E. Jones, October 12, 1934.

[12]Zora Neale Hurston to Franz Boas, March 29, 1927.

[13]Hurston, "Folklore and Music," pp. 875, 892.

[14]Hurston, *Mules and Men* (New York: HarperCollins, 1990), p. 2.

[15]Zora Neale Hurston, "Characteristics of Negro Expression," Nancy Cunard, ed., *Negro: An Anthology*, (1934), abridged edition, Hugh Ford, ed. (New York: Ungar, 1970), p. 27.

[16]Zora Neale Hurston, *Mules and Men*, p. 3.

[17]Hemenway, p. 111.

[18]Richard Wright, "Between Laughter and Tears," *New Masses*, October 5, 1937; Alain Locke, review of *Their Eyes Were Watching God*, *Opportunity*, June 1, 1938.

[19]Hurston, *Dust Tracks on a Road*, pp. 129, 128.

[20]Hemenway, p. 109.

[21]Louise Thompson, as quoted by Hemenway, p. 107.

[22]Contract between Charlotte Osgood Mason and Zora Neale Hurston, December 8, 1927. Alain Locke papers, Moorland-Spingarn Center, Howard University.

[23]Contract between Zora Neale Hurston and Charlotte Osgood Mason; Zora Neale Hurston to Langston Hughes, March 28, 1928; and April 12, 1928.

[24]Zora Neale Hurston to Dorothy West, November 1928; Zora Neale Hurston to Franz Boas, December 27, 1928; Zora Neale Hurston to Langston Hughes, spring/summer 1929; Zora Neale Hurston to Langston Hughes, October 15, 1929.

[25]Zora Neale Hurston to Langston Hughes, October 15, 1929.

[26]Zora Neale Hurston to Langston Hughes, October 15, 1929; Zora Neale Hurston to Franz Boas, October 20, 1929.

[27]Zora Neale Hurston to Langston Hughes, April 30, 1929.

[28]Hemenway, p. 133.

[29]Akua Duku Anokye, *Linguistic Form and Social Function: A Discourse Analysis of Rhetorical and Narrative Structure in Oral and Written African American Folk Narrative Texts*, Ph.D. dissertation, City University of New York, 1991, p. 161. Dr. Anokye has done an extensive analysis of some of the folktales from this manuscript. I am grateful to her for her generosity in sharing her dissertation and her own story of authenticating Hurston's manuscript along with Professor Sally McLendon and James Glenn, then senior archivist of the National Anthropological Archives at the Smithsonian.

[30]I am grateful to John Homiak, archivist of the National Anthropological Archives, and to his staff, for gracious assistance with this manuscript and its history.

A Note to the Reader

As a fierce advocate of the folklore animating the lives of what she called "the Negro farthest down," Hurston believed that black people had wonderful stories that the world needed to hear. The manuscript she left was titled *Negro Folk-tales from the Gulf States*. The title under which it is now published, *Every Tongue Got to Confess*, comes from a short tale in her section of Preacher tales. "Every tongue got to confess; everybody got to stand in judgment for theyself; every tub got to stand on its own bottom," a preacher tells his congregation. Dissatisfied with being told what she's "got to" do, "one little tee-ninchy woman in de amen corner" snaps back: "Lordy, make my bottom wider." "Every Tongue Got to Confess" can be read in different ways. On the one hand, it suggests that everyone *has* something *worth* confessing, just as every tongue has a tale to tell. On the other hand, it begs for an ironic reading since Hurston did not believe in forced confessions—the coercions of preachers, politicians, and authorities. The phrase "Every Tongue Got to Confess" works as one of her many inside jokes about gender as well. "Don't you know you can't get de best of no woman in de talkin' game?" it asks. "Her tongue is all de weapon a woman

---

Mules and Men (New York: HarperCollins, 1990), p. 3.

got.''* Any reader who expects to best Hurston in the talking game of her people has just been both fairly warned and also invited to play.

Hurston's undated manuscript appears to have been prepared for publication but not yet edited. It is evident that Hurston shuffled and reshuffled the material, adding a Table of Contents later (which is replicated on page three). The manuscript contains as many as six different pagination schemes, and her marked paginations do not generally correspond to those typed on her contents page. With few other exceptions, the manuscript is published here exactly as Hurston left it, in the order in which it was found. Hurston titled many of her tales, then crossed the titles out. This symbol † is used to indicate titles and/or text that Hurston had marked to be deleted in her original manuscript. When tales are included twice in the volume, in identical versions, the second version has been omitted and a footnote indicates where it appeared. Lists of Hurston's sources and a listing marked "Stories Kossula Told Me," originally placed at the front of the volume, have been moved to the appendices of this book. Hurston's underlined words are now replaced with italics. Editorial changes indicated by Hurston are typed in the manuscript and explained in footnotes. No corrections have been made to grammar, spelling, punctuation, syntax, or dialect. The language of the tales is reproduced exactly as it appears in Hurston's manuscript. Whenever possible, Hurston's own glossaries and footnotes—published elsewhere—have been used to annotate folk expressions and slang.

Negro Folk-tales from the Gulf States

TABLE OF CONTENTS*

*On her manuscript, Hurston—or someone else—crossed off titles of four sections: "Massa and White Folks Tales" (originally, seventh); "Tall Hunting Tales" (originally, ninth); "Mosquito and Gnat Tales" (originally, tenth); and "Hidden Lover Tales" (originally, fourteenth). The "Tall Hunting Tales" are scattered within "Tall Tales."

God Tales

WHY GOD MADE ADAM LAST†

God wuz through makin' de lan' an' de sea an' de birds an' de animals an' de fishes an' de trees befo' He made man. He wuz intendin' tuh make 'im all along, but He put it off tuh de last cause if He had uh made Adam fust an' let him see Him makin' all dese other things, when Eve wuz made Adam would of stood round braggin' tuh her. He would of said: "Eve, do you see dat ole stripe-ed tagger (tiger) over dere? Ah made. See dat ole narrow geraffe (giraffe) over dere? Ah made 'im too. See dat big ole tree over dere? Ah made dat jus' so *you* could set under it."

God knowed all dat, so He jus' waited till everything wuz finished before he made man, cause He knows man will lie and brag on hisself tuh uh woman. Man ain't found out yet how things wuz made—he ain't meant tuh know.

—JAMES PRESLEY.

When God first put folks on earth there wasn't no dif-ference between men and women. They was all alike. They did de same work and everything. De man got tired uh fussin 'bout who gointer do this and who gointer do that.

So he went up tuh God and ast him tuh give him power over de woman so dat he could rule her and stop all dat arguin'.

He ast Him tuh give him a lil mo' strength and he'd do de heavy work and let de woman jus' take orders from him whut to do. He tole Him he wouldn't mind doing de heavy [work] if he could jus' boss de job. So de Lawd done all he ast Him and he went on back home—and right off he started tuh bossin' de woman uh-round.

So de woman didn't lak dat a-tall. So she went up tuh God and ast Him how come He give man all de power and didn't leave her none. So He tole her, "You never ast Me for none. I thought you was satisfied."

She says, "Well, I ain't, wid de man bossin' me round lak he took tuh doin' since you give him all de power. I wants half uh his power. Take it away and give it tuh me."

De Lawd shook His head. He tole her, "I never takes nothin' back after I done give it out. It's too bad since you don't like it, but you shoulda come up wid him, then I woulda 'vided it half and half!"

De woman was so mad she left dere spittin' lak a cat. She went straight tuh de devil. He tole her: "I'll tell you whut to do. You go right back up tuh God and ast Him tuh give you dat bunch uh keys hangin' by de mantle shelf; den bring 'em here tuh me and I'll tell you whut to do wid 'em, and you kin have mo' power than man."

So she did and God give 'em tuh her thout uh word and she took 'em back tuh de devil. They was three keys on dat ring. So de devil tole her whut they was. One was de key to de bed-room and one was de key to de cradle and de other was de kitchen key. He tole her not tuh go home and start no fuss, jus' take de keys and lock up everything an' wait till de man come in—and she could have her way. So she did. De man tried tuh ack stubborn at first. But he couldn't git no peace in de bed and nothin' tuh eat, an' he couldn't make no generations tuh follow him unless he use his power tuh suit de woman. It was-n't doin' him no good tuh have de power cause she wouldn't let 'im use it lak he wanted tuh. So he tried tuh dicker wid her. He said he'd give her half de power if she would let him keep de keys half de time.

De devil popped right up and tole her naw, jus' keep whut she got and let him keep whut he got. So de man went back up tuh God, but He tole him jus' lak he done de woman.

So he ast God jus' tuh give him part de key tuh de cradle so's he could know and be sure who was de father of chillun, but God shook His head and tole him: "You have tuh ast de woman and take her word. She got de keys and I never take back whut I give out."

So de man come on back and done lak de woman tole him for de sake of peace in de bed. And thass how come women got de power over mens today.

—OLD MAN DRUMMOND.

God done pretty good when He made man, but He could have made us a lot more convenient. For in-stance: we only got eyes in de front uh our heads—we need some in de back, too, so nuthin' can't slip upon us. Nuther thing: it would be handy, too, ef we had one right on de end uv our dog finger (first finger). Den we could jest point dat eye any which way. Nuther thing: our mouths oughter be on top uv our heads 'stead uh right in front. Then, when I'm late tuh work I kin just throw my breakfast in my hat, an' put my hat on my head, an' eat my breakfast as I go on tuh work. Now, ain't dat reasonable, Miss? Besides, mouths ain't so pretty nohow.

—GEORGE BROWN.

One day Christ wuz going along wid His disciples an' He tole 'em all tuh pick up uh rock an' bring it along. All of 'em got one, but Peter happened tuh be sorta tired dat day, so he picked up uh pebble an' toted it.

When Christ got where He wuz going, He stopped under de shade of uh tree an' ast de disciples where wuz they rocks. They all showed 'em an' He turned 'em all tuh bread an' they set down an' et. Peter didn't have nothin' but uh pebble, so he didn't hardly have uh bite uh bread, an' he wuz *hungry*. He didn't lak de way things wuz goin' uh bit, neither.

Another time after dat, Jesus tole 'em all, "Well, we'se goin' for another walk t'day, an' I wants you all tuh bring long uh rock."

Peter wuzn't goin' tuh get left dis time, so he tore down half a mountain. He couldn't tote it, so he moved it along wid a pinch bar, but he wagged all day wid it till way after while Christ rested under uh tree. Then Christ said, "All right, now, everybody bring up yo' rocks." They did, and here come Peter wid his half a mountain. He turned round an' looked at all de rocks de disciples had done brought, an' He smiled when He saw de big, fine rock Peter had done toted, an' He said: "Peter, on *dis* rock I'm gointer build my church . . ."

Peter said, "Naw you ain't, neither! I be damned if you is. You gointer turn *dis* rock intuh bread."

Christ did it, too. Den He took de leben other rocks an' stuck 'em together an' built His church on it, an' that's how come churches split up so much t'day (built on a pieced-up rock).

—CLIFFERT ULMER.

People wuz on earth uh long time, den God says He reckon He better give 'em something tuh do tuh keep 'em outa mischief. So He put two boxes down 'bout uh mile up de road and tole 'em, says they could race for de prizes. De nigger out run de white man, but he wuz so tired dat he run fell up 'ginst de big box an' says: "Ah got it! Ah got de biggest one! Dis'n's mine! Ah got here first."

De white man says, "All right, I'll take yo' leavin's." He went and picked up de little box. He opened it an' it had uh pen an' ink an' some writin' paper. De nigger opened his an' it had uh ax an' grubbin'-hoe an' plow an' sich ez dat. De nigger been workin' hard ever since an' de white man been settin' down bossin' 'im.

—LARKINS WHITE.

WHY NEGROES HAVE NOTHING[†]

After God thew makin' de world an' rested Hisself uh little He called all de different nations uh people (races) up tuh Him an' ast 'em all whut dey wanted. De white man said he wanted tuh be pretty an' tuh boss everything; de Jew said he wanted all de money an' wealth; de Indian said he wanted tuh know all about rovin' de woods an' huntin' an' sich. De nigger didn't even come up tuh ast fuh nothin'. He wuz off somewhere restin'. Finally, God got tired uh waitin' an' sent one uh His angels tuh wake 'im up an' tell 'im tuh come on up an' git his, whutever he wanted.

He went on up an' God ast 'im, say, "Negro, whut do you want? Ah'm givin' de nations whutever dey wants, but dis is yo' las' chance. Now you better look all roun' an' see whut you want me tuh give yuh."

De nigger never moved out his tracks. He said, "Ah don't want nothin'," and went on back tuh sleep.

Thass how come we ain't got nothin'.

—LARKINS WHITE.

WHY NEGROES ARE BLACK[†]

The reason Negroes are black is because in the beginning God told everybody to be there at a certain time and get they color. Everybody went back at the right time but the Negroes. They went off somewhere and went to sleep. When they did get there they wuz so skeered they wouldn't get waited on they started to pushing and shoving and acting crazy, and God pushed them back and said, "Get back!" They misunderstood and got black.

—CHARLEY BRADLEY.

UNCLE IKE IN DE JUDGMENT[†]

Once an old man named Ike died and went to judgment. It was the great day and all the people in the world were coming up to be judged; but they were being judged by races—the whites, the yellow, the Indians and the blacks.

Ike used to work for some particular white folks and they had always taught him to be on time; so he was up at the throne dead on time. He saw the whites judged and sent to their doom or reward, then Gabriel turned over a new page for the Chinese and so on till everybody had been judged except the Negroes. They hadn't got to judgment yet. Gabriel turned over a new page for Negroes and called for them to come to the throne. Uncle Ike, he went on up and told the Lord that his race wasn't there, but he wanted to be judged; but the Lord told him he would have to wait until his race got there. He didn't judge by individuals. So Ike stood one side and waited.

God had two hours to wait; then he saw a great cloud of dust and He pushed Ike to one side so that he could see better. It was the colored folks coming to judgment. When they got up to the throne, God breathed on them and they said: "Just give us anything you got—hell or heaven, but let us all go on together."

Us Negroes are just like crabs, you know. One can't get away from the rest; do, they'll pull him right back.

After they got quieted down, God judged them and said that He was sorry, but He had to send them all to hell because they were so late. Some of them cried; some of them begged Him to change His mind; and some of them said that they didn't care one or the other. When Ike heard the judgment he made God remember that he had been there on time, even before anybody had been judged; and God said that He thought He would have to give Ike some consideration, but He was wondering what to do with Ike when all the rest of the Negroes would be gone to hell.

Then all the Negroes began to holler and shout, "Let him come on wid us! He's a nigger just like us. How come he don't want to come on to hell with us? That's just like some old niggers—always trying to get away from their race! He come up here way ahead of time trying to pass for white, and if he ain't trying to pass, he's trying to act like white folks. Make him come on wid de rest of us, God."

God told them that Ike was on time and so He felt that He must fix him some place in heaven; but the colored folks set up such a racket that they woke up saints that had been sleep for thousands of years—way back in the back rooms of heaven, and they came out to see what was the trouble. God couldn't stand all that racket so He told them all to go on to hell where He had assigned them, but they didn't want to leave Ike up there. God sent a band of angels to shoo them on out, but some of the last ones grabbed Ike and dragged him on with them.

So you see, even on judgment day Negroes won't let one another get nowhere. We are too much like crabs.

—LOUISE NOBLE.

God made de cabbage and stood dere wid de hoe over his shoulder. And de Devil saw him, so he said he was going to make him a field of cabbage just like God. So he made it, but he couldn't git it straight and it made tobacco. So that's how come we got tobacco today.

—MRS. ANNIE KING.

Dere wuz once uh man an' he didn't count* nobody, not even God. So one day his son wuz out in de field and de lightning struck 'im. De man come running out de house hollering, "Don't come killing my son, pick on me, my shoulders is broad. I bet I'll take an . . ." Jes about dat time he got struck himself—not uh big stroke, jes enough tuh burn him uh little and skeer 'im. So he said, "Umph! God don't stand no joking dese days.

—JULIUS HENRY.

TWO BOYS, A SWEET POTATO AND GOD†

Two lil boys went tuh play in de woods once stayed too long, an' dark caught 'im, an' dey got lost in de woods.

So one uv de boys got down and prayed: "Dear Lawd, if you help me find de way home, I'll give you dat great big sweet potato we got home."

De lil brother got tuh cryin' when he heard dat and said: "Brother, you stop telling God dat, cause I want dat sweet potato myself."

—MARY DASH.

---

*"did not listen to anyone"; "did not account for others."

A man who was down on his knees praying for God to forgive him for stealing hogs said: "You might as well forgive me for that big ole turkey gobbler dat roosts in de chinaberry tree, too, Lord."

—EDWARD MORRIS.

Preacher
Tales

Once upon a time it wuz ah man and wife. Man wuz name Isaac and wife named Daphne. There wuz a convention going to be in town and the preacher ast Isaac to care for some of the delegates. He tole him he wasn't able. So de preacher tole him to trust in de Lord and whatsoever he ast de Lord for in faith that He would give it to 'im. So he tole him all right, he would take two delegates. The night before he went to church he tole his wife Daphne: "Lest make out an order for some groceries." So the Lord would have plenty time to have it here by morning. He tole her to call it out whilst he write it down.

"Lord, send us a sack of flour, a ham of cow, and a ham of hog, a bushel of meal, a barrel of black pepper, one barrel* of sugar, one barrel of lard."

So they went on to church to service and when service was over he brought the two preachers home that was to stop with him and taken them in the room. And then when they came out, him and Daphne went in de kitchen to see had they order

---

*Originally typed "package" but changed in the manuscript.

came. It wuzn't there, so they lied down. The next morning before day he went in agin to see had it come. It wasn't there. He got angry then and he got down on his knees and prayed agin.

"Say, Lord, I have these two brothers here and nothing for them to eat and you didn't do what you promised, and furthermore you are not a man to your word. So from this on, you be damned sho to tend to yo' own bizness and let Isaac tend to his own."

So de preachers heard him prayin' so loud they tole Sister Daphne to talk to him—that they think he wuz losin' his mind and she said: "Isaac ain't crazy. He's just a plain man. If uh man don't treat 'im right, Isaac 'll tell to dey teeth." Bout dat time I left.

—VIOLA BALLON.

GABRIEL'S TRUMPET[†]

One time uh preacher had uh church an' his members wuz pretty wicked, so he made up his mind tuh give 'em uh strong sermon tuh shake 'em up. So he preached on judgment day.

Somebody's parrot had done got away and had done flew up in de loft uh de church, but nobody didn't know it. So de preacher preached on till he got down to where de angel Gabrill would be blowin'. He said, "Brothers an' sisters, when Gabrill shall plant one foot on sea an' one on de dry land wid his trumpet in his hand an' shall cry dat Time shall be no mo'—whut'll you poor sinners do? When blows his trumpet, 'Tooot toot', whut *will* you do?"

Every time he said 'toot toot' de parrot would answer him; but he wuz so busy preachin' he didn't notice nothin'. But some of the people heard de parrot an' dey begin slippin' out a de church one an' two at uh time. Dey thought it wuz Gabrill sho nuff. He kept on preachin' in uh strainin' voice wid his eyes shet tight, till he hollered 'toot, toot' and de parrot answered him so loud dat everybody heered 'im, an' everybody bolted for de door, de preacher, too. But he wuz way up in de pulpit and so he wuz de very las' one tuh reach de door. Justez he wuz goin' out de door de wind slammed it on his coattail and he hollered: "Aw naw, Gabrill, turn me loose! You 'low me de same chance you 'lowed dese others."

—JAMES PRESLEY.

A preacher wuz preaching and one ole woman kept on hollerin', "Let de Holy Ghost ride, let de Holy Ghost ride!"

When they went to lift collection de preacher says, "Now all y'all dat enjoyed de sermon so much, come up and put a dollar on de table."

De ole woman says, "Let de Holy Ghost walk."

—L. O. TAYLOR.

DE PREACHER AN' DE SHEEP'S TAILS†

Dere wuz uh man had uh pretty wife, an' de preacher wuz hangin' round her; but she wuzn't tumblin' fast.

He studied how tuh make her, so he started tuh spreadin' his flannel (his tongue) tuh make her think he had plenty power—so he up an' tole her one time dat he could change de color uh her baby from black tuh white, cause he wuz uh man uh God.

Her husban' wuz jus' outside an' heard 'im, but he didn't say nothin'—he jus' let dat ride.

De preacher had uh whole heap uh sheeps, so he jus' went on over tuh his place an' cut off de tails uh de sheeps an' put 'em down by de gate-post an' come on home an' went tuh bed.

De nex' day de preacher wuz all uhround rearin' an' cussin'

'bout his sheep. "If I jus' knowed who cut off my sheeps' tails I'd fix him. I'd give uh thousand dollars tuh know de seben-sided son of uh gun dat did it."

When he come tuh de man dat did it an' said dat, he tole 'im: "Well," he says, "if you kin turn black babies white, look lak you could tell who cut off yo' sheeps' tails."

—W. M. RICHARDSON.

A man and his wife had a colt that they thought a lot of. So they bought him a pretty new halter. Next Sunday they went to church and the preacher's text was: "There was an angel come down from heaven with a pair of tongs and taken a live coal from the altar."

The old lady said, "Come on, old man, let's git home just as quick as we kin."

He ast her why she wanted to leave the service and she said: "Didn't you hear what he said? He's preachin' 'bout our colt. He says 'There was a wild Indian from New Hampshire come and caught the colt by the tail and snatched his head out de halter.'"

TESTIMONY[†]

Dere wuz once uh woman who b'longded to de church an' she uster git up an' tell de greatest experience of anybody. No matter whut nobody said, she always carried it past 'em. So one Sunday when de Love-Feast wuz red hot, she got up and said: "Brothers and sisters, I jes been tuh heben in mah vision."

Chorus: "Amen."

Sister: "An' Gawd wuz in de beanpatch pickin' beans."

Chorus: "Amen."

Sister: "An' He tole me tuh go in de house and make myself tuh home. An' I went in de house in de many mentions (mansions) an' made myself tuh home. An' when He come in, He tole me, says: 'Liza, Liza, go git yourself a long white robe.' I got it and put it on, and praise God, it fit.

"Den He tole me tuh git myself some golden slippers, and I put 'im on an' He says: "Liza, you sho looks good.'

"Den He tole me to go git myself uh starry crown. I put it on and, praise God, it fit.

"Den He tole me, He says: 'Liza, go get yourself some long white wings.' I got dem and put 'em on and flew and flew and flew so fast till I flew into God's tombstone an' knocked it down an' God stopped pickin' beans, an' pushed back His hat an' looked up an' He says: 'AHHH-HHHAHHAHH, didn't dat nigger fly-hi?'"

Uh man in de back uh de church says, "Yes, and didn't dat nigger lie?'"

An' dat broke up de meetin' in uh fight.

—MATTHEW BRAZZLE.

There was a great Sunday-school boy. He went to Sunday-school every Sunday. The boy was named Willie. Willie was very active about asking and answering questions until no one else could ask or answer a question. One Sunday his mother said, "Son, you want to give the others a chance and let them talk."

So the next Sunday the subject was Jacob's ladder. So Willie sat quietly until they was almost through. Willie saw the picture of Jacob's ladder and the angel going up and down. The superintendent said, "If there is nothing else we will close."

Willie held up his hand and said, "Mr. Superintendent, what in the hell does the angel need with a ladder when he's got wings?"

—CLIFFERT ULMER.

One time dere wuz a preacher wanted everybody to jine church and he went roun', my Lord, aroun'. He tole each an' everyone be down tuh de Economical River. Sunday evening he gwine tell you whut one of God's chillun gwine do.

Everybody dat heard about it was dere. He tole two deacons tuh build 'im a scaffold all de way cross de river under de water. De deacons only built it half way cross. He thowed up his hands and said, "All right, chillun, I'm gwinter sho you whut one of God's chilluns is gwinter do."

All right, he stepped out and went tuh singing his song, "I'm uh walkin' on de water, I'm uh walkin' on de water to be baptized. Oh water, to be baptized." About to de end of de scaffold dese deacons done built, he fell in. "I tole dem deacons tuh build dis scaffold all de way cross." (Gesture of swimming laboriously.)

—James Brown.

Once there wuz a preacher. He sent his boy over to a man name Paul to git him a half pint of shinny.* Boy stayed so long till when he got back his father wuz gone.

So he goes on over to the church and his father had taken his text in Paul. He wuz teaching about Paul and he ast: "Whut did Paul say?"

Little boy peep round de door every time he would say "What did Paul say?" Kept on asting whut did Paul say and de boy thought he wuz talking to him. The boy hollered out and tole him, "Paul say he wuzn't goin' send him a damn bit more till he pay for dat he got."

—Will Thomas.

---

*"Shine" or "moonshine."

There wuz uh woman who wuz always in church. Whenever her husban' looked for her she wuz there. One day she locked up de kitchen an' went on. She wuz in uh hurry tuh git dere cause dey wuz holdin' protracted meetin'. When her husban' come home she had him locked way from his rations, so he went down tuh de church an' peeped. He couldn't see her, but he knowed she wuz dere. He heered 'em singing': "Git on board, lil childen", so he answered 'em wid de nex' verse, "An' if my wife is in dere, jus' tell her this fuh me, jus' send dat doggone kitchen key an' stay on board, lil childen."

She had 'im locked way from his eatin's an' he wuz mad.
—LARKINS WHITE.

Once there was a man and the preacher came to his house to take dinner. Preacher saw the rooster on the yard and the man went into the garden to pick some greens. He cooked them and called the preacher to dinner. The preacher came to dinner and looked at the greens and said: "Uh! Say, I thought you were going to have chicken for dinner?"

The man said, "I be doggone if you are going to eat my rooster so I won't have any more eggs on my yard."
—ARTHUR HOPKINS.

Once an ole preacher was up preaching. An ole man sitting in the amen corner said, "God grant it!" to everything the preacher would say.

"What do you think about these fast trains running at the rate of one hundred fifty miles a hour?"

"God grant it!"

"What you think about these automobiles running at the rate of two hundred fifty miles a hour?"

"God grant it!"

"What you think about these ships on the water going at the rate of three hundred fifty miles a hour?"

"God grant it!"

"What you think about these airplanes going at the rate of four hundred fifty miles a hour?"

Old man died down and he said, "God damn it."

—ARTHUR HOPKINS.

Once there wuz an ole lady died and her name wuz Aunt Dinah. Being she wuz so ole they thought they would have a prayer over her. So de ole deacon he call all of 'em round him and went down in prayer. He said, "Send your power down here and wake up dese cold, frozen hearts. I can't hear a moan and neither a groan." So he called again and nobody still didn't say nothing.

So he raised up and looked and everybody wuz gone but him and Aunt Dinah. She wuz sittin' up on de coolin' board, and so he called her. He said, "Aunt Dinah?"

She said, "Huh?"

He said, "Is dat you?"

She says, "Uh hunh."

He says, "Don't you move a damn peg, do I'll knock you dead on de coolin' board."

—WILL THOMAS.

Once there wuz another ole preacher. He wuz talkin' to some boys one day and de boys ast him would he be ready when Gabriel blow his trumpet. He told 'em, "Yeah, he'd be ready if Gabriel wuz to blow his trumpet dis minute."

So dat night he went on to church and he wuz asting de members, "Will you be ready when Gabriel blow his trumpet?" So whilst he wuz preaching, de boys begin to blow on a horn back of a church and dey blowed de second time. He says, "Hush, I think I hear Gabriel blowing now. If it's him he'll blow de third time." So they blowed de third time. He stopped and said, "Wait dere, Gabriel, I ain't ready to go yet."

So he runned on home, told his wife to open de door. She wuz so slow 'bout opening de door he run round to de back. She ast him what wuz de matter. Says, "Gabriel begin to blow dat damn trumpet down yonder."

She says, "I speck you cussed, didn't you?"

He says, "Yes, you damn right I cussed and ain't thew cussin' yet."

—WILL THOMAS.

You know, too many folks is preaching dese days. Jes lak one man, he wuz grubbin' and cuttin' new ground, an' one day de sun got so hot, an' he got so tired. So he went and laid down on de shady side uh de log an' says: "Now, God, if you don't pick me up and throw me over dis log, I'll know you done called me tuh preach." De Lord never did, so he went and tole people he wuz called tuh preach.

—DAUGHTER SARAH SEWELL.

JUST DONE DAT TUH TRY YO' FAITH†

It wuz uh big revival meetin' goin' on and many souls wuz saved. De preacher really likes his women, you know. And there wuz one good-lookin' kinda plump-like girl at de mourner's bench he wuz likin'. You know, way back when folks uster lay under conviction, they uster stay at de church prayin' and singin' over de mourners all night long, 'specially them whut wuz layin' under conviction.

Dis girl wuz under conviction and she done fell out in de floor in front de altar rail all stretched out dere, and you could see her fat legs. Way in de night when nearly everybody done went home, and them whut wuz dere wuz mostly bowed down sleep, de preacher looked all round and looked at dem legs, and eased on down out de pulpit and started tuh feelin' her legs.

It skeered her and she hollered out, "Oh, stop dat! Who dat grabbin' me by my leg?"

Dat skeered de preacher cause everybody woke up and begin lookin' right at 'im. So he started on back in de pulpit singin': "Oh, Ah jus' done dat to try yo' faith, Ah jus' done dat tuh try yo' faith."

—CLIFFERT ULMER.

Uh preacher wuz up preachin'. He reared an' he pitched an' he had de church wid 'im, too. He says, "Ooooh, brothers an' sisters, when all de saints come marchin' up under de blood-stained banner uh Jesus Christ; when they go marchin', marchin', marchin', marchin', trompin', trompin', up tuh glory in dat ma-a-awni-ing; when Gabrull shall place one foot on de sea an' one on de land an' shall draw in de win' from de four corners uh de earth; when de rocks an' de mountains shall skip lak lambs; when de sun shall go down in blood and de moon shed tears lak uh weepin' woman; when Jesus Christ de Lamb of Gawd shall lead forth de forty-an'-four thousand dat's been redeemed by de blood uh de blood shed on Calvary for de sins uh de world; when de sinner man, de sinner woman shall run tuh de rocks and de mountains cryin', 'Who, who, who whoooo shall save me from de wrath of an angry God?'; when de rocks shall cry, 'Awwahhh! Git away! Ah'm burnin', too.'; when God shall step down from His throne an' say dat Time shall be no more—brothers an' sisters, will you be dere?"

Response: "Yes!"

Preacher: "Some of you got mothers gone on before."

Response: "Yes, Lord."

Preacher: "Some of you got fathers gone on tuh glory."

Response: "Yes, Yes."

Preacher: "Some of you got one child gone on before."

Response: "Yes, preach it!"

Preacher: "Some of you got two-oo children gone on before."

Response: "Yes, my God."

Preacher: "Some of you got three children, some got four."

Response: "Yes, I mean tuh see 'em, too!"

Preacher: "Some of you got seben children gone on tuh heben."

Response: "Lawd! I can't stand it!"

Preacher: "Some got ten children waitin' in glory."

Response: "My God, ain't it de truth!"

Preacher: "AN' DEY *ALL* GOT DIFFERENT DADDIES!"

You could uh heered uh pin drop in dat church. Not uh soul said amen on dat.

—LARKINS WHITE.

Preacher wuz going down to the water wid his candidates and uh sister wuz upon de bank and de people wuz singing: "Gimme dat ole time religion, gimme dat ole time religion, gimme dat ole time religion, it's good enough for me."

De sister upon de bank saw a big ole 'gator out behond de preacher, but the preacher didn't see him. So she wuz singing: "I don't lak dat red-eyed 'gator, I don't lak dat red-eyed 'gator, I don't lak dat red-eyed 'gator."

De preacher looked round and said, "No, by God, and I don't neither; he's too big and black for me."

—CARRIE MCCRAY.

De preacher was up preaching and he said: "Every tongue got to confess; everybody got to stand in judgment for theyself; every tub got to stand on its own bottom."

One little tee-ninchy* woman in de amen corner said: "Lordy, make my bottom wider."

—REBECCA CORBETT.

There wuz two deacons of de church, one Methodist and one Baptist. They went out sailing one night in a little boat and in de late watches of de night de water begin to git rough and stormy, and de tides begin to rise, and de boat begin to wheel and rock to ketch water; and de Methodist deacon said to the Baptist deacon: "Say dere, brother, we better git busy and begin to dip dis water out de boat wid a bucket."

So de Baptist deacon decided dat dipping de water out wid a bucket wuzn't gettin' much results. So de Baptist deacon decided dey better pray. So he said, "We better say our prayers."

The Methodist deacon said, "No, dem little God damn Our Fathers prayers ain't gointer do us any good, dip water."

—CARRIE MCCRAY.

A man wuz cussin' and damnin', an' a preacher come along and says tuh him: "Son, it's wrong tuh be talkin' 'bout fightin'. Let God fight your case."

So de man says: "All right." An' so he didn't fight.

'Bout uh week after dat de man met de preacher, an' he wuz all scratched up, an' his clothes all tore up. He said to de preacher: "God maybe all right in uh man fight, but He ain't worth uh damn in uh bear fight."

—GEORGE BROWN.

---

*"tiny."

A man wuz hongry and he ast de preacher to help him out. De preacher tole him just ast de Lawd for whut he wants and he'll git it. So de man went home and got down and ast de Lawd, says: "O Lawd, send me down a barrel of flour, a barrel of meal, a barrel of sugar, a tub of lard, ten hams, a side of meat, a barrel of pepper—hold on, dere a minute, God. Dat's too damn much pepper."

—NAT JAMES.

This was a great big woman. So she had done got religion and was going to be baptized in de river de next Sunday. So she went round and tole her friends she had better religion than anybody ever joined dat church and they better come see her baptized. So they did.

De preacher was a lil man, and de river was full of holes, and he got fretted when he heard how this big portly sister was going to rear and pitch out dere in dat water, so he got to studying 'bout dat thing.

So dat Sunday he tole de deacons to make her de last candidate and to stand close and give him aid and assistance wid her case. All de time he was baptizing others, she was rearin' and pitchin' and hollerin' so de people on shore could take notice. When he got to her he said de words right quick and ducks her under and holds her under till she swallows a little water. She was so full when she come up she couldn't git her wind. She was steppin' out on de bank before she got straight to open her mouf, but she seen all de folks upon de bank she had done tole to come so she had to say something; but all she could git out was "Chris'mus gift".

—L. O. TAYLOR.

Two men wuz hoboing round an' come tuh uh town. They had done caught three pigeons an' wuz 'bout tuh kill 'em an' eat 'em when dey heard somebody say de church needed uh preacher. So they made it up for one of 'em to preach an' git holt uh some money.

They went on to de church house an' one of 'em took de pigeons an' clammed up in de loft, an' de other one took his seat in de pulpit.

When de people come, he tole 'em he wuz uh preacher an' uh God-sent man: so they let 'im preach.

Him an' his partner had done made it up dat everytime he call for uh pigeon from heben, de one up in de loft would send down one so de people would think it come from heben. Dey knowed dey wuz going tuh get uh good collection after that.

De one dat wuz preachin' reared an' he pitched. De church got all warmed up. After awhile he thowed back his head an' hollered, "If I be uh God-sent man, send me down uh pigeon from heben!"

De one up in de loft sent down uh pigeon. De people begin tuh shout.

He preached on awhile an' he hollered agin, "If I be uh God-sent man, send down another pigeon!"

Down come another pigeon. De people wuz goin' wild. Some of 'em even got skeered an' crep' out de church.

He preached some more, den he hollered de third time, "If I be uh God-sent man, send down another pigeon!"

De pigeon didn't come. He hollered agin, but no pigeon. He figgered his buddy mus' be sleep so he hollered still louder. De one up in de loft wuzn't sleep. Dat last pigeon had done got loose an' he wuz tryin' tuh ketch 'im, so when his buddy kept on hollerin', he hollered down, "You kin wait till I ketch 'im, cantcher?"

—CLIFFERT ULMER.

There was a church at my home that couldn't keep a pastor. So they changed pastors as regular as jumping checkers. So at last one of the deacons said, "I've found the man."

So on Saturday he come to preach Sunday, so the deacon advised him to be particular for he had a peculiar people to deal with.

He said, "Oh, I'll suit the people all right."

So on Sunday everybody was in a hurry to get to church. When he got up to address the congregation he said: "Brothers and sisters, it affords me no small source of pleasure of being with you today."

So his favorite deacon whispers to him and says, "Be careful, for God's sake! Don't tell a lie."

The preacher said, "I want to sing one of my favorite songs suited to common meter." So he gave it out—"O for a thousand tongues to sing my Great Redeemer's praise!"

One old deacon back in the corner said, "Come on down! Come on down from there! You have lied to start with—got a thousand tongues singing a song I can sing with one tongue. Come on down."

And that's all he got to say in that church, and when I left home they were still pastorless.

—JOE WILEY.

Once there wuz an ole lady so par'lyzed tuh not do nothing. One day she wuz in church, so de preacher put a man in de loft of de church and told him, when he say, "De Lawd is coming by", to go tuh tearin' off de shingles and make uh fuss.

He begin to preach. He said, "De Lawd is coming by," man begin to tear shingles and make a fuss. Everything begin to run, and this par'lyzed lady led de crowd hollerin', "De Lawd is coming by."

—EDWARD MORRIS.

There were once an old fellow, a farmer, and he had cleared some new ground, and he had a lil son and when he went to cultivate this land he put his son out to plow it with a very contrary mule; and de boy was plowing and de mule was going contrary, and de boy begin to curse and rear at de mule. So a preacher was passing at de time to revival meeting, and he heard the boy cussing and he ast de boy why did he cuss so bad and why didn't he pray. And de boy told him that a man couldn't pray and plow new ground, and so de preacher begged de boy to come to church dat night—which he did.

De preacher says, "You never hear me cuss, smoke, drink or lie, and if you ever hear or see me doing any of those things— you just whistle."

De preacher talked on and said, "Nothing could pick the grass as close to the ground as a goose," and when he said dat the lil boy raised up in de back of the church and whistled.

The preacher remembered that he had told the boy right immediately and after he finished preaching he ast de boy whut did he lie 'bout.

De lil boy tole him, "I heard you say dat nothin' could pick grass as close as a goose; but I must say dat a gander can pick it just as close as a goose."

—JERRY BENNETT.

Man loved preachers an' uster always have uh heap uh stump knockers* round all de time. He had uh boy dat wuz kinda mis*chee*vous an' one time he made de ole man so mad he tole 'im to git out an' go where he couldn't never see 'im no more. De boy jus' wanted tuh be aggravatin', so he ast 'im where he must go. De ole man wuz so mad he tole him tuh go tuh hell, cause he didn't keer whut become of 'im.

---

*"preachers."

De boy went on off an' thought he would jus' travel roun' an' see de world while he wuz on his way tuh hell. He traveled on till he come tuh de land uh de molly-moes (mile-or-mores). They is great big birds dat sticks they heads down in de ground when they see somebody comin' an' shake they feathers, an' you kin hear de wind whistlin' thew 'em fur uh mile or mo'.

He got by dem all right an' traveled on till he got tuh Head-and-Belly land. Dere all you had tuh do wuz tuh set down on de side uh de road an' wait, an' anything you want tuh eat would come by yuh. Uh baked hog wid uh knife an' fork in his side would come trottin' long an' all you had tuh do wuz tuh stop 'im an' eat all you want—then tell 'im tuh go on tuh de nex' one dat wanted some meat. Fried chickens an' everything come long, an' tater pies an' he et all he wanted; den he went on where he wuz gwine.

Way after while he got tuh hell, but everybody wuz back in de kitchen, an' so when he hailed he didn't git no answer. He didn't see no dogs, so he went on round tuh de back an' heered somebody talkin' in de kitchen an' he got skeered. He thought whut uh bad boy he uster be an' he wuz skeered de devil wuz gointer ketch 'im an' chunk 'im in de fire, but he didn't see de fire. Way after while he got up nerve tuh peep thew un crack an' he seen de devil settin' tuh de table playin' skin wid two or three preachers. One of 'em said: "Seem lak Ah hear somebody outside. Better go look."

De devil played on. De preacher tole 'im agin he thought he heered somebody outside, but de devil got mad an' tole 'im: "Say! you tryin' tuh git me tuh go outside so you kin shuffle dese cards tuh suit yo'self. But Ah ain't goin' no damn where till you fall."

De devil had uh big open fireplace wid taters roastin' in de ashes an' slices uh country cured ham broilin' on sticks an' uh big jug uh likker settin' on de table. Bad Boy wanted tuh git in dere so bad! He wanted de devil tuh ketch 'im after he seen all dat, so he made some noise wid his feet. Afterwhile de devil says: "B'lieve I *do* hear somebody out dere, but it ain't nobody but uh preacher an' I got too many uh dem here now tuh eat up my rations an' drink up mah likker. He sho ain't gointuh git in. B'lieve I'll go sick de dogs on 'im."

De boy went on way from hell an' kept on travelin' fuh uh year uh two, den he come tuh uh place an' some crackers got 'im. They had uh way uh ketchin' niggers an' keerin' 'em cross on uh island an' makin' 'em work two or three years, an' den if youse uh good nigger, they'd give yuh uh pass an' let yuh go. They paid yuh all right, but you couldn't leave.

Well, de boy staid over dere three years an' saved all his money. Den he got intuh uh crap game an' won uh whole heap uh money, so he made up in his mind he wanted out. So he went on down tuh de boat an' de white man dat run de boat wuz settin' dere readin' uh paper wid his gun layin' on de groun' beside 'im. He had jus' cleaned it. He wouldn't eben look up at de nigger.

He say tuh de man: "Cap'n, Ah'd lak tuh go cross here tuh-day."

De white man didn't look up, still he jus' retched out his hand fuh de pass an' de boy says: "Ah ain't got no pass, cap'n, but Ah'm liable tuh give yuh uh couple hunded dollahs fur keerin' me cross."

De white man put down his paper an' looked at 'im an' said: "Oh, you got to, got to lick Venus, got to lick Venus an' her puppies (pistol and six bullets) or you can't cross here." (Sung to the tune of "You must have dat true religion.")

De boy reached in his shirt an' tole 'im, "Ah got uh thirty-two-twenty; b'lieve tuh mah soul it's uh doggone plenty. If dat ain't enough Ah got uh forty-four-forty an' uh pocket full uh cartidges an' Ah'm goin' cross here." (Sung to same air.)

Dat white man looked at dat pistol, begin tuh clap his hands an' says: "Oh, git on board, lil childen, git on board lil childen, git on board lil childen, dere's room for many uh mo'." (Chorus of "Git on board".)

De boy come on cross an' kep' on travelin'. Way afterwhile he come home. He had done been off seben years when he got back. It wuz uh cold night when he come tuh de door an' knocked an' de ole man said: "Who is dat?"

An' de boy said: "It's me, John." De ole man let 'im in an' he looked so well de ole man wuz glad tuh see 'im, so he ast 'im where he been all dis time, an' he says: "You tole me to go tuh hell, didn't yuh? Well, Ah went." He looked round an' seen six preachers settin' tuh de fire.

"Naw! Whut wuz hell lak?"

"Jus' lak here. Ah couldn't git tuh de fire fuh de preachers."
—James Presley.

UNCLE JEFF AND THE CHURCH

During slavery there was an old slave named Jeff and he used to serve his old master so well that he used to give him his old clothes once in a while.

One time he gave Jeff a good pair of pants that he didn't like for some cause and Jeff decided—now that he had something nice to wear—to join the church, but he wanted to join the white church. So when Sunday came, he went and took a seat in the back of the church, and when they opened the doors of the church, he got up and told them he wanted to join.

You know they didn't want him in the church; but the preacher didn't exactly know how to turn him off; so he asked him, he said: "Jeff, do you think the Lord intended for you to join this church?"

Jeff said, "Why sho, He tole me to go unite myself wid a church, an' de niggers ain't got none; so He musta meant for me to join dis one."

"Jeff, I think you are mistaken. You didn't understand Him. I tell you what to do. You go back and ask him again, and if He tells you to come here again—why, then you can join."

Jeff knew that the preacher had just taken a way to get rid of him, so he waited a long time before he went back; but finally he did go, and when the doors of the church were opened, he went up again.

The preacher said, "Well, Jeff, what did the Lord tell you this time?"

"I went back and ast de Lawd agin lak you tole me about joinin' dis church."

"Well, what did He say, Jeff?"

"He say dat a good Christian lak me oughter been 'shamed of myself for even comin' here thinkin' 'bout joinin' dis church. He says He ain't never even joined here hisself. Fact is, He don't think He could git in if He wuz to try."

Then Jeff walked on out dat church and never came back.

—LOUISE NOBLE.

Preacher had a son that was just crazy 'bout card playin and gamblin. So one Sunday he was at it wid some of his friends and his old man come in. The boy was scared to let his pa ketch 'im so, you know in them days, preachers used to wear long dusters. So he had one hanging long side de wall. So de boy just stuck de cards in de pocket of de coat and make out he wasn't doing a thing. So de preacher put de coat on and went on down to de river to baptize some converts. De boy and his mama went too.

So when de preacher got out waist deep out come de ace. Next thing a king, next a queen and jack. Then de deuce. (A good poker hand)

De boy's mama hollered: "Oh, my husband done lost!" (She meant his soul, thinking he had taken to gambling.)

Boys says: "Well, mama, if papa lose wid a hand like that he don't deserve no sympathy."
—MACK C. FORD.

Once there was a preacher in the pulpit that had a handkerchief in his pocket. A man slipped a lamp eel in his pocket. The preacher reached his hand in his pocket to get his handkerchief, and grabbed the lamp eel by the head. He went to hollering and said, "What is it, what is it, what is it?"

An old sister in the church said, "I don't know what in the hell it is, but don't throw it on me."
—JOE WILEY.

There was a man went to church every Sunday and he would shout and run all over the church. One of the deacons of the church told the man if he would stop shouting and running around all over the church he would get him a pair of boots. The man stood it for about two Sundays. When the preacher was preaching, the man got happy and said: "Boots or no boots!" and started to shouting.
—DAVID LEVERETT.

Too many people say step out on de *word*. But all dem words don't say preach. Sometimes God writes and just as soon as God git to de letter P—they run off and go preach. God wuz gointer say 'plow', but they don't wait tuh see.

Now, one time uh jackass sent uh man tuh preach. They wuz two brothers and both of 'em wuz preaching and one always had big charges, so de other one went down in de woods and prayed to de Lord to know if he wuz called. About a mile or more through de woods uh man had a jackass and he wuz hungry, so just as de man ast de Lord dat, he whickered: "Wa-a-anh Wanh! Go preach, go preach!"

De man jumped up and went and tole folks he wuz called to preach. But look like he never could git no good charges. He wuz always on turpentine stills and sawmill camps. So one day he met his brother and ast him how come, and his brother tole him, says: "You sho de Lord done called you to preach?" He tole him yeah, he heard de voice distinct. Says, "You better go ast Him agin."

So he went back to de same praying ground, but de woods wuz cut down. So when he ast de Lord dis time, de jackass whickered agin and de man looked up and seen him, and says: "Yes, youse de son of a gun* sent me off to preach last time."

—EUGENE OLIVER.

There was a little boy lived on a hill and it was a thicket between his home and the schoolhouse. One day he was coming from school. He was going up the hill and met a bear. The boy came running back down the hill and he met a preacher. The preacher saw him running and asked, "What's the matter, son?"

The boy told him that a bear got after him. The preacher asked him why didn't he stop and pray, and the boy said, "I didn't have time."

The preacher said, "I am going up there—watch me."

The boy watched the preacher. After while the preacher came running down. The boy asked what was the matter. The preacher said, "A bear got after me, son. A prayer is all right in prayer meeting, but it ain't worth a damn in bear-meeting."

—EDWARD MORRIS.

---

*Originally typed "son of a bitch," but changed in the manuscript.

My daddy was a great preacher. One Sunday he got to preaching and said: "When I get to heaven, I am going to fly around awhile, then I am going to put on my golden slippers and walk around awhile."

There was a bunch of boys standing around the church house peeping in the windows. So the preacher said, "I am going to see God for myself. I am going to tell him how you treated me. I am going to be on Hallelujah Street, and then I am going to have some fun." And he wanted to show the people how he was going to have fun. He started to sit down in the window, but it was up and he fell out on the ground. The boys came running around the church house to see what had happened. The preacher said, "What in the hell is you all coming around here for? The fun is all over now."

—L. O. TAYLOR.

There was two colored preachers went to Mississippi to run revival and ran their meeting for two weeks.

At the end of the meeting they had gained a lot of souls. So on their way back to Alabama they stopped to count money, and to their surprise they had a hundred bucks a-piece.

The younger preacher said to the old one, "Let's shoot some craps."

The older one said, "No, no, I've quit all that for twenty years."

So the younger one kept on persuading him until finally the game started. The younger preacher had a sharp shot they called the Hudson; the older preacher had the shot they call the Up-and-Out.

So him and him! The old preacher losing all the time. So when he got to his last dollar he opened his knife—(Soliloquy): "And as soon as the younger one make that point I am going to take my money back."

The younger one was watching him all the time, so he continued to shoot. As soon as the point was made the old one fastened him around the neck and said: "Give me my money! I've 'hark from the tomb around your neck," not noticing the thirty-two–twenty the younger preacher had in his side. So the young preacher said, "Yes, but I've got the doleful sound."

So the old one looked and saw the gat and said, "The doleful sound gets it." So I being there, I asked the bushes to go my bond.*

—Joe Wiley.

❧ I had the occasion of leaving Alabama and going to Georgia. While being in Georgia I attended a meeting runned by Reverend Fullbosom. So the meeting lasted one week.

So all the time meeting was going on, nobody wouldn't bow down, neither say "amen" to nothing said.

So the church had only one door and one window, and the window was in the pulpit behind the preacher. So the last night of the meeting, Reverend Fullbosom carried his fifty-six special; so when church begin Reverend said: "Brothers and sisters, we are about to end our meeting, so Brother Sexton, lock the door and bring me the key." So he did, the sexton being peg-legged.

About that time I was a mourner.

Reverend Fullbosom said, "I've preached to all of you one week and not a one of you have even bowed down." So he opened his grip and out with his fifty-six special and said: "Now, all of you thieves, and robbers, hoboes, cut-throats, and rounders, BOW DOWN!"

So they begin to bow. So the peg-leg man thought it was impossible for him to bend that peg, so he said: "Brother Pastor, me too?"

---

*As in, "headed for the hills."

Reverend said, "Yes, you peg-leg son of a gun, BOW DOWN!"

So when I looked around the sexton was on both knees singing: "If my wife is in this church, tell her to come here please; if she ain't got time to come, tell her to send me them keys."

So Reverend made three shots in the church and everybody went to run and made for the side of the church, and running so fast they carried it twenty-eight miles before they thought to turn it loose.

—JOE WILEY.

"Say, boy, where have you been?"

"I been to hell and everywheres else, mister."

"What did you see there?"

"I saw a preacher and some boys. The boys was shooting crap on Sunday. The preacher scolded them and told them they ought not to do that. So the boys told the preacher that they were going to find Jesus next Sunday. So the boys had dirty* under a hat and covered it up. The preacher was standing up and they all said, 'We have found Jesus.'

" 'Where is he,' said the preacher?

" 'You pick it up,' said the boys.

"So the preacher picked the hat up and said, 'Well, boys, Jesus done defecated and gone.' "

—EDWARD MORRIS.

---

*"incriminating evidence."

Devil Tales

The' passed the communion cup to a woman and she turned it up to her head and drunk it all up. She rubbed her belly and hand de cup back to de deacon and says: "Hah! I could drink uh quart uh dat wine for my sweet Jesus."

Baptis' and Meth'dis' always got a pick out at one 'nother.

One time two preachers—one Meth'dis' and de other Baptis' wuz on a train and de engine blowed up. When they started up in de air de Baptis' preacher hollered: "I bet I go higher than you."

A man had two sons. One was name Jack and de other one was name Frank. So they got grown and their father called 'em one day and says, "Now, y'all are grown. Here's five hundred dollars a piece. Go out for yourself."

Frank took his and went and bought him a farm and settled down.

Jack took his and went on down de road. He got into a crap game and bet his five hundred dollars and won. He bet five hundred more and won agin.

He went walking on down de road and met a man. "Good morning, my boy, what might be your name?"

"My name is Jack. Who are you?"

"Lie-a-road to ketch meddlers."

Jack says, "I speck youse de man I'm looking for to play me some five-up."

"All right, let's go."

So they set down and played and Jack lost. "I got five hundred more that says I'll win." They played and Jack lost agin. "Well," he says, "I got five hundred more." He lost dat.

Den de man says, "I tell you what I'll do. I'll play you a game for your life against all the money."

Jack lost again. So the man he says, "My name is the devil. My home is across the Atlantic ocean. If you gets there before this sun rises and goes down again I'll save your life. If not, you'll have to die."

Jack was down by de road crying and a ole mast ast him, "What you crying for?"

Jack says, "I played five-up wid de devil and he have won my life. He's gone back across the Atlantic Ocean. He told me if I'm not there before the sun rises and goes down again he's bound to take my life. I don't see no chance of getting there."

Old man says, "Youse in a pretty bad fix, all right. There's only one thing can cross de ocean in twelve hours. That's a bald eagle. She comes here every morning and dips herself in de ocean and walks out and plucks off her dead feathers. Now you be here tomorrow morning with a bull yearling; when she get through plucking her feathers she'll be ready to go. You mount her back wid dis bull yearling and every time she hollers, you put a piece of meat in her mouf and she'll carry you straight across de ocean by nine o'clock."

Jack was there de nex' morning wid de bull yearling and saw

de eagle when she dipped herself in de ocean and come out on shore to pick off her dead feathers. She dipped herself the second time and shook herself. When she rocked herself and made ready to mount the sky, Jack mounted her back wid his yearling.

After while she hollered, "Hah-ah! one quarter cross de ocean. I don't see nothing but blue water." Jack tore off one de hams of dat yearling and stuck it in her mouf and she flew on.

After a while, "Hah-ah! half way cross de ocean—don't see nothing but blue water, hah!" He give her de hind quarters and she flew on.

After while, "Hah-ah! mighty nigh cross de ocean—don't see nothing but blue water, Hah!" He give her de rest and pretty soon she landed. Jack hopped off and met an old black man with red eyes and ast him if he know where de devil live at. He told him, "Yeah, he live in de first little house down de road."

He knocked on de door and de devil opened it. "Well, you made it, didn't you? Come in and have breakfast with me."

After breakfast he says to Jack. "I got a lil job for you to do and if you do it, you can have my youngest daughter; but if you fail I'll hafta take yo' life. I got seventy-five acres of new ground—never a bush cut on it. Every bush, every tree, every stump got to be cut and piled up and burnt before twelve o'clock."

Jack went on down there and went to work; then he begin to cry and de devil's youngest daughter come down wid his breakfast. She says, "Whut's de matter, Jack?"

"Your father gimme a hard task. I can't clean all dis off by twelve o'clock."

"Eat yo' breakfast, Jack, and lay yo' head in my lap and go to sleep."

Jack done so, and when he woke up every bush, every tree, every stump was cut and piled up and burnt. So Jack went on back to de house.

"I got one more little hard task for you to do. If you do, you kin have my daughter; if you don't, I'll hafta take yo' life. I got a well three thousand feet deep—I want every drop of water dipped out and bring me whut you find on the bottom."

Jack went to dipping the water out de well, but it run in faster then he could dip it out; so he set down and went to crying. Here come de devil's daughter and ast him, "Whut's de matter, Jack?"

"Your father have give me another hard task. I can't do this work."

"Lay down and put your head in my lap and go to sleep."

Jack done so and after while she woke him up and hand him a ring and tole him: "Heah, take dis to papa. That's whut he want. Mama was walking out here de other day and lost her ring."

Devil says, "I got one more task for you to do and you kin have my youngest daughter. If you don't, I'll hafta take your life." De devil had some coconut palms three hundred fifty feet high. He tole Jack, "You kill these two geeses and go up dat palm tree and pick 'em and bring me back every feather."

Jack took de geeses and went on up de tree and de wind was blowing so strong he couldn't hardly stay up there. Jack started to cry. Pretty soon here come de devil's daughter. "Whut's de matter, Jack?"

"Your father have give me too hard a task. I can't do it."

"Just lay your head in my lap and go to sleep."

Jack done so and she caught the feathers that had got away from Jack and when he woke up she hand him every feather and de geese and says: Heah, take 'em to papa and let's get married."

So de devil give them a house to start housekeeping in.

That night the girl woke up and says: "Jack, father is coming after us. He's got two horses out in the barn and a bull. You hitch up de horses and turn their heads to us."

He hitched up de horses and she got in and off they went.

De devil misses 'em and run to git his horses. He seen they was gone, so he hitched up his bull. De horses could leap one thousand miles at every jump and de bull could jump five hundred. Jack was whipping up dem horses but de devil was coming fast behind them and de horses could hear his voice one thousand miles away. One of 'em was named Hallowed-Be-Thy-Name and the other one Thy-Kingdom-Come.

De devil would call, "Oh, Hallowed-Be-Thy-Name, Thy-Kingdom-Come! don't you hear your Master calling you? Jump Bull, jump five hundred miles." Every time he'd holler de horses would fall to their knees and de bull would gain on 'em.

De girl says, "Jack, get out de buggy and drag your heel nine steps backward and throw dirt over your left shoulder and git back in and let's go."

They did this three times before de horses got so far off they couldn't hear their master's voice. After dat they went so fast they got clean away. De devil kept right on coming and so he passed an old man and ast: "Did you see a girl black as coal, with eyes of fire, wid a young man in a buckboa'd?" He tole him yeah. "Where did you hear 'em say they were going?"

"On de mountain."

"I know 'tain't no use now, I can't ketch 'em. (Chant) Turn, bull, turn clean around, turn bull, turn clean around."

De bull turnt so short till he throwed de devil out and kilt him and broke his own neck."

That's why they say, "Jack beat the devil."

—JERRY BENNETT.

THE WOMAN AND THE DEVIL[†]

There was one man and his wife who always lived lovin'. They never had fussed since they had been married. Devil didn't like dat so he decided to break 'em up. He tried and tried, but he was about to give up one day when he stopped a woman's house to get a drink of water. So she ast him why he looked so downhearted and he tole her he been trying to break up a couple for two years and they just wouldn't fuss.

So she says, "If you will gimme a new pair shoes, I betcher I kin git 'em to fussin' and quarrelin'."

So he tole her he would. So she quit whut she was doin' and went on over to de couple's house. De woman was sweepin' and singin'. De woman says, "You so happy, I'm sorry I come."

"How come? Don't you like to see folks happy?"

"Yes, thass how come I wish I hadn't come here. Youse too good a woman to have such a deceitful man. I ain't goin' tuh tell you whut he done, so don't ast me."

De woman says, "Nobody can't make me b'lieve my husband ain't right. Not even de devil hisself couldn't break us up."

"Oh, I ain't trying, thass how come I ain't goin' to tell you nothin'. But if you jus' watch you'll see for yourself. Nobody won't have to tell you if you keep yo' eyes open."

Then she left de woman and went on down in de fiel' where de man was plowin'. "Hello, brother, you sho is a smart man. That's whut makes me sorry to see a man like you wid a woman that keeps secrets from him."

"My wife ain't got no secrets from me. Thass one thing we don't do, is keep things from one 'nother."

"Well, all I got to say is, long as a person don't open up a box you can't tell whut they got in it. You jus' got to take they word for it. A secret wouldn't be a secret if ever body knowed it. Don't think I come to talk about nobody. I wouldn't tell you nothin', not even if you paid me. But if you keep yo' eyes open an' yo' mouf shet and nobody won't have to tell you nothin'."

So she went on 'bout her business. Devil hung round where he could watch. De man come in and never said a word. De wife got busy wid de cookin' and she never spoke. He took

down de wash pan and started to washin' his hands. She come
snatched de towel out his hands and wiped her face with it. He
set on de stoop and wouldn't ast her wuz dinner ready. She
took de broom and swept all over him and wouldn't ast him to
move.

He says, "Looka heah, ole nigger 'oman, whut de hell's de
matter wid you? If you wanta know, I kin knock some uh dat
hell out you anytime you git too high."

She up and tole 'im, "Looka here, Mr. Nappy-chin, I kin
make out without you any day in the week. Gwan, hit me! I
dare you!"

So they fought all over de house before they thought to git
de thing straight. So de devil went on and give de woman de
new pair of shoes.

—GENEVA WOODS.

Once I wuz travelin' huntin' uh job tuh work, and met
uh man wid two horses. He ast me if I wanta work. I
tole 'im, yes suh. He said, one of de horses was swift ez de
wind and de other wuz a little bit swifter.

He tole me tuh go tuh his house and git his shotgun and
one shell tuh kill enough birds to build uh bridge across de
devil's trussle (trestle). I didn't do lak he tole me. I went an' got
uh whole handful uh shells. He tole me after I build dat bridge
dat I could have his daughter.

I went out dere and shot up one tree and all de birds flew
out dat tree intuh another one. Went over and shot in de other
tree, and by dat time the devil's daughter come out dere where
I wuz. She ast me couldn't I kill 'em. I tole her naw.

She took de gun and shot and here come a bundle of birds
fallin' down and she took de toes fur de nails, and she took de
thighs fuh de logs to cross de bridge, and she took de backs fur
de boards (floors), so she bilt de bridge and she tole me: "Papa
ain't gointer let me go wid you." She tole me, "When you

come up dere tonight, when he snore so loud—he ain't sleep. Wait till he breathes easy. Then, you ketch dem two horses," says, "an' we'll go."

She give me one-half uh banana, and tole me to put dat in my pocket. She give me one-half uh peanut, and tole me to put dat in my pocket. She give me uh egg, and tole me to put dat in my pocket. And so she tole me, "When we go to my grandma's house, she got a lil fice (dog) and ef he kiss me, I won't see you no mo', and ef he kiss you, you won't see me no mo'."

He had an ole jumpin' bull jump five thousand miles every time he jump. De horses wuz named Three Color and Changeable. Every time you say "Changeable" he be changing states dat quick.

So when we saw her daddy coming, she tole me to han' her de egg. She threwed it crost her left shoulder and it made a great big river, and he had tuh go back home tuh git his blood hounds to drink up all de water so he could come on across.

Look back agin and saw him comin' on his bull, and so she tole me tuh hand her dat half uh banana. She threwed dat crost her left shoulder, and dere come a great big banana field. She said, "Papa love bananas, an' I know he'll hafter stop and git some of those."

He stopped and turnt roun' and carried some bananas back to de house. While he was carrying those bananas back to de house, we dodged him. So we got dere and we stopped and went in, an' so we wuz setten down talkin' and de lil ole fice come dere to play with me, and I pat 'im on de head. When I know anything, he had done kiss me "bap" in de mouth, and I ain't seen my gal no mo'.

—JULIUS HENRY.

WOMAN SMARTER THAN DEVIL†

There was a young man, very nice young man, raised nice, and he married a very nice girl and they loved one another dearly. And they lived so happy together and de Devil didn't like it, so he put in to break 'em up.

Every scheme the Devil would figure out their love would overcome. So de Devil met a woman named Sarah one day and she was barefooted. De Devil said to her: "Whut you doin barefooted?"

She says: "I ain't able to buy no shoes."

Devil says to her: "I got a job for you and if you 'complish dat job I'll give give you a pair of new shoes."

She says: "All right."

Devil says: "You know dat young man and his wife?"

She says: "Yes."

Devil says: "I been trying a long time to break 'em up, but every scheme I have don't take no effect. I give it up."

Woman says: "I'll break 'em up if you gimme dem shoes."

So de woman went to de house, de man was in de field plowing and she seen him before she got there. He had a mole on his neck. So she went to de house. Before he got there de woman was bragging about the husband. She says: "He is handsome, but there is one thing I don't like him. Dat mole on his neck. You cut dat off and he will be perfect."

So the wife ast: "How kin I cut it off and he won't know it?"

Sarah says: "Wait till he go to sleep and you take his razor and cut it off."

Wife says: "He is pretty now, but if anything will make him more pretty, I'll do it."

So after dinner de man went on back down in de field and went to plowing. So when de woman left she went on down in de fiel and she tole de man: "You know I found out something today."

He says: "Whut?"

She says: "You and yo wife been living together a nary a year and you love her, don't you?"

He says: "Yes".

"And she make out she love you, too, but tonight when you go to bed you stay wake and cover up yo' head and when she start to pull de cover off yo' head she gointer have yo' razor in her hand to cut yo' throat. Now don't say I told you. Don't call my name, but you'll see whut I'm tellin you is true."

So dat evening when he knocked off she had supper ready, he eat and went on to bed and covered up. When she thought he was sleep she went to easing the cover off and he looked up and saw de razor in her hand. He says: "Whut you doing wid dat razor. I done heard it today you was going to cut my throat. Good as I been to you, long as we been living together, too."

She says: "I just wanted to cut dat mole off yo' neck to make you mo' pretty."

"Oh, naw, you wuzn't—trying to cut my throat."

He put her out.

Next morning the woman she went over to the devil's house. He says: "Is dat you, Sarah?"

She says: "Yeah. I done whut I tole you. I done broke 'em up. I want my shoes."

Devil says: "All right, wait a minute."

He went down to de swamp and cut a long pole and tied de shoes on to it.

Says: Here's yo' shoes, but anybody slicker than me, I don't want 'em close to me. Git back. I don't want you close to me."

—M. C. FORD.

Once there was a man going with the devil's daughter and wanted to marry her. The devil told him he could, if he could tell her from the rest.

So he put all her seven sisters in a line with her and they were all exactly alike. But Mary had done told him she would move her feet, so he could tell her from the rest. So she did.

So he took her and married her and she used to fuss with him. One night in the bed he asked her what make her fuss so much when he was nice and kind to her and she said: "Honey, that's the devil. I got seven devils in me."

So he took a sledge hammer and knocked her on the head, and six devils jumped out, but one stayed in her. That's how come all lady people got the devil in them, because that one was left in her.

—ARTHER HOPKINS.

These people was vast rich. De devil had taken posses-sion to such an extent dat all of 'em had died but de man and his daughter. So dey left de mansion and built another one not far off and made an offer to give any man de daughter to stay over night in dis*. Several tried it and couldn't stand de racket. At last two niggers came along and taken de job. They went upstairs and made them a fire. One sent de other down to get a couple of chickens. He stayed so long he went to look for him and found him dead at the foot of the stair. John didn't stop. He stepped over him and went on out to the coop and got de chickens and went back upstairs and picked 'em. By time he got in a good way picking 'em, in walked a man with a greasy sack and beard to waist. He ast John what's he doing.

"I'm picking my chicken."

He ast, "Kin I help you?"

Reply was, "Yes, if you behave yourself."

This party was de devil and he had sharp claws and he was

_____

*Marked to supply missing word (probably "mansion") but word was not supplied.

tearing the chicken up. The man grabbed the chicken, taken it away and picked and cooked it. Devil ast, "Whut you going to do now?"

"Cook my chickens."

After cooked, "Whut you going to do now?"

"Eat."

"Kin I eat with you?"

"Yes, if you behave yourself." So they ate together; after supper they smoked. Now this sack dat devil had in his hand was full of imps. After they went to bed de devil turned 'em a-loose. They begin running all over de bed and house and in de meantime John had hid a hatchet under the pillow. He up wid it and lammed one of dese imps wid it and dat intempered de devil; so he jumped up and made a break for John and John made a break for de door and round de house, de woodshed and into de workshop, John on one side of de work bench and de devil on de other. Devil was reaching over after John and his whiskers got caught in the vice and John screwed up on them. He had him.

"Now you've got me, Now I'll not bother you, but stay off dat hill yonder. Don't you never come up dat hill."

So John won and married de girl. They gave him the girl and made him vast rich. One evening they went out driving in a buggy with a horse and saw a little white rabbit. Girl says, "Oh dear, git dat for me."

He spring out de buggy and run after de rabbit and de rabbit run right up dat hill. When he got up dere he turned back to de original devil. "I got you now. I tole you not to come upon dis hill."

"When I had you, I granted your request; now there's one request I want you to grant me—I want to go down and tell my wife good-bye—and you see her down dere in de buggy."

He goes down and got his wife and wrapped her in de rug and put her under his arm and walked on back. De devil saw him coming, ast him: "Whut's dat you got under your arm?"

"My vice." Devil tole him to gwan back—he didn't need him. Some years later John died and went to hell—devil looked through the iron gate and saw him. Give him some matches and tole him to go on back and build a hell of his own.
—L. O. TAYLOR.

A Negro and de devil had a bet of one thousand dollars to tell which one was the strongest. They brought out a five-ton hammer, placed it on the ground, and going to see which one could throw it the farthest. Devil picked up de hammer at nine A.M. and threw it. Turned to the Negro and said: "We'll go home—the hammer won't return until three days later."

On the third morning at nine A.M. the hammer fell. Knocked a hole in the ground big enough to place three counties in it. They took the hammer out and placed it on level again and it was then the Negro's time to throw it. The Negro looked straight towards the clouds and said: "Stand back, Rayfield (Raphael); move back, Abraham; watch your step, Jesus."

The devil walked up to the Negro and said to him: "Don't you throw my damn hammer up there. Some of my tools was left there when the Lord threw me down, and I ain't got 'em yet."
—JONATHAN HINES.

You know de devil don't do everything they say. One day uh man wuz on his way tuh church an' he wuz late, so he cut crost uh pasture. When he wuz gettin' under de barb-wire fence he snagged his pants, an' he said: "Oh shucks! de devil done dat."

Soon's he said dat he heard somebody snufflin' an' cryin' an' he looked up an' seen uh man settin' on uh fence post justa cryin'. De man wuz sayin': "Ah sho do have uh hard time. Now there goes another man lyin' on me."

It wuz de devil!

—W. M. RICHARDSON.

WHY WE SAY "UNH HUNH"†

 A widow lady had jus' one chile and it was a girl. She was mighty pretty. A man next door had four children.

So one day de Devil come stole 'em all. He put two chillen under each arm and put de pretty girl in his mouf.

De widow looked up and saw him flyin off wid her pretty daughter in his mouf so she thought up a way to git her back. So she hollered and ast: "Hey, old Satan, is you comin back after more?"

He says: "Yeah." Kerdap! De girl fell out his mouf and run back to her mama.

Next time he got somebody in his mouf they (the people) hollered and ast him: "Hey, Satan, is you comin back for more?"

He said: "Unh hunh" and kept right on.

—MACK C. FORD.

Witch and Hant* Tales

---

*"Hant" means "haunt" or "ghost."

DE WITCH WOMAN[†]

There was a witch woman wid a saddle-cat who could git out her skin and go ride people she didn't like. She had a great big looking-glass. When she git ready to go out she'd git befo dat glass naked. Jus befo she shake herself she would go and lay all her clothes out—stretch em out on de bed so she wouldn't have no trouble when she git back.

Then she'd go back befo de glass and shake herself and she'd say: "Gee whiz! Slip 'em and slip 'em agin!" And de old skin would slip off and she'd git out on her [illegible] and she'd look back and say "umph!! I forgot sumthin." And she'd go back to her keyhole and she blow and say, "Open door, lemme come in agin." And she'd go back and spread de old skin out at de fire place and tell de skin, "So remember who you are."

And one time her old use-to-be she used to love so hard was eave-dropping her and when she got away he slipped in and salts de hide wid pepper and salt. She couldn't find her old use-to-be at his house so she could ride him nowhere at no struggle of sleep, so she made her way back home. Says, "Umph! I'm de witch woman, but I b'lieve I'm done lost out."

So she goes and blows to de key hole in de door and de do'

got tighter. She squinch herself and blow, say: "Witchcraft, won't you let me in?"

Her old use-to-be come from behind de house and de door cracked and in she went. She looked all around. Everything looked all right. She said to de old skin, "Less go agin." When she tried de old skin on, de old skin begin to burn and sting. She laid it back down and looked at it. She picked it up agin and said: "Skin, oh skin, old skin, don't you know me?"

She tried it agin and it burned and stung her agin. Said: "Gee whiz! old skin, dis is me. I been goin and goin, but I think dis is my old use-to-be (who has conquered me)."

Her old use-to-be spoke behind de house and says: "You used to have me, but I got you now."

—A. D. FRAZIER.

THE FOUR STORY LOST LOT[†]

In Bullard County, Alabama, there was a haunted house and you had to spend the night so as you could tell whut happened during de night. The first guest come in had music to console him, gamblers and preachers, drunkards and other dissipated class to amuse one another and see whut happen.

The first thing come in at twelve o'clock was a big black cat and he would come sit by de hearth with his back to de fire and his face to de guests. Den for one hour de wind would blow and de lights would go out just as fast as you light 'em. So de guests would get skeered and run out and they couldn't tell nothin but "de black cat come in and de lights went out."

Some more guests come. This cat come in agin—back to fire and his face to de people. They begin to start de music to stay till day. De wind begin to blow and all de lights went out agin. They stood de hour through and de lights come on. When de wind riz de do' wuz already locked and thumb bolted, but it flew open. In come a pair of white feets and stood before de fire wid de heels to de fire and they toes to de people. When de door opened again, de legs come in and joined to dem feet. De do' wuz still locked. Nex' time de thighs come in and joined to de legs. Nex' when de do' open agin in come de body and join on to de thighs. Nex' time in come de arms and joined on to de body. When de do' open agin, head come in and said: "Now, by God, we got de man."

Guests of people whut wuz there said: "No, by God, you got a hell of a run."

Next time five people tried it a old woman and her two daughters and the son-in-law and de baby. All four had a package but de baby. They set out on de porch wid they feets on second step from de top. Look at each other and every now and then the baby would cry. He was in de house on de bed. They would go and quiet de baby and go back on de porch.

Old lady said: "Lemme me go git de baby and git some water for it."

They all went out to de well, catch hold of the rope and begin to pull. Old lady said: "Lawd, dis bucket must be hung, it pulls so hard. Whut we goin do now?"

All drilled* back to de porch and set down agin. Come a big white man round de corner of de house. Old lady looks at him and say: "Lawd, whut you want here?"

He said to her: "Good that you spoke, If you hadna spoke I'd a 'stroyed de crowd." And he said to her, he said: "Y'all git up and follow me."

They followed him on down cross de weedy field. Old lady right behind de white man, and so on to de youngest. Carried 'em up in de pine thicket where there was a old chestnut tree and he caught on to one of de saplins and bent it down. After he got it down he told de old lady to tell her youngest girl to

---

*"walked," probably derived from militant marches.

come here. He said: "Now, before I tell y'all whut I want you
to do", he says to de young girl, "come ketch hold of de tip
top of dis sapling." He said: "Now lissen, at de root of dat tree
where dis saplin growed upon, I buried years and years of
money. You go to my old barn when I'm gone and you'll find
a bunch of tools tied up with chains. Everything I took (used)
to bury dis money is in dat chain. You'll find a steel box with
keys and you take it and get dis money for yourself. My home
is yo' home as long as you all live." Dat time de wind riz and
de lil girl holdin to de saplin top hit straightened in a flash of
wind and de old lady looked for her and she said: "Now, dat's
hell agin. But this is my home." They ain't never seen de girl
no more.

    —A.D. FRAZIER.

THE ORPHAN BOY AND GIRL
AND THE WITCHES[†]

An orphan boy and girl lived in the house with their
grandmother, and one day she had to go a journey and
left them there alone. The little girl was sick and the boy went
to search for food for them both.

After he was gone, the girl felt stronger so she got out of
bed. She was walking in the house when he came back.

"Why do you get out of bed?" he asked her.

She said that she got out of bed because she smelt the
witches about. He laughed at her and persuaded her to eat
some yams. While they were eating, sure enough in came three
witches.

The witches wanted to eat them at once, but they begged to
be spared until their grandmother returned at sundown. The
witches didn't want to wait, so they said that they would not
eat them if they would go and get some water from the spring.
The children gladly said that they would go.

The witches gave them a sieve to fill with water, and told them that if they did not return at once with it, they would be eaten immediately.

The boy and girl went to the spring for the water and dipped and dipped to try to fill the sieve, but the water always ran out faster than they could fill it. At last they saw the witches coming. Their teeth were far longer than their lips.

The boy and girl were terribly frightened. He seized her hand said, "Let us run. Let us go across the deep river."

The children ran as fast they could. They saw the witches behind them coming so fast that they made a great cloud of dust that darkened the sun. The little girl stumbled and the witches gained so fast that they saw they could not reach the river before the witches, and so climbed a great tree.

The witches came to the foot of the tree and smelt their blood. They came with a broad-ax and began to chop down the tree. The little girl said: "Block eye, chip, block eye chip!" and the pieces that the witches chopped off would fly back into the witches' eyes and blind them.

The boy called his dogs. (Chant) "Hail Counter! Hail Jack! Hail Counter! Hail Jack!"

The witches at the foot of the tree chopping away said, (chant): O-ooo! Whyncher, whyncher! O-ooo! Whyncher, whyncher!" (Here it is understood that each actor in the drama is speaking, or chanting his lines without further indications.)

"Hail Counter, Hail Jack!"

"O-ooo! Whyncher, whyncher!"

"Block eye chip, block eye chip!"

The tree was toppling and the children was so scared, but the boy kept on calling: "Hail Counter, hail Jack!"

"Block eye chip, block eye chip!"

"O-ooo! Whyncher, whyncher!"

The little girl asked her brother: "Do you see the dogs coming yet?"

He said, "Not yet. Hail Counter! Hail Jack!" He didn't see the dogs coming and he began to sing: "I'm a little fellow here by myself for an hour."

"Block eye chip, block eye chip."

The dogs was tied at home. They heard his voice and wanted to come, but they were tied. The grandmother was asleep. She was very tired from her journey. She wondered where her grandchildren were. She did not hear the dogs whining to go to the aid of the boy. But a black fast-running snake heard the boy and ran to the house and struck the grandmother across the face with his tail and woke her, and she loosed the dogs.

"I'm a little fellow here by myself for an hour."

"Block eye, chip! Block eye, chip!"

"Hail Counter, hail Jack!"

"O-oooo! Whyncher, whyncher!"

By that time here come the dogs. The tree was falling. The boy and girl was so glad to see the dogs. He told one dog: "Kill 'em!" He told another one, "Suck their blood!" He told the last one, "Eat the bones!"

By that time I left. (Favorite way of ending a story.)

—Hattie Reeves, born on Island of
Grand Command.

The old fortune-teller woman, you know. Dis old man and woman had been married for fifty years. And they lived a long ways from town and dis old fortune teller woman she lived on de road to town.

De old folks raised rice and hawgs and lived pretty good all they life.

Dis old fortune-teller woman she got out of produce so she figgered uh way to cut dis old man off on his way to town and git something off him to go upon.

She sees him comin down de road wid his team uh oxen so she got herself out where she could stop 'im. So she says to 'im:

"Brothah Ishum, I been dreamin bout you every night and de Lawd done tole me to tell you to watch yo wife. Cause she's gointer cut yo' th'oat when you git back—thinkin youse wid other wimmen when youse in town. Whilst youse in town doin yo' shoppin think of me. When you start back home think of me."

Soon's he drives on off she gits her basket and sack and lights out to his house to see his old lady. She gits down to his Hannah's house and sets down and talks wid her and asts her why she don't never go to town wid her husband no time.

She tole her: "Lawd, chile, I ain't been to town in twenty year and I ain't feel like takin dat ride. I stay heah and take keer everything and have him a hot supper ready when he git back."

De old fortune-teller woman she say: "Lawd, Sister Hannah, you don't know Brer Ishum. He got a gal uptown. Thass how come it take him so long to go and come, and it wouldn't be *me*, Lawd, puttin up wid such."

So she gathered up her things and went on over to de fortune teller's house. She ast her: "Whut you do to yo' husband?"

Dat put de fortune teller in uh strain so she took her and carried her over to a neighbor's house.

Brer Ishum had done got lonesome for de old lady so when de witch woman got back home he wuz dere. He ast her: "Is you seen my old 'oman?"

She tole him: "No, I ain't seen 'em."

—A.D. Frazier.

A man sold hisself to de high chief devil. He give 'im his whole soul and body to do as he please wid it. He went out in dis drift of woods and lied down flat of his back beyond all dese skull heads and bloody bones and said: "Go way, Lawd, and come heah Devil, and do as you please wid me, cause I wanta do everything in de world dat's wrong and never do nothin right."

And he dried up and died away on doin wrong. His meat all left his bones and de bones all wuz separated. And at dat time High Walker walked upon his skull head and kicked de old skull-head and kicked and kicked it on ahead of him a many and many times and said to it: "Rise up and shake yo'self. High Walker is here."

Old skull head wouldn't say nothin. He looked back over his shoulder, cause he heard a noise behind and said: "Bloody Bones, you won't say nothin yet."

Den de skull-head said: "My mouth brought me here, and if you don't mind, yours will bring you here."

High Walker and Bloody Bones went on back to his white folks and told de white man dat a dry skull-head wuz talkin in de drift today. White man say he didn't believe it.

So: "Well, if you don't believe it, come go with me and I'll prove it. And if hit don't speak you kin chop my head off right where hit at."

So de white man and High Walker went back in de drift to find dis old skull-head. So when he walked up to it, he begin to kick and kick de ole skull-head and it wouldn't say nothin. High Walker looked at de white man and de white man cut his head off. And de old dry skull-head said: "See dat now—I told you dat mouf brought me here and if you didn't mind it'd bring you heah."

So de Bloody Bones riz up and shook they selves and de white man said: "Whut you mean by dis?"

Bloody Bones say: "We got High Walker and we all bloody bones now in de drift together."

—A. D. FRAZIER.

HIGH WALKER AND BLOODY BONES[†]

This was a man. His name was High Walker. He walked into a boneyard with skull-heads and other bones. So he would call them: "Rise up, bloody bones and shake yo'self."

And they would rise up and come together and shake their selves and part and lay back down. Then he would say to hisself: "High Walker" and de bones would say: "Be walkin."

When he'd get off a little way he'd look back over his shoulder and shake hisself, say: "High Walker and bloody bones." And de bones would shake their selves. He knowed he had power.

—A. D. FRAZIER.

Heaven Tales

THE FIRST COLORED MAN IN HEBEN[†]

The first colored man that went to heben was John. So
John goes up there walking. So he knocked. They ast
him who he was. He said, "John."

"From where?"

"Alabama."

"Riding or walking?"

"Walking."

"Don't allow any walkers here."

So on his way back to Alabama he met a white man walking. He said, "Cap, where you going—to heben?"

He said yes.

"They don't allow no walkers there, so you ride me up there
and we both will get in." So he rode John on up to heben and
knocked.

"Who's that?"

"White man."

"From where?"

"Mississippi."

"Riding or walking?"

"Riding."

"Hitch your horse and come in."

Left John still out. Says the Good Book in heben no filth is found. So there was some old sacks outside of heben where they had been scrubbing the streets and the floors. So John began to study. So he taken one of the sacks and throwed it just as far in heben as he could. So the angels called him in to get that sack out of heben. So he goes in like he was going to get the sack (gesture of swift flight). And down Hallelujah Street! So down Amen Street picking them up and laying them down! So he come to Jerusalem Street and down the street! Throwing them in and curving round! So at the foot of Jerusalem Street was the Sea of Glass. Out on the Sea of Glass John went— breaking glass. The Lord was out there skating and asked, "What's the matter? What's the matter?"

They said, "This nigger throwed a sack in here and we was after him to make him take it out again."

The Lord said, "Never mind 'bout the sack. Just leave that nigger alone before he tear up heben."

—JOE WILEY.

DE FLYING NEGRO†

One time five niggers went tuh heben at one time, which is something don't happen often. Soon's dey got dere Gabull (Gabriel) fixed 'em all up wid robes an' wings an' everything, an' set 'em down in some golden cheers.

Four of 'em set dere; but one nigger tole 'em: "Shucks, Ah got tuh git up an' try out dese wings."

De others tole 'im, "You betta set down lak Gabull tole us. He'll tell us whut tuh do nex'."

"He don't need tuh tell me whut tuh do. He done gimme de wings, ain't he? They mine now, an' Ah'm gointer *use* 'em. Watch me skim roun' dat tree uh life thout tetchin' uh leaf."

He got up an' he flew thisa way an' thata way. They had a whole heap uh lights an' big vases settin' roun' an' de other niggers says tuh him, "You betta be keerful, cause you liable tuh knock down some uh dem hangin' lamps uh knock over some uh dem fine vases!"

"Oh naw, I won't neither." He flew round an' round. He'd go way up, den fold his wings lak uh buzzard an' drop straight down; he'd dart under dem hangin' lights an' round dem vases. After while he says, "Watch me skim right cross de Sea uh Glass an' round de throne an' right cross God's nose thout tetchin' it. Jus' watch me."

He zipped off an' knocked down two or three lights an' fell intuh uh row uh dem vases an' knocked 'em all down an' skidded right upon de throne befo' he could git straight. God didn't say nothin'. He just looked at him. But Gabull knowed what to do. He come over tuh 'im an' snatched off his wings an' set 'im down so hard till it almost bust his robe, an' tole 'im: "Now, you set dere till I tell yuh to move, an' you ain't gointuh git no mo' wings neither."

His friends say, "Unhunh! We tole you you wuz gointuh keep on till you break somethin'. Now look at yuh. Ain't got no wings. Everybody got wings but you."

"Oh, I don't keer," he says, "but I sho wuz uh flyin' fool when I had 'em."

—Cliffert Ulmer.

When all the prophets died and all of them went to heaven and they all got wings, one day one of the angels opened the door and let Simon Peter and all the rest out and told them to be back at two o'clock. All of the rest of the prophets came back at two o'clock except Simon Peter. At three o'clock Simon Peter came back and knocked at the door of heaven. The doorkeeper asked who it was. Simon Peter said, "Simon Peter." The doorkeeper told him that he couldn't come in and asked him where had he been. Simon Peter told him that he had been flying around. The doorkeeper asked him then why didn't he come back with the others and told him that he had come too late and couldn't get in.

Simon Peter said, "I forgot what time to come back and I don't care if you don't let me in for I was a flying fool when I was in there."

—Ed Morris.

Once a stingy man died and went up to heaven. When he got to the gates Peter ast him whut good had he ever done. He thought awhile then he says: "One time I saw a little girl crying and I ast her whut's de matter, and she says I lost my neckel, so I give her three cents and went on."

Peter says, "John, look on de books and see if that's on dere."

John looked and says, "Yes, he done it."

Peter says, "Is dat all de good ye ever done?"

Says, "No, another time I seen a little boy crying and I ast him whut wuz de matter, and he said I lost my nickel, so I give him two cents and went on."

"John, see if that's dere." So it was.

"So dat all you ever done good?" So he said yes.

John says, "Is you goin' let him in, Peter?"

Peter thought a while, "No, give him his damn nickel back and let him gwan to hell."

—Christopher Jenkins.

Said there wuz a white man had a girl and she died, but he told her he would meet her in heaven. So after a while he went on up, but he couldn't git in.

Said there was a nigger up there flying around outside of heaven trying out his wings. So he met the white fellow. Tole the nigger boy, says, "Here's some dice. Let's shoot some for a dollar."

So the boy says he didn't have no dollar. White man says he'll shoot each wing for fifty cents. So he won the first fifty cents; so he decided to shoot again, so he lost that one, too. So he says, "Guess I'll try my wings again," so he throwed twelve. So he says, "Didn't I win?" and the white fellow says, "No, you know damn well you crapped." So de poor boy lost—that's all of that.

—CHRISTOPHER JENKINS.

You know, when folks die an' go up tuh heben, they has tuh keer long uh piece uh crayon an' God got uh great big blackboard an' He makes you go tuh de blackboard while John reads off yo' sins out de Big Book, an' you has tuh write 'em down. Den God looks over 'em an' if they ain't many an' ain't too bad, He lets yuh stay in heben. If not, you get sent on tuh hell.

Well, my uncle died 'bout twenty years ago an' went on up. He wuz uh big preacher an' everybody said he sho wuz gointer git uh good seat on de right hand side, right up tuh de throne. But last week somebody died an' went up an' met my uncle on de way back to de earth tuh git some more chalk.

—LARKINS WHITE.

There was a man went to heaven and a man told him if he start to stealing he would go to hell. And he said, "Each person in the world has a lamp, and if your lamp is low you are going to hell."

The man seen that his lamp was low, and he went to stealing oil out of the people's lamps, puttin it in to his—and he went to hell.

—DAVIS LEVERETT.

One time a man died and had uh brother, and his brother loved him uh whole lots.

So after he wuz dead, his brother called up heaven on the

telephone and ast tuh speak tuh his brother. Peter tole him tuh wait uh minute cause he didn't remember nobody of dat description, so he tole him tuh hold de line uh minute.

He tole John tuh look on de book an' see if dat nigger wuz dere. John looked but he said he couldn't find no trace uv him.

So he tole him he had better call up hell and see ef he wuz dere. So he called up hell and ast if his brother wuz dere, and de devil tole him, yes, he wuz dere, and had done got tuh be de head fireman.

—CLIFFORD ULMER.

Uh nigger died and went tuh heben de same day dat President Harding died. He walked up to heben and knocked on de door. Ole Peter says, "Who comes?"

An' he tole him, "One."

An Peter ast him, "Walking or riding?"

An' he said, "Walking."

They tole him, "We can't take nobody in here walking, you hafter come ridin'." So de nigger turnt round and went back.

Soon after dat he met President Harding going up tuh heben. So he tole him, "You can't get in dere walking, so you might just as well turn back an' git something tuh ride."

Harding stopped a minute, den he said tuh de nigger, "I got uh good scheme, you let me ride you on up tuh heben, and when dey ask me if I'm ridin' or walkin', and I tell 'em I'm ridin', and they'll tell me to come on in, an' I'll ride you on in an' we both will be there."

So he rode de nigger on up dere, and de Lord ast him, "Ridin' or walkin?"

An' he tole him, "Ridin'."

So God said, "Hitch your horse on de outside an' come on in."

—CLIFFORD ULMER.

John and Massa Tales*

---

*Hurston's original title for this section was "John De Conqueror." John the Conqueror is a mythic figure, famous for his skill in outwitting his master or the Devil.

During slavery time Ole Massa had uh nigger name John an' he wuz uh faithful nigger an' Ole Massa lakked 'im, too.

Somebody got tuh stealin' Ole Massa's corn, so he sent John tuh ketch'im. John saw de somethin' in dere breakin' off de years uh corn an' kep' droppin' 'em on de groun'. It wuz uh bear, an' yuh know uh bear can't hold but three years at de time. If he break any mo' he'll drop all over three. John saw 'im keep breakin' corn an' droppin' one, so he walked up an' picked up one uh de years an' says: "Jus' you break another one now and see whut I'll do tuh yuh!"

He thought it wuz uh man all dis time. De bear thowed down de corn an' grabbed John, an' him an' dat bear! John finally got 'im by de tail an' de bear wuz tryin' tuh git tuh 'im, so dey walked roun' in uh ring all night long. He wuz skeered tuh turn de bear loose cause if he did, de bear would git 'im. He wuz holding de bear's tail an' de bear's nose jus' almost tuh tetch 'im in de back.

Daybreak Ole Massa come out tuh see 'bout John an' he seen de bear an' John walkin' roun' in de ring so tired dey wuz jus' creepin'. He run up an' says: "Lemme take holt of 'im, John, whilst you run git help."

John wuz so tired, he says: "Come here, Massa, now you run in quick an' grab 'im jus' so."

Ole Massa took holt uh de bear's tail an' tole John tuh hurry. John staggered off an' set down on de grass an' fanned hisself wid his hat. He wuzn't studyin' 'bout goin' fur no help. He wuz too tired.

Ole Massa looked over dere at John on de grass an' he hollered: "John, you better gwan git help or I'm gwinter turn 'im loose."

"Turn 'im loose, den. Dat's whut I tried tuh do all night long, but I couldn't."

—JAMES PRESLEY.

Once in olden times Ole Marster had two niggers, one named John and the other one, Bill. John was his favorite nigger. He was worth twice as much as Bill.

One day Bill ast his Marster for five dollars and Marster told him he ought not to did dat—he ought to ast for two dollars and a half, because he had to give John ten.

Then Bill ast Ole Marster for a suit of clothes and he said: "Bill, you ought not to ast for a suit of clothes—you ought to ast for a pair of pants or a coat, because now I have to give my favorite, John, two suits."

Bill went out into the crib and went to shelling corn and said: "Lord, tell me something to git away wid Ole Marster." He prayed a whole hour, but de Lord didn't tell him a thing. He went off and he said: "I know what I'm going to do. I'm going down amongst the cattle." And he said, "O devil, tell me something to git away wid Ole Marster."

De devil popped up right away and said, "Oh, hell! Tell Ole Marster to knock out one uh yo' eyes, and you know damn well he'll hafter knock out both uh John's."

—JOE WILEY (variant of tale from Chaucer).

In slavery time Ole Massa had uh nigger an' his name wuz John. He uster go stan' in de chimbley (chimney) corner of nights an' listen tuh whut Ole Massa say, den he'd go nex' day an' tell de other niggers whut tuh do. Ole Massa had done made 'im his foreman anyhow.

One night he heered 'im say, I'm gointuh have dem niggers plow dat bottom tuhmorrow." Soon ez John got out nex' mawnin' he tole de colored folks, "Well, Ole Massa wants y'all tuh plow dat bottom land dis mawnin'. Hit de grit."

In uh few minutes Ole Massa come out tuh give de orders fuh de day an' he said: "Well, John I wants you tuh have 'em plow dat bottom land tuhday. He says, "Dat's jus' whut I done tole 'em."

They all looked at one 'nother cause they couldn't understan' how John knowed whut Massa wuz gointer say. Massa didn't know hisself, an' John kept on doing dat till finally Massa ast John how he done it. John made b'lieve he could tell fortunes an' read de mind, an' Ole Massa b'lieved 'im.

One day he says tuh John, "John, looka here. I done bet mah whole plantation on you. Me an' one uh mah frien's got tuh arguin' 'bout you cause I tole 'im you could tell *anything*. He said he bet he could fix somethin' you couldn't tell thout seein' an' so we got it fixed. He's gointuh be here in uh few minutes an' if you make me lose mah plantation, Ah'll kill yuh."

Well, after while they called Ole John an' they had somethin' under uh turnt-down wash-pot, an' Ole Massa says tuh John, "Now, John, you tell us whut's under dat wash-pot."

John didn't have de least idee whut wuz under dat pot. He walked round an' round dat pot an' scratched his head an' tried tuh see if he could hear anything tuh give 'im uh lead; but he couldn't git de slightes' thing. So finally he give up an' said, "Well, you got de ole coon dis time."

He thought sho he wuz gointer git killed, but Ole Massa give uh whoop an' kicked over de pot and hollered: "I wins, I knowed he could tell. John you gointuh git yo' freedom. Now I got two plantations 'stead uh one."

It wuz uh coon under de pot—but John didn't know it.

—Larkins White.*

After Massa winned offa John, he wanted tuh go way off on de water, an' he wanted John tuh stay wid Ole Missus; but John went tuh New York some way an' so when Massa stepped offa de train, dere wuz John waitin' fuh 'im in de station. He ast 'im, "How did *you* git here, John?"

"Ah run behin' dat train."

Massa wuz so took wid dat he didn't whup John. He jus' tole 'im tuh gwan back home an' stay wid Ole Miss. But John slipped on de boat an' hid hisself an' slipped off befo' Ole Massa did, an' wuz waitin' fuh 'im on de dock.

Ole Massa's eyes nearly popped outa his head when he saw John on de dock. He ast 'im, "John, how did you git cross de water?"

"Ah swimmed behind dat ship."

Massa called all de folks roun' dere to come see his John. He wuz wringin' wet jus' lak he been swimmin', but he had done wet hisself in de edge uh de water. Whilst they wuz all talkin' an' makin' 'mirations. John seed uh man out in de water uh swimmin' roun' an' cuttin' up. John hollered tuh 'im he said, "How long you been in dat water?"

Man tole 'im three hours. He said tuh Massa, "Massa, dat man can't swim none. Git me uh stove an' some wood an' rations cause Ah'm gointuh cook an' eat an' stay in dere uh month. Uh month ain't nothin' uh tall fuh me tuh swim."

He hollered tuh de man an' challenged 'im tuh swim wid

---

*In 1935, on a folklore expedition with Alan Lomax and Mary Barnicle, Hurston recorded John Davis's rendition of this tale.

'im. De man says he'll swim wid 'im cause he's de champeen over dere. Den John hollered back tuh ast 'im how much money he'd swim fuh an' de man says two thousan' dollars. By dat time Ole Massa b'lieves John kin do some swimmin' so he raises de man in de water tuh fifty thousan' dollars an' tole John tuh git ready an' if he lost his money he wuz gointuh kill 'im sho.

"Aw, Ah ain't gointuh lose yo' money, Massa. Jus' you git me de things Ah tole you, an' Ah'll beat 'im."

By dat time John wuz skeered tuh death cause everybody went tuh makin' preparations fuh de big swimmin' match, an' he couldn't swim uh lick. He hollered out tuh de man in de water, "Say, you betta git yo' self some vittles cause dis ain't gonna be one uh dem lil baby matches, jus' gittin out in de water an' playin' round six or seben hours. Cain't hardly git wet thew in dat lil time. Git yo' self some vittles tuh cook cause we gointuh be swimmin' fuh months, maybe uh year or two."

De man come out de water tuh look at John and he quit. He said he couldn't swim no whole day even—so John winned agin fuh Ole Massa on uh bluff.

—LARKINS WHITE.

There wuz a man in slavery time always meddling in everything he see. So finally de master said to him, "John, I want you to stay in this room all day and take keer of this box for me. Now, don't tetch it—don't bother it in no way, and I'll give you yo' freedom."

Ole Master had done put a young turkey under dat box, and left de window open so John could git some air. De box wuz restin' on a table.

Well, Master locked John up in de room and went off and set where he could watch.

John set there a little while, then he got to worrying about what wuz under dat box. First he come set side of de box.

Then he set on de box; last he got under de table trying to find out what's in de box.

Finally he couldn't stand it no longer and he lift up de box and out flew de turkey and right on out de window. John didn't know what to do.

After a little while Master came on in and said, "I see you can't mind yo' own business; so git back to hoeing."

—GEORGE MILLS.

BEAR IN DE CANE PATCH†

During slavery time Ole Master had uh cane patch and uh bear uster come stealing his cane. One night Ole Master see him himself. He had John along wid 'im, so John says, "Marsa, lemme go kill dat bear fer yuh."

"No, John, you might git hurt an' I don't want you all hurt up. You know I thinks uh whole heap uh you."

De nex' night ole John goes down dere atter dat bear unbeknownst tuh Ole Master. He had never seen uh bear up close, an' he didn't know how strong he wuz.

Dat bear grabbed John and wuz wearing him out er dis world, till John broke his holt and put out fuh de big house hollering "Ole Master" at every jump. Round and round dat house, John wid de bear right behind him. Ole Master heered de rookus and looked out and seed de bear an' shot 'im. Jes as soon as he done dat, John come on in de house and said, "Master, did yo' see de fine bear I brought you?"

"Why, John, I just killed uh bear I seen running round de house."

John made out he wuz so sorry. "Oh Master, you didn't kill mah bear, didja?"

"Why yes, John, why?"

"Why, Master, I had done conquered dat bear and wuz

bringing him up here tuh de house tuh be a plaything for yo' chillun."

—ROBERT WILLIAMS.

In slavery time Ole Marsa bought Jack an' took 'im home. Jack played green tuh everything.

While they wuz ridin' long they passed uh haystack an' Jack ast Ole Marsa whut it wuz. Marsa says, "Why, dat's my high tall mountain I feeds my cattle on."

When they got tuh de house de cat run out tuh meet Ole Marsa an' Jack ast 'im whut wuz dat. "Oh, dat's my red balls uh simmons, Jack."

They went inside de house an' dere wuz uh fire in de fireplace an' Jack ast 'im whut wuz dat. "Why, dat's my flames uh flapperation tuh keep me warm."

Ole Marsa went an' put on his bedroom slippers an' Jack ast 'im whut they wuz. "Why, dese are my flying trapeze."

Night come an' Jack saw Ole Marsa go tuh his bed an' he ast 'im whut wuz dat. "Why dat's my flowery beds of ease where I sleep. I ain't goin' tuh take you down tuh de quarters t'night. You kin sleep right in front uh my flames uh flapperation till mornin'—den I'll fix fuh yuh."

He made Jack down uh pallet on de floor in front uh de fire an' went on tuh bed. Jack went tuh sleep an' way afterwhile de cat come got on de pallet wid Jack an' he hauled off an' kicked her intuh de fire, an' she caught on fire an' shot outdoors an' right intuh dat haystack. Jack got up an' called Ole Marsa tuh tell 'im de haystack wuz on fire, so he said: "Marsa, Marsa!"

"Whut you want, Jack?"

"You better git outa yo' flowery beds uh ease, an' put on yo' flying trapeze, cause yo' red balls uh simmons done carried yo' flames uh flapperation tuh yo' high tall mountain."

"Whut you say, Jack?"

"I say you better git outa yo' flowery beds uh ease an' put on yo' flyin' trapeze, cause yo' red ball uh simmons done fell intuh yo' flames uh flapperation an' done carried it intuh yo' high tall mountain."

"I didn't understand whut you sayin', Jack."

"Aw, I said you better git out dat bed cause dat damn cat done set dat haystack afire."

—EUGENE OLIVER.

In slavery time Ole Massa wuzn't very good tuh John, so John got tired. So one day he made up a plot wid his buddy to fool Ole Massa. So dey put a whole heap uh groceries up a sycamore tree, so when Ole Massa come out tuh de field and started fussin' at John, John said:

"Ole Massa, I am tired de way you treats me. You works me befo' day an' after dark. I specks you gwinter be workin' me by de light uh de moon nex' thing. You don't half feed me. I'm gwine tuh God fur whut I want after dis."

"Well," said Ole Massa, "I feed you, don't I? God don't feed you, do He? So ef you don't do lak I say, you gwinter git plenty on yo' back an' starve, too."

John tole him, "No, I won't neither. I'm gwinter quit work right now an' go ask God for some rations."

So John went on over under de sycamore tree and fell down on his knees. His buddy wuz already up de tree. John begun tuh pray. He hollered, "O Lord, if I be your servant, send me down a sack uh flour." Down come de sack uh flour. "Now, Lord, please send your humble servant a side uh meat and a bag uh rice." Down come de rice and bacon. "Now, Lord, if I ask you tuh throw me down a sack uh meal and a sack uh sugar and a can uh lard and uh ham, if it be Thy holy and righteous will." Down come everything he ast fur.

Ole Massa's eyes wuz poppin'. He didn't know whut tuh do. John got up off his knees and tole Ole Massa, he said: "I'm gwinter git back down on my knees and ast 'im tuh lam dis place wid uh bolt uh lightnin' and kill all dese weeked white folks. B'lieve I'l ast 'im to 'stroy de world."

Ole Massa got skeered and tole John, "Now, don't do dat, John. Ef you don't ast 'im dat, I'll give you your freedom and forty acres an' uh thousand dollars." So he give it tuh 'im and that's how niggers got they freedom.

—FRED COOPER.

BIG SIXTEEN[†]

Back in slavery time Marster had a Negro named John. John was such they named him Big Sixteen. He told Big Sixteen one morning to go down in his pasture and ketch him dat wild hawg and bring him to him. He run dat hawg down and brought him to him. Marster thought that wuz pretty good, so he thought he'd try him out agin.

So next morning he wanted to put some new blocks under his house, and he had some twelve by twelves in his cow lot and tole him to go bring him one. Big Sixteen goes and puts dat twelve by twelve on his shoulder and brings it to the house, and next morning Ole Marster decided to try him agin. He tole him to go ketch up all his chickens and he caught all dat was roosting in yard and tree. How many?—two thousand.

"That was all, John, I believe you can ketch de devil."

John tole him, "Yeah, Marster, I kin ketch him."

Nex' morning Marster tole him to go ketch de devil. John tole him, "All right, Marster. Gimme a shovel and a ten eb hammer."

Marster gits him de shovel and de ten eb hammer and John walks out about two hundred yards in front of de house and commenced digging in de dirt—digging dis hole. Finally he come to de devil's house and knocked on de door and his wife ast him who was it and he told her Big Sixteen. He ast her was Jack de Devil dere and she said, "Yes."

"Tell him I wants to see him."

Devil cracked de door and peeped out and John tapped him in de forehead wid dat hammer and kilt him, and run in and grabbed him up and threw him crost his shoulder and carried him back to Ole Marster. His Marster tole him say, "I don't want dat ugly thing—take him back."

Big Sixteen took him back and threwed him in dat same hole dat he had dug and buried him. 'Bout two weeks later Big Sixteen died and he went to hell. Devil's wife and chillun saw him comin' and de chillun begin to run and hide, and de wife saw him coming so straight till she slammed de door herself. Big Sixteen walks up and knocks on de door and she ast who was it. He tole her Big Sixteen. She tole him, "Go way! Go back! We don't want you down here—you're too bad."

Big Sixteen goes on back. He goes to heben. When he got to heben he knocked on de gates. They ast who was it. He says Big Sixteen. They says, "Go on way from here. We don't want you here—you're too bad."

It was nowhere else for Big Sixteen to go. He had to come on back to de earth. His soul changed to a ball of fire. He is wandering round on de earth and they calls him Jack-o-Lanten; but it's nobody but Big Sixteen.

—JERRY BENNETT.

JOHN[†]

❧ In slavery time there was a colored man by the name of John. One day him and his Ole Master was going along and John said, "Ole Massa, I can tell fortunes." Ole Massa didn't pay him no attention.

They went on to the next plantation and he told the owner, "I have a nigger that can tell fortunes."

He said, "I bet you my plantation and all my niggers against yours that he can't tell fortunes." So they called a notary public and signed up the bet.

John was in misery all that night for he knowed he couldn't tell no fortunes. Every morning John used to get up and saddle his mule and Ole Massa's horse. Ole Massa had to get him up that morning. Going over to the plantation where the bet was on, John had been riding side by side with Ole Massa; but this time he rode behind.

So the man on the plantation had went out that night and caught a coon and had it sealed up in a box. So there was a many one there to hear John tell what was in the box.

They brought John out and he pulled off his hat and scratched his head and said: "Well, white folks, you got the old coon at last."

He meant himself, but everybody hollered, "It's a coon sure enough. John sure can tell fortunes!" So he won for Ole Massa.

Going back home he said, "Ole Massa, I am not going to tell any more fortunes."

Massa said, "I don't care if you don't, because you have made me a rich man. Now I am going to New York and leave everything with you. So in the fall you can sell or keep everything until I come back."

Him and his wife left for the train, went to the next station and got off.

So John told what niggers that was there to get on the mules and one to ride three miles north, the other one to ride three miles south, one to ride three miles west and the other to ride three miles east. "Tell everybody to come here; there's going to be a ball here tonight. The rest of you go into the lot and kill hogs until you can walk on them."

So they did. He goes in and dressed up in Ole Massa's evening clothes, put on a collar and tie, got a box of cigars and put under his arm and one in his mouth. When the crowd come that night and begin to dance, John told them he was going to call figures.* So he got the big old rocking chair and put it up in the bed and got up in the bed in the chair and began to call figures. "Hands up four! Circle right! Half back! Two ladies change!"

He puffed his cigar. When he went to say "Hands up four", Ole Massa walked in and said: "John, look what you have done. You have on my evening suit, up in my bed, done killed all my hogs, and got all these niggers in my house. I am going to take you out to that persimmon tree and break your neck."

"Ole Massa, can I have a word with Jack before you kill me?"

"Yes, but have it quick."

So he called Jack and told him, "Ole Massa is going to break my neck. Get three matches and get in the top of that persimmon tree. When I pray and ask God to let it lightning I want you to strike the matches."

So he got to the tree. Ole Massa had the rope around John's neck and put it over a limb.

"Now, John, have you anything to say before I hang you?"

"Yes, sir. I want to pray."

"Well, pray and pray damn quick."

"O Lord, here I am at the foot of the persimmon tree. If you are going to destroy Ole Massa tonight, his wife and all he has, I want to see it lightning."

Jack striked a match. Ole Massa said, "John, don't pray no more."

"Oh, yes, turn me loose so I can pray. O Lord, here I am at the foot of the persimmon tree. O Lord, here I am tonight calling on thee. If thou are going to destroy Ole Massa tonight, his wife and all he has, I want to see it lightning again."

Jack struck another match and Ole Massa started to run. He

---

*As in "figure-eights"; to call out moves for square dancing.

run so fast till it took an express train running at the rate of ninety miles an hour six months to bring him back home.

—JOE WILEY.

During slavery time Old Marsa had uh slave name Jack an' his desire wuz chicken. Dere wuz one ole rooster uster jump upon de fence right in front uh Jack an' crow jes' 'bout time he wuz knockin' off. Jack wuz layin' for 'im, too, but he couldn't git uh good chance 'cause somebody wuz around. Old Marsa wuz watchin' *him* whilst he wuz watchin' de rooster, but he didn't know it.

At las' one evenin' Jack got de ole rooster, and he said (sang): "Dat ole rooster sittin' on de fence, got 'im in mah arms at las'."

Ole Marsa come up an' said, "Yes, an' dat ole whip wuz hangin' on de wall, Ah got it in mah hand at las'."

—JAMES PRESLEY.

Ole John, you know, been stealing Massa's hogs. Ole Massa said to 'im: "John, somebody been stealin' my hawgs. I'd give a thousand to know who done it."

"Massa, it musta been a bear. I goin' ketch 'im."

So next night ole Massa missed another hog. "John, I missed another hawg."

"Massa, I sho goin' git dat bear." So dat night when John went out tuh git him a pig an' there was a panter after *him* uh pig. John said, "Whut you doin' down there after Massa's pigs?" So de panter took after John.

John run round and round de crib, and de door were open and John run under de crib, and de panter thought he went in, so he darted in after. John shut de do' on 'im.

John run tuh de house, called his master up. He ast, "Whut is it, John?"

"I caught dat thing been stealin' yo' hogs."

"Whut wuz it, John?"

"It was a panter."

"Whut you do with 'im?"

"I put 'im in de barn."

"O, gwan, John, you ain't caught no panter."

"I be damn if I didn't caught 'im."

His wife said tuh 'im, "Git up and go an' see. John wouldn't cuss befo' me dat way ef it wuzn't something." So he went and looked. Sho nuff, dere wuz de panter. So he went round nex' day and told all his neighbors about it, whut his nigger, John, did. So dey didn't bleve it, so, "I will show you dat John will go in an' ketch 'im an' bring 'im out."

So dey betted so many thousand on John. His master betted his plantation and all his niggers. Then he tole John: "Now, John, you go in and git 'im and bring 'im out and I'll set you free."

John keep uh standin' round de crib dere and Ole Massa kept uh urgin' 'im to gwan in. Say, "Massa, wait till I git fixed."* (He went in.) As John opened de do', de panter made a leap at John and struck his head ginst de do' facin' an' broke his neck. John seen dat and grabbed 'im an' wrasseled wid 'im. "Oh, I got yo! You varmint. I'm bringin' 'im out, Massa. Oh, I done break his neck."

"John, I didn't mean for you tuh kill 'im."

"Well, Massa, you ortu been fuh tell me."

Well, Massa won de bet. One man says, "I will bet yo' a million I knows where's a wile man John can't handle."

"I'll betcher two million John kin whip 'im."

John knowed where de fightin' groun' wuz gointer be. He goes down an' cut de roots uh de oak trees. So dat nex' day de

---

*"prepared" or "ready."

fight wuz to come off. (John wuz tuh ride his master's horse down. So he tuk an' cut de bridle reins, so when he pulled on it, it would break.) So nex' day dey went down at de fightin' groun'. It wuz late when John come. De man said dat betted against John: "Look lak John ain't comin'."

"Yes, John be here in a few minutes." Tureckly*, here come John just whut he could come on de horse. He rared back on de bridle-reins and dey broke. Dat wild man looked. John jumped down. John looked round and said: "Looka here, Massa, is dis de fightin' groun'?"

His master tole him, "Why yes, John, what's de matter wid it?"

"Whuss de matter wid it? Can't yo' see 'tain't 'nough room for uh man tuh move roun' in? We better clear it off uh little."

John begin tuh grab up de trees by de roots an' toss 'em roun'. De wile man looked on, got skeered (gesture with hands as of a quick departure.) John winned agin for his master so he give 'im a thousand dollars and set 'im free."

—DELLA LEWIS.

JOHN IN THE SMOKE-HOUSE†

Some one continued tuh steal Mister George's meat out of the smoke-house. The rogues had cut uh hole in de wall for their convenience. Mister George keep er missin' his meat, so he sided he'd watch and ketch de nigger dat is stealin' his meat. He tole his wife tuh give him his gun and his sharpest hatchet. (His wife gave him the gun and hatchet.) Away Mister George went for the smoke-house. Mister George got dere and waited for one, two and three hours. After while he heard de rogues comin'. De rogues come nearer and nearer till dey got to de smoke-house, and den dey laid down

---

*"directly."

right by dat hole. Dese rogues wuz a white man an' a nigger named John.

Mister George heard de white man say, "John, you put your hand through and git a ham, and den I'll put mine through and git a ham."

John put his hand through and jerked it out quickly, placing it behind him and said: "Now, Master, I got a big one. Now you put yours through and git another one."

The white man put his hands through and jerked it out quickly and said: "I'll be damn if it ain't cut off."

John said, "Mine is, too, Massa."

The white man said, "Well, why the hell didn't you tell me?"

John said, "I wanted you to git just whut I got, so I didn't tell you nuthin."

—Della Lewis.

JOHN AND DE HORSE†

Ole John, he wuz working fur Marster. You see, Master had uh horse an' had gi' John uh horse. John uster always hit Master's horse, but never hit his own horse. So then some white folks tole Master about John hitting his horse an' never hitting his own horse. So Master tole John if he ever hear tell of him hitting his horse, he wuz gwinter kill his (John's) horse. John tole 'im, "If you kill my horse, I'll beatcher makin' money."

One day ole John hit Marster's horse again. Dey went and tole Master about it. Marster come down dere wid a great big ole knife and cut John's horse's throat. John jumped down off de wagon and skint his horse and put de hide upon a stick and throwed it cross his shoulder.

John went downtown calling it a fortune teller. (He was a fortune teller hisself.) A man tole him, "Say, make it talk some,

John, an' I'll give you a sack of money and a horse and a saddle, and five head of cattle."

And John pulled out de stick and hit cross de horse hide and hold his head down dere. "Dere's a man in your bedroom behind de bed talking to your wife."

He went inside to see and come back out and said: "Yeah, John, you sho telling de truth. Well, make 'im talk some more."

"No, Master, he's tired now."

Then he said, "I will give you six head of sheep and four horses and four sacks of money."

He pulled out de stick an' hit down on it and held down his head to listen, and it said, "It's a man in de kitchen opening de stove." (De man went out tuh look.)

John went on by his Master's house driving his horse and sheeps an' hollering, "Yee! whoo pee! Crack! (Whip)

Master said, "John, where did you git all dat?"

John said, "I tole you if you kilt my horse, I'd beatcher makin' money."

Said tuh 'im, "Reckin if Ah killed my horse, I'd make dat much?"

"Yes, Master, I reckon so."

So Master went out and cut his horse's throat and took it to town. "Horse hide for sale! Horse hide for sale!"

One man said, "I'll give you twenty-five cents to put some bottom in some chairs."

Master said, "Youse crazy," an' went on.

Another man said, "I'll give you twenty cents to put bottoms in some chairs."

Master said, "You must be crazy, this hide is worth five thousand dollars." De people just laughed and he couldn't sell de horse hide.

So John, he's already rich, he didn't have to work, an' he went to driving horse and buggy for Master, and John let his grandma ride in dat buggy, and his Master said: "De nex' time I ketch your grandma in dat buggy, I'm goin' kill her."

John tole him, "If you kill my grandma, I'll beatcher making money."

Some white folks tole Master John wuz taking his grandma to town and hitting his horse, an' showing out wid 'im, so Master come out dere an' cut John's grandma's throat.

So John went and got his same ole horse hide and keered it uptown again. So John went uptown talking about, "Fortune teller! Fortune teller!"

One man tole 'im, "Why make 'im talk some, I'll give you six head of goats, six sheeps, an' a horse an' saddle to drive 'im wid."

John went on back by his master's house on his horse driving his sheeps and cattle. He jes' went by so Master could see 'im. So his Master said to 'im, "Oh, John, where did you git all dat?"

He said, "I tole you if you kill my grandma, I'd beatcher makin' money."

Master said, "You reckon if I kill mine, I'll make all dat?"

"Yes, Master, I reckon so."

So Master runned out dere and cut his grandma's throat and went uptown hollering, "Grandma for sale!"

Wouldn't nobody say nothin' to 'im. Dey thought he wuz crazy. He couldn't git nuthin' fur his grandma, so he tole John, "You made me kill my grandma, now I'm gwinter throw you in de river."

He got ole John in de sack and carried him down to de river, but he forgot his weights and while he wuz goin' after his weights uh toad frog come by dere and John tole 'im, "If you open dis sack and let me out, I'll give you uh dollar."

Toad frog let 'im out, so he got uh soft shell turtle and put it in de sack and two big ole bricks. So Master got his weights an' come back an' put 'em on de sack and throwed it in de river.

So ole John went back and got his ole horse hide and went back again calling it, "Fortune teller! Fortune teller!

One rich man said, "Make it talk some, John."

So John pulled out de stick and hit it an' said, "Uh man's in your kitchen in your meat safe."

De man went in de house and come back and said, "You sho kin tell de truth, make 'im talk some more, John."

"No, Master, he's tired now, I got tuh cair 'im home."

So John went back by his Master's house wid his horse an' uh sack uh money tied on de side of his horse. So ole Master said, "Oh John, where'd you git all dat?"

Say, "I tole you if you throw me in de river, I'd beatcher makin' money."

So he said to 'im, "Reckon if I let you throw me in dere, I'll make dat much money?"

John say, "Yes, Master, I know so."

John got Master in de sack an' carried 'im down to de river. John didn't ferget his weights. Put de weights on Ole Master, and just befo' he thowed 'im out, he said: "Good-bye, Master."

And dat wuz de last of Ole Master, cause he wuz crazy enough tuh let John throw 'im in de river.

—JULIUS HENRY (variant of a tale from
    Hans Andersen).

Master had got kinder good tuh Jack, an' let ole Jack stay in de house; an' he decided he'd go tuh town dat night—an' left Jack dere wid his wife.

While he wuz gone, Jack got in de bed wid his wife. Master forgot his pocketbook an' decided he wouldn't go dat night—he'd wait till tomorrow morning. So he turnt roun' an' came back an' hitched de horse an' knocked on de do', an' Jack says: "Who dat?"

"It's Marster."

Old Jack jumped up out de bed an' says: "Master, kin I have one of dem sweet potatoes?" He says, "Yes, an' one of dem buttered biscuits?" "Yes." He walked past an' said to Master's wife: "Wuzn't dat uh sharp turn?"

Master said to 'im: "Whut kinder sharp turn is dat yo' talkin' about?"

Jack says, "Nuthin, Master, just dropped mah biscuit and de butter side turned up."

—JULIUS HENRY.

Massa and White Folks Tales

SAMBO

One time Master had a nigger named Sambo. He had been working Sambo pretty hard. Sambo played sick for seven years and every time dey carried Sambo something tuh eat, he'd tell 'im, "Put de pan uh peas up, an' hand me down mah banjo. I done fooled Master seven years and specks tuh fool 'im seven mo'."

Sambo would have 'im up dere doin' de buzzard lope* and dancing, and den he'd have dem tuh pick de banjo and let 'im do de buzzard lope.

De people got tired uh totin' Sambo grub and tole Master 'bout it. Tole Master, Sambo wuzn't sick. Master didn't b'lieve it. He jes knowed Sambo wuz sick, and they tole him Sambo wuzn't sick cause he had dem up dere dancin' every day and picking de banjo, and tole 'im, say, "Ef, you don't b'lieve it, you go up dere tomorrow when we go tuh cair Sambo's dinner, and stand on de outside and listen."

So Massa went up dere and evedropped Sambo and heard him in dere dancing. So Massa walked in and Sambo stopped

_____

*A plantation slave-dance imitating a buzzard in flight.

dancing and said, "Is dat you, Massa? I'm gwinter ketch de mule now."
—CHRISTOPHER JENKINS.

Another nigger and his sone stole some meat from de white folks. So they caught 'em. Ole Massa says, "I'm going to whip you niggers till you own up."

De ole nigger says to his boy, "Take two hundred and keep you mouf." They lit in on de boy and they lashed him. His daddy kept on hollern, "Stand up to him and don't talk." So de boy took two hundred lashes and never cheeped.

Then they grabbed de ole man and tied him down and begin to lay it on him. When they hit him five licks he says, "Untie me, white folks, and I'm gwine git your meat for you."
—BABY-FACE TURL.

Once in slavery time Ole Massa had his niggers out workin'. Man, he uster work his niggers, too. So one day when he wuz out in de fiel' uh big rain come up. They all run into de barn, Ole Massa wid 'em.

Massa says, "I hates dat rain come up. I wants tuh git uh heap uh work did tuhday."

Ole John over in de corner say, "Mo' rain, mo' rest."

Ole Massa say, "Whut you say, John?"

John say, "Mo' rain, mo' grass."
—EUGENE OLIVER.

Dis nigger wuz workin' for a white man down in de new ground cuttin' up logs for wood. He set down all day long till he hear de boss man coming, den he hit on de log wid de heel of de axe. "Clunk, clunk, clunk, clunk—think I'm working, but I ain't."

De white man seen 'im, but he didn't say nothing. Sat'day night Sam come up to git his wages. White man took out a handful of silver dollars and shook them in de nigger's face and says, "Unh hunh—clank, clank, clank—think I'm goin' pay you, but I ain't."

—JERRY BENNETT.

OLE MASSA'S GUN

Once in slavery, Ole Massa had uh nigger he uster pet. He tole 'im once tuh go out and get 'im a deer. Some more niggers went long wid him, but Ole Massa let his favorite take his best gun.

When dey got out in de woods, dey sprung uh deer. De man dat had Massa's new gun waited down de hill, and another went up de hill and headed de deer down. He hollered tuh de one wid de new gun, "Here he come, shoot 'im!"

De nigger didn't pay no 'tention tuh him. He hollered again, "Sam, he's coming down, shoot 'im!"

Still he didn't make uh move. De deer run on past 'im and got clean away. De other nigger come running down de hill and ast, "Say Sam, why didn't you kill dat deer?"

Sam say, "Nigger, is you crazy, think I'm gointer sprain Massa's gun shooting up hill wid it?"

—WILLIE ROBERTS.

Ole Massa took uh nigger deer-huntin' an' posted him in uh place an' tole 'im, he says, "Now, you wait right here an' keep yo' gun ready. Ah'm goin' roun' de hill an' skeer up de deer an' head 'im dis way. When he come past, you shoot 'im."

De nigger said, "Yessir, Ah sho will, Massa." He sot dere an' waited wid de gun all cocked an' after while de deer come on past. Pretty soon de white man come on round de hill an' ast 'im did he kill de deer. De nigger says, "Ah ain't seed no deer pass here yit."

"Yes, you did, too, cause he come right disa way. You couldn't he'p but see 'im."

"Well Ah sho ain't seed none. All Ah seed wuz uh white man come long by here wid uh pack uh cheers on his head an' Ah tipped mah hat tuh 'im."

—LARKINS WHITE.

Once there wuz an old colored man and he walk long one day and he found a gold watch and chain. He didn't know whut it wuz, so the first thing he met wuz a white man and he ast de man whut wuz it. White man told him, "Lemme see it."

He give it to him and de white man put it in his own pocket and told him next time he found one like dat it wuz a gold watch, and the next thing he find kicking in the road put it in his pocket and sell it.

So he walked on down de road a piece further and walked upon a tarrypin kicking in de road. So he picked him up and tied a string on to him and put him in his pocket and let de string hang out.

So he met another colored fellow and fellow ast him, he says: "Cap, whut time you got?"

He pulled him out and told him, "Quarter to leben and kicking lak hell for twelve."

—WILL THOMAS.

Once uh white man took his nigger wid him tuh see his girl. He lef' de nigger outside in de buggy an' he went inside an' called on his girl. When he got ready tuh leave he ast fuh his hat, an' when he got tuh de door, he ast her fuh uh kiss. She acted lak girls do an' tole 'im: "Ah can't do so now; but maybe when you come agin Ah'll be able tuh gratify yo' wishes."

He said good-bye tuh her an' got in de buggy an' de nigger drove 'im on home; but he had done noticed whut de white man done. De nigger gal dat dressed de white girl, she wuz listenin', too, an' she heered all her mistis had done tole her feller; so when dis coachman come tuh see her an' he set uh while, an' when he got his hat tuh go, he ast her fuh uh kiss. She tole 'im: "Ah can't do so now, but nex' time you comes Ah hopes tuh be able tuh grabble in yo' britches."

—LARKINS WHITE.

DE WHITE MAN'S PRAYER[†]

Well, it come uh famine an' all de crops wuz dried up an' Brother John had prayed last year for rain an' it rained; so they all 'sembled at de church an' called on John tuh pray, an' he got down an' prayed:

"Lord, first thing, I want you tuh understand that dis ain't no nigger talking tuh you. This is uh white man talking tuh you now an' I want you tuh *hear* me. I don't worry an' bother you all de time like dese niggers, an' when I do ast uh favor I want it *granted*. Now, Lord, I want some rain. Our crops is all burnin' up, an' I want you tuh send rain. I don't mean fuh you to come in uh hell of uh storm lak you done las' year. You kicked up as much racket as niggers at uh barbecue. I mean fuh you tuh come quiet an' easy. Now, another blessing I want tuh ast of you, Lord. Don't let dese niggers be as sassy as they have in the past. Keep 'em in their places, Lord. Amen."

—JAMES PRESLEY.

You know, niggers is so skeered uh white folks dat one time two men wuz roofin' uh house an' one of 'em slipped an' fell off de house. When he wuz half-way tuh de groun' he give up tuh die; but he seen he wuz 'bout tuh fall on uh white woman—so he turnt right roun' and fell back upon dat house.

—LARKINS WHITE.

'Twuz uh white lady walkin' cross de street. Uh colored man stood looking after her as she passed by. She looked nice tuh him, so he said: "Long dere's life dere's hopes."

He didn't see a white man standing right behind him. So de white man said, "Yes, an' long as dere's a limb, dere's ropes."

—RAYMOND MCGILL.

In Mississippi a black horse run away with a white lady. When they caught the horse they lynched him, and they hung the harness and burnt the buggy.

—ARTHUR HOPKINS.

A HUNTER

Uh man wuz hunting before hunting season. De game warden slipped upon 'im and said: "I hafter arrest you fer killing game dat you oughten tuh. No need looking so wild and so fear, I have a thirty-two hanging right here."

Dis is whut de nigger told him: "Mister Game Warden, would you 'rest me fur dat?"

"I'll hafter 'rest you. I know jest where you wuz at. I could have 'rest you when you wuz comin' through towm, but I knowed damn well I'd have tuh run you down."

He taken him up to de courthouse and de gam warden said: "I have uh man fur killin' uh squirrel."

Judge: "Yes, we're not going to give him a whirl."
Game Warden: "We have uh man for killing a deer."
Judge: "We'll just have to give him one year."
Game Warden: "We have uh man fur killin' a quail."
Judge: "Dat's white folks' meat. We'll put him under de jail."
—FLOYD THOMAS.

Durin' slavery time they didn't 'low niggers tuh eat biscuit bread; but Ole Miss had uh cook dat uster steal biscuits an' eat 'em. Ole Miss had uh parrot dat roosted out in de kitchen an' tole her all dat went on.

One day, jus' as she taken some biscuits out de pan, she heard Ole Miss comin' so she hid de biscuits under de cushion in de cheer an' made out lak she wuz busy doin' somethin' else. De parrot saw her, but she wuzn't payin' him no mind. Ole Miss started tuh set down in de cheer an' de parrot hollered: "Hot biscuits, Ole Miss! Burn yo' behind*!" He kept dat up till she looked under de cushion an' foun' de bread. Then she had forty lashes put on dat cook's back.

Dat made de cook mad wid dat ole parrot, so one day when Ole Miss wuz gone away, she turned her clothes up over her head an' backed up tuh de parrot an' it skeered 'im so bad till he dropped dead. Ever since den, if uh parrot sees uh naked behind he'll drop dead.
—BERTHA ALLEN.

BIG TALK†

During slavery time two ole niggers wuz talkin' an' one said tuh de other one: "Ole Massa made me so mad yistiddy till I give 'im uh good cussin' out. Man, I called 'im *everything* wid uh handle on it."

---

*Originally typed "buttocks" but changed in the manuscript.

De other one says, "You didn't cuss *Ole Massa,* didja? Good God! Whut did he do tuh yuh?"

"He didn't do *nothin'*, an' man, I laid one cussin' on 'im! I'm uh man lak dis, I won't stan' no hunchin! I betcha he won't bother *me* no mo'."

"Well, if you cussed 'im an' he didn't do nothin' tuh you, de nex' time he make me mad I'm goin' tuh lay uh hearin' on him."

Nex' day de nigger did somethin', Ole Massa got in behind 'im an' he turnt round an' give Ole Massa one good cussin'. An' Ole Massa had 'im took down an' whupped nearly tuh death. Nex' time he saw dat other nigger he says tuh 'im: "Thought you tole me you cussed Ole Massa out an' he never opened his mouf!"

"I did."

"Well, how come he never did nothin' tuh yuh? I did it an' he come nigh killin' uh *me*."

"Man, you didn't go cuss 'im tuh his face, didja?"

"Sho I did. Ain't dat whut you tole me you done?"

"Naw, I didn't say I cussed 'im tuh his face. You sho is crazy. Man, I thought you had mo' sense than dat. When I cussed Ole Massa he wuz settin' on de front porch an' I wuz down at de big gate."

De other nigger wuz mad, but he didn't let on. Way after-while he 'proached de nigger dat got 'im de beatin' an' tole 'im: "Know whut I done tuhday?"

"Naw, whut you done—give Ole Massa 'nother cussin'?"

"Naw, I ain't never goin' do dat no mo'. I peeped up under Ole Misses drawers."

"Man, hush yo' mouf! You knows you ain't looked up under Ole Misses clothes!"

"Yes I did, too. I looked right up intuh her very drawers!"

"You better hush dat talk! Somebody goin' hear you an' Ole Massa'll have you kilt."

"Well, I sho done it an' she never done nothin' neither."

"Well, whut did she say?"

"Not uh mumblin' word; an' I stopped an' looked jus' as long as I wanted tuh an' went on 'bout my business."

"Well, de nex' time I see her settin' out on de porch I'm goin' tuh look, too."

"Help yo'self."

Dat very day Ole Miss wuz settin' out on de proch in de cool uh de evenin' all dressed up in her starchy white clothes. She had her legs all crossed up an' de nigger walked up tuh de edge uh de porch an' peeped up under Ole Misses clothes. She took an hollered an' Ole Massa come out an' had dat nigger almost kilt alive.

When he wuz able tuh be about agin he said tuh de other nigger: "Thought you tole me you peeped up under Ole Misses drawers?"

"I sho did."

"Well, how come she never done nothin' tuh *you*? She got me nearly kilt."

"Man, when I looked up under Ole Misses drawers they wuz hangin' out on de clothes line. You didn't go look up in 'em while she had 'em on, didja? You sho is uh fool! I thought you had mo' sense than dat, I 'clare I did. It's uh wonder he didn't kill you dead. Umph, umph, umph! You sho ain't got no sense atall."

—CLIFFORD ULMER.*

MOUFY EMMA†

During slavery there was a girl who tattled to the white folks. If the Negroes said just the smallest thing, she would run and blab it, so they named her Moufy Emma.

When she was sent to the well for water, she would stand

---

*In 1935, on a folklore expedition with Alan Lomax and Mary Barnicle, Hurston recorded John Davis's rendition of this tale.

around to hear what the other slaves had to say so she could tell it when she went back to the big house. But one thing—she was crazy about pomegranites.

She had got some slaves whipped to death and some others beat up pretty bad; so they decided to get rid of her before she killed any more—so they poisoned a pomegranite and laid it on the well.

As soon as she came to the well and saw the pomegranite, she took it and ate it. By the time that she got back to the house she tried to tell Ole Miss that some of the Negroes had been picking her pomegranites, her lips began to turn wrong side out and she died.

The next day, when they took her to the place where slaves were buried, they began to sing a little song:

"Same way you done Brother Jefiries
    Same way come back to you.
        Mouf is de cause of it all.

There's Brother Johnson laying over yonder
    Same way come back to you.

There's Sister Clue, too, laying over yonder
    Same way come back to you.
        Oh, mouf is de cause of it all."

They sang about all the graves of the people Moufy Emma had got killed, then they buried her still singing; and when they threw the last lump of dirt on her they said: "Mouf is de cause of it all."

—LOUISE NOBLE.

Once in slavery time Ole Master had a slave named John. One day John stole one uh Ole Master's sheep and took 'im home. Befo' he could git it on de fire he seen Ole Master coming. So he took it an' hid it in de baby cradle, an' when Ole Master got dere he wuz sitting down rocking de sheep, making out it wuz uh baby.

Ole Master come on in de house. He seen John when he tool dat sheep but he didn't let on. John wuz juster rockin' away. Ole Master ast him, "John, whut you got in dat cradle?"

John kept on rocking away and tole him, "It's us baby, Massa, it's uh new baby we got."

"Lemme see 'im, John."

"Naw, Massa, I can't let you see 'im. De doctor say not tuh take de cover offen him till he say so."

"You better let me see 'im, John. I might kin cure 'im."

"Naw, you can't, Master. De doctor says not."

"Well, John, I don't care whut de doctor says, I'm gwinter see dat baby uh yours."

John got up ready tuh run, an' he says to Massa: "Well, Massa, I put dat in dere uh baby. I don't give a damn whut it done turnt to."

—JAMES MOSELEY.

Tall Tales

THE UGLIEST MAN[†]

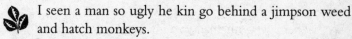 I seen a man so ugly he kin go behind a jimpson weed
and hatch monkeys.
—ARTHUR HOPKINS.

I seen a man so ugly he had to take a hammer to bed to
break day.
—JOE WILEY.

I seen a man so ugly he could git behind a tombstone
and hatch hants (ghosts).
—F. BRADLEY.

I seen a man so ugly they threw him in Dog River and
they could skim ugly for six months.
—ARTHUR HOPKINS.

I saw a man so ugly he didn't die—he uglied away.

—GEORGE HARRIS.

 I saw a man so ugly till at night when he get ready to go to bed he have to take a gatling gun with him to keep ugly from sittin' on him and killin' him.
—ARTHUR HOPKINS.

 Hey, fellow, I am going to tell you the truth. I saw a man so ugly until he could turn sweet milk into cherry wine.

 There wuz uh man so ugly dat he could crack all de lookin' glasses in uh town as soon as he got off de train.
—CLIFFERT ULMER.

THE MEANEST MAN†

 A man was so mean he greased another man and swallowed him whole.
—GEORGE HARRIS.

 I seen a man so bad till he had to tote a pistol to the pump with him to keep from getting in a fight with himself.
—EDWARD MORRIS.

I seen a man so bad till every time he set down he print "dangerous" in red on the chair.
—LORENZO MORRIS.

 I know a man was so hungry that he never ate no food, because it never would fill him up. He had to eat iron and bricks for his dinner, you know he was hungry.
—ARTHUR HOPKINS.

 No, man, that man wasn't hungry. I know a man was so hungry that he salted and peppered himself and swallowed himself and left nothing but his shadow.
—EDWARD MORRIS.

 I saw a man shoot another with a gun and the bullet worked de man twice before he died and three times after. If you hold it high, it sweep the sky; if you hold it level, it will kill the devil.
—ARTHUR HOPKINS.

 Once I wuz an engineer on a train and I had a friend and his nose wuz so big I thought it was a tunnel, and I ran up his nose and ran into another train, and it was switching box cars in his nose.
—F. BRADLEY.

 I knowed a man so smart he had the seven year itch and scratched it out in three months.

Whut's de fastest man you ever seed run? I seen uh man running so fast (away from de white folks) he turnt roun' and got in his own hip pocket, running so fast.
—Mae Oliver.

I've seen a man run so fast till de sheriff had to wire ahead tuh de people tuh hold 'im till his shadder got dere.
—F. Bradley.

Once there was a man so lazy until he would pray to God if there was any work around his heart, please cast it into the river of forgetfulness where it would never rise to condemn him.
—Arthur Hopkins.

THE TALLEST MAN†

Whut is de tallest man you ever seen? De tallest man I ever seen could stand knee deep in hell an' shake hands wid Gabriel.
—Eugene Oliver.

Whut's de biggest man you ever seen? Dat drives over me. I know a man so big dat when he went to whip his boy, de boy runned under his stomach and stayed hid under dere six months.
—Mae Oliver.

THE SHORTEST MAN†

I seen a man so low he had to git on a ladder tuh pick sweet potatoes, an' den he tuh reach up an' pull 'im wid a hoe.

—JULIUS HENRY.

Whut is de shortest man you ever seen? I seen uh man so short he had tuh get upon uh box tuh look over uh grain uh sand.

—ARTHUR HOPKINS.

THE STINGIEST MAN†

There was a man so stingy he used to climb upon top of the house and chunk the wood down the stove pipe to keep from wearing out his stove door.

—WILL HOUSE.

I know a man who wouldn't walk on moonshine nights to keep from wearing out his shadow.

I seen uh man so stingy dat he wouldn't eat uh ham sandwich out in de sunlight—skeered his shadow might ast him fur some.

—WILLIE CLARKE.

I seen a man so stingy when he killed uh hawg, he throwed uh sack over his head to keep him from squealing. Said he wuz losing pork.

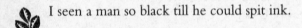 Whut's the stingiest man you ever seen? I seen a man so stingy he wouldn't give God uh honest prayer without snatching back amen.
—Eugene Oliver.

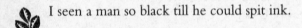 I knowed a man and he was foreman and he was so stingy that when three of his men on the job got blowed up, he docked 'em for the time they was up in the air.
—Joe Wiley.

THE BLACKEST MAN[†]

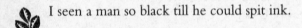 I seen a man so black till lightning bugs followed him at twelve o'clock in the day—thinking it's night.
—David Levritt.

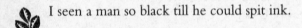 I seen a man so black till he could spit ink.

—Lorenzo Morris.

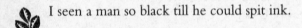 I seen a man so black till he could go naked and every-body would think he was dressed in deep mourning.
—David Levritt.

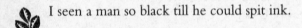 Ah seen a woman so black dat her husband had to spread a white sheet over her at night so sleep could slip upon her.
—Floyd Thomas.

A man had a wife and she was so small that she got in a storm and never got wet because she stepped between the drops.
—FLOYD THOMAS.

My old man had a cow. She give so much milk they had to build a platform under de calf to keep him from drowning.
—J. WILLIAMS.

I seen a cow so swaybacked that she could use de bushy part of her tail for a umbrella over her head.
—FRED COOPER.

THE FASTEST HORSE†

My father owned uh fast horse—I mean uh fast horse. We lived in Ocala. Mah mother took sick an' my father come an' said: "Skeet, you oughter wired yo' sister in St. Petersburg."

I tole 'im I just wired her an' he ast me whut I put in it, an' I tole 'im. He says: "Dat ain't right. I'm going ketch it."

He went out in de pasture an' caught de horse, shod 'im, curried 'im and breshed 'im and put de saddle on 'im, an' got on 'im an' caught de telegram, read it and took it tuh mah sister.

Mother said: "You chillun make uh fire in de stove an' fix somethin' for de ole man tuh eat." Befo' she could git de word out her mouf, him an' mah sister rid up tuh de do' an' said "whoa!"

That time uh flea ast me fur uh shoeshine—so I left.
—"NIGGER" HENRY BIRD.

My dad had a mare wid a lil colt and one day it come up a rain wid thunder and lightning and de lightning struck de mare and kilt her and run dat colt four days and nights and couldn't ketch him.

—JERRY BENNETT.

Dat same colt when he got bigger, my ole man hitched him to de plow to plow up some new ground, and he was so fast till he turned ten acres outside de fence.

—JERRY BENNETT.

THE POOREST HORSE[†]

Whut's de poorest horse you ever seen? I seen one so poor dat he had to stand in one place twice to make a shadder.

Oh, dat wuz a fat horse. I seen one so poor until de man drove him up in town in front o' de post office, an' got 'im uh letter and went round one side of de horse to read it in secret, looked roun'—twuz uh man on de other side de horse readin' de letter fast as he wuz.

—JULIUS HENRY.

I seen a horse so poor the man had to squat down to see if he wuz moving.

—JOE WILEY.

I seen a horse so poor you could wash clothes on his ribs and hang 'em up on his hips to dry.

—F. BRADLEY.

I seen a mule so poor they had to feed him on muddy water to keep from seeing through him.
—RUSSELL SINGER.

 I saw a horse so poor they had to tie a knot in his tail to keep him from slipping through his collar.
—CLIFTON GREEN.

 Wonce (once) there was a hen. She cakel (cackled) so much that she give the rooster the blues.
—WILL HOWARD.

Whut is the biggest chickens you ever saw? My father had some chickens so big you couldn't feed 'em on earth. You had tuh shoot their food up to 'em wid uh britch-loader (breechloading gun).
—JAMES PRESLEY.

"What's the best trained mule you ever seen?"
"I seen one so sensible he would carry letters, you didn't have to tell him where—he'd read de address and deliver it to de right place.

"I seen a mule could sit down and write letters to another mule and ast him how much corn he got."

"My paw had a mule working upon a fifty-story building and mule hauled off and fell off and got nearly to de ground. I said 'whoa' and he stopped right dere in de air and stood right there till somebody come rescued him."
—N. A. JAMES.

THE BIGGEST PUMPKIN[†]

Dis pumpkin wuz raised off of mosquito dust. My father went out in de woods tuh cut some timber, him and two three mo', an' uh rain come up. So dey went up under uh oak tree tuh keep out de rain.

It wuz uh great big ole tree. So big dat it took five or six men tuh reach round it. Well, my father wuz leaning up sidder de tree and uh big ole mosquito come upon de other side uv dat tree an' bored right through dat tree intuh my father's back an' got blood.

Dat made my father mad, so he bradded dat mosquito's bill right tuh de tree. By dat time, it had done stopped raining, so dey all went home.

De next day dey went tuh de woods and dat mosquito had clean up ten acres, dying. Dey went on home again, and about uh week after dat, my father went tuh de tree again an' he got enuff bones frum dat skeeter tuh fence in dat ten acres. An' dere wuz enuff dust frum dat skeeter tuh furtelize it.

So my father planted pumpkins de first year. He raised one pumpkin so big till he never could tell how high it wuz, an' we never did find how big around it wuz; even though we sent telegrams all round de world, nobody never did see de edge of dat pumpkin.

'Bout dat time my father lost uh fine brood sow wid leben pigs, an' we searched all over Florida and Georgie, and Alabama, an' everywhere, but we never could find her, till one day my father tole us boys tuh hitch up de double wagons and go haul one uv dem seeds to plant de nex' year.

When we dropped dat seed offen de wagon it bust and dere wuz dat sow an' two mo' broods, and everyone uh her pigs had pigs in dere.

—JULIUS HENRY.

My daddy raised a punkin so big we wuz six years building a shed over it. One day I dropped my hammer down in it and went down to look and I looked for two days. Then I went to a man and he ask me whut I wuz doing in dere and I tole him, and he said I might as well go back because he had been hunting for a mule and wagon for four days in dere and hadn't got no trace of 'em yet.

—N. A. JAMES.

My grandfather said that when he was a farmer he raised sugar cane so large that he would have to get an axe to cut it down; and that his watermelons would be so large until he would have to get a saw to saw the rind in two; and a pumpkin so large that Uncle Sam bought it to have the United States training camp in.

—JERRY BENNETT.

My father wuz a farmer and de most he raised wuz watermelons. He raised one so large he had to build a railroad down through de patch to load it on flatcars. When they got it loaded they sent it to Mississippi where it wuz awful dry. In unloading de melon out there it burst and the juice out of it caused the river to flood and drown all 'em people you read about.

—WILL HOUSE.

Whut's de biggest apple you ever seen? My pa raised a apple so big till they was shipping it out west and it fell in de Mississippi River, and it run cider for six months.

—JERRY BENNETT.

THE BIGGEST CABBAGE†

Whut is de biggest cabbage you ever saw? Ah seed one so big that it took de southern train twelve years tuh run round it. My papa growed dat cabbage.

Yes, an' my daddy built uh pot tuh hold dat lyin' cabbage yo' paw raised.

—NORA LEE AND LARKINS WHITE.

My daddy raised uh sweet potato so big they had to make a sawmill job out of it, an' all de houses was made outa tater slabs an' whut you reckon they did wid all dat sawdust? Made tater puddin'.

—JAMES PRESLEY.

THE BIGGEST TREE†

Dis William M. Richardson spreading his mess.

Whut's de biggest tree you've ever seen? Tell you 'bout one I saw. My ole man went out to clear some ground, and they wuz a tree out dere so big dat him and fo' mo' men wuz cutting on it uh week and hadn't got thew de bark; so he stopped chopping to rest a spell, and he went round to de other side and found ten men round dere been choppin' fuh six months and wuzn't half thew yet.

My other brother wuz a carpenter, and one day he went out in de woods and chopped down uh tree an' sawed it intuh timber and hauled it and built uh hundred story building, an' de man had done furnished it, and wuz suing some uh de people for back rent befo' de tree hit de ground.

—SODDY SEWELL.

In the year eighteen hundred my great-grandpa bought some land. And the land had a big tree on it. And my great-grandpa paid two men to saw the tree down. Before he died he gave it to my grandpa and the men was still a-sawing on the tree. Before grandpa died he give the land to my pa and the men was still a-sawing on the tree, and I got a letter today saying that the tree just fell.

—CLIFFERT ULMER.

RICH GROUND[†]

I have ground so rich until one day my father's mule died and he buried him out in the field. The next morning, guess what happened? The mule had sprouted little jackasses.

—JOE WILEY.

We wuz plantin' us crops very late dis year. Everybody had they stuff, but we wuz planting a mighty rich piece of ground. So he wuz a-dropping de corn and I wuz coming behind covering it, and by time we made one round a stalk de corn wuz coming up. I put my brother on it to hold it down. So de next day he drops me back a note, says: "Don't worry 'bout me cause I passed through heben yesterday at twelve o'clock selling roasting ears."

—LONNIE BARNES.

I seen ground so rich till dey plant corn on it and in a week's time, it done come up and have roasten ears on it. Roasten ears step down off de stalk and go tuh de mule lot and ketch de mules and hitch 'im up tuh de plow and lay by their ownself.

—CHRISTOPHER JENKINS.

This is T. Williams strowin' it.

Another time my ole man walked cross his farm wid uh cucumber seed in his pocket, and de land wuz so rich dat de air blowing over it sprouted dat seed in his pocket, and befo' he could git back in de house he had ripe cucumbers hangin' off 'im.

This is T. Williams strowin' it.

My father had a farm an' uh man give 'im uh grain uh corn tuh plant an' he took it an' planted it at de end of uh row, den he stuck uh stick dere fuh uh marker. Dat land wuz so rich dat nex' mornin' when he went out tuh look over de place, it wuz uh stalk uh corn wid ten ears on it an' three ears had done growed on de stick.

—T. WILLIAMS.

My daddy had some land an' it wuz so rich that one time he planted watermelons an' de vines growed so fast till they drug out de little melons.

—FLOYD THOMAS.

Down on Mississippi River I and my wife going fishing and it's a awful rich place on de river side. While fishing on one side, looking crost at de other, seen some good places to fish. But being there no way to get across, jes' thought of a seed I had in my pocket; so I dropped it into the rich soil and, going back after muh hooks jes' a few steps up de river, left my wife standing there where I dropped the seeds. When I got back to her, the seeds had come up and grown clear crost de Mississippi River and she had walked across de vine. When I got over dere on it too, she wuz over dere in de punkin on de vine; inside, lying down looking up de neck thinking about a sweet punkin tree.

—LONNIE BARNES.

THE POOREST GROUND

Ole Mitchell Field was de poorest land I ever seed. Dey bought uh lot on it tuh build a church. Built uh church, select de pastor, an' deacons, de members all together had to phone back to Jacksonville for ten sacks Commercinal to fertilize de ground befo' de could raise a hymn on it.—That's all.
—R. T. WILLIAMS.

I know an old colored man that had a plantation so poor it taken nine partridges to holler "bob white".
—JOE WILEY.

I seen a land so poor till dey had tuh put soda on people breast when dey bury dem so dey could rise in judgment.
—FLOYD THOMAS.

I saw a country so hilly till the squirrel had to put on britches to keep from breaking they neck.
—ARTHUR HOPKINS.

I saw a country so hilly till they had to shoot the corn into the hillside with a britch loader.
—ARTHUR HOPKINS.

HARD GROUND[†]

My daddy had a field where de ground wuz so hard dat one day he planted some peas, and a week later he went dere tuh see if de peas wuz growin', but he didn't see no peas; he went de next week, still no peas; and still no peas de third week; so de fourth week he went again and still he see no peas. But while he wuz standing looking around he heard something making a noise and he looked down, and it wuz de peas grunting, trying to git out of de hard ground.
—FLOYD THOMAS.

HARD WIND[†]

Seen de wind blow so hard whilst travelin along it blowed de crooked road straight and blowed a wash-pot wrong side outwards.
—WILL HOUSE.

One day de wind blowed so hard, till it blowed de sun four hours late.
—N. A. JAMES.

Another time it blowed so hard till it blowed South up North and had de North way down in Dixie.
—N. A. JAMES.

Another time it blowed so hard till a man had de catarrh and hadn't blowed his nose in fifteen years and it blowed his nose.
—N. A. JAMES.

What is the hardest wind you ever seen? I seen wind so hard till it blowed a man's nose off his face and onto the back of his neck and every time he sneeze, blow his hat off.
—N. A. JAMES.

One day on de West Coast sich uh hard wind come up dat it blowed uh wash-pot wrong side out, an' scattered de days uh de week so bad till Sunday didn't come till late Tuesday evening.
—CHARLIE JONES.

I seen it rain so hard a barrel settin' in de yard wid no head in it swell up and burst.
—LONNIE BARNES.

I seen it rain so hard till a buzzard wuz up in de air flying and his shadder wuz on de ground barking.
—CATHERINE HARDY.

I seen it so dry the fish came swimming up the road in dust.
—LONNIE BARNES.

DE DARKEST NIGHT†

My daddy had a forty-five high-powered rifle. I heard a rumblin' in de woodpile. Stepped tuh de do', shot out. I heard somethin' zooning aroun' de house all night. Got up real soon de nex' mornin' tuh see whut it wuz. Jes as day began tuh break, I seen whut it wuz. It wuz de bullet goin' roun' de house waitin' fur day tuh see which way tuh go.
—R. T. WILLIAMS.

THE HOTTEST DAY[†]

 I seen it so hot dat de li'dwood knots wuz crawling off in de shade.

 I seen it so hot till you had to feed the hens cracked ice to keep them from laying hard-boiled eggs.
—RICHARD EDWARDS.

 Whut's de hottest day you ever seen? I seen uh day so hot dat when de train from Miami pulled intuh Tampa, two blue serge suits got off de train. De men whut wuz in 'em had done melted an' run out.
—W. M. RICHARDSON.

 It wuz so hot once uh cake of ice walked away from de ice house and went down de street and fainted.
—RAYMOND McGILL.

THE COLDEST DAY[†]

 I seen it so cold till de fire wuz goin' somewhere to git warm.

I seen it so cold till dey had to build a fire under de cow to warm de tits.

The coldest I ever seen it, while being the age of twenty-four I saw de moon toting a light for de sun to keep it warm and show it de way to go home.
—WILL HOUSE.

Hey, boy, how cold have you know it to get?
Big boy*, I have known it to get so cold that you would have to carry a bucket along so when some one talked to you, you would have to put the words in the bucket and carry them home and put the bucket on the stove and let the words melt.

That wasn't cold at all. I have known it to be so cold that the fire in hell would freeze and the sun froze so hard that the ice just melted today.
—EDWARD MORRIS.

Once it wuz so cold dat when people talked, de conversation froze up. My brother wuz down to de jook and dey wuz all skinnin' an cussin', an' damnin', but de words all froze up and fell tuh de floor lak hail.

My brother got 'im uh crocus sack and gathered up all dem frozen words and took 'em home and poured 'em out in front of de fire, an' when they commenced tuh thaw out, his wife up and left 'im.
—ROBERT WILLIAMS.

---

*In her "Glossary of Harlem Slang," Hurston defines "Big boy" as "stout fellow. But in the South, it means fool and is a prime insult."

What is the biggest gate that you have seen? I have seen a gate so big that it took a train six days to pass, and the train was running a hundred sixty miles an hour.
—JOE WILEY.

THE BLACKSMITH

My brother wuz uh blacksmith. An' one day he saw uh horse runnin' away. He wuz comin' straight towards my brother's blacksmith shop at de rate uv ninety-thousand miles uh hour, and my brother measured him and heated some iron and made uh shoe and put in on dat horse fo' he could pass de do'.
—SODDY SEWELL.

My father made a boiler so big dat when he dropped his hammer, de handle had done rotted out befo' it hit de bottom.
—SODDY SEWELL.

Ah wuz passin' long uh fence an' Ah heered uh turrible racket in uh fence corner an' whut you reckon it wuz? It wuz uh seed-tick down dere wid uh splinter in his toe an' uh red-bug wuz pickin' it out wid uh fence-rail.
—LARKINS WHITE.

Whut is de workenest pill you ever seen? I'm gwinter tell you whut kind of a pill it wuz and how much it did work. It wuz an ole man one time an' he had rheumatism so bad de po' boy didn't know whut to do. I tole 'im to go tuh town and git some uh dem conthartic pills. As he wuz coming on back, he come through new ground where dey wuz clearin' up land. He opened his box and went to lookin' at his pills. He dropped one of dem down dere in his field. He got to de house and say, "Ole lady, look down yonder whut a big smoke," say, "whut is dat?"

She said, "I don't know."

"Well," he said, he guess he'd walk down dere and see what dat big smoke is down dere. He come back and says, "Guess whut it is? One of dem conthartic pills done worked all dem roots out de ground an' got 'em burning."

—JAMES BROWN.

Talking about fishing—I went to fishing the other day and set out my line. The water was very high; so that night the water fell and left two of my hooks and bait out of the water. And when I got there the next morning, a catfish had jumped up at the bait until he was washed down in sweat.

—JOE WILEY.

Once John D. Rockefeller and Henry Ford was woofing* at each other. Rockefeller told Henry Ford he could build a solid gold road around the world. Henry Ford told him if he would he would look at it and see if he liked it, and if he did he would buy it and put one of his tin lizzies on it.

—ARTHUR HOPKINS.

---

*In her "Glossary of Harlem Slang," Hurston defines "woofing" as "aimless talk, as a dog barks on a moonlight night."

My daddy went fishing one day and caught so many fish that he could not carry them home. And he was so bad that he called a alligator out of the water and made him carry him and those fish home. When he got home he told the alligator: "Now, rascal, you can go back."

—Louis Robinson.

My brother was so swift that the governor got him to work for the United States. And his job was sitting on the front of a train and turning the switch while the train was running.

Once we wuz on a train with some more boy friends and they got to talking about how fast the train wuz running which we didn't think it wuz running very fast; so I poked my head out de window to see how fast it wuz running and the steam from the locomotive wuz milking cows five miles from the railroad.

—Arthur Hopkins.

I got on the train in New Orleans and ast the boys wuz the train running fast.

"Sho, sho."

"Why, no," I says, "this train ain't running fast."

We jumped off the train and run to Mobile and ast the ticket agent wuz we ahead of time. He says, "Why, yes."

We jumped up and run back and met the train half way and rode on back to Mobile.

—Gennie Murray.

We seen the Alabama River running so fast till the fish had to back paddle with their fins to bite the people's hooks in Magazine Point.
—ARTHUR HOPKINS.

 On a hobo trip out in Texas one rainy night we were going down de track thout orders and we had passed de station where we wuz stopped to get our orders. When we found we had passed de engine blowed for de orders at de next station. When we got to de next station it wuz too late for de engineerman to get them, so the conductor and de caboose got 'em, wondering how he wuz going to get 'em to the engineerman without stopping. So the brakeman told the conductor, "You got to go round dis bend." The engineer met de caboose at de other end and got de orders.
—WILL HOUSE.

 I seen a railroad so crooked till de fireman be throwing coal in de headlight instead of de fire-box.
—ARTHUR HOPKINS.

 My father sent me and my brother tuh de grist mill. We gits tuh de mill, but so much corn ahead uh us till it overlaid us and caused us tuh be night gittin' home.

On our way back home dat night, we passed a cane patch. I repeated tuh him, "Ooo brother, whut nice cane!" I said to 'im, "Say, looka here, we want some of dat cane."

He said, "We must have some," and we 'cided we'd go dere an' we went in. We cuts us a great turn of dat cane apiece, an' we started back into de car wid de cane. And between de cane patch and de highway, there wuz a mud-mash, and goin' thew dis mash de man fired uh gun, and firin' uh dis gun, we made such uh dash forrunnin' dat us bogged down an' breaks our legs off even wid our knees. But we didn't stop—we kept right on runnin'. We built a fire an' we chewed thirty-five or forty stalks of cane apiece. After chewin' it, we decided tuh lie down, rise soon in de mornin' by de four o'clock whistle. Then finally we had missed our feets when we reached down tuh git our shoes—we had run so hard dat we had lost our feets in de mud-mash.

—ROBERT BAILEY.

I wuz gwine long one day cross de wood. I seen two blocks of ice come running and they were gatherin' li'dard knots to make up uh fire and warm. I had tuh go he'p 'em cause I wuz 'bout to freeze tuh death.

—JOHN BIRD.

There was once a man had a plantation up de country and de houses wuz built on each side of de creek, and they had a burning there—houses on both sides caught fire— and de creek got so hot, after the burning you walk along and pick up done (cooked) trouts.

—JOE WILEY.

Went down to the river today, took one match, set the river on fire. Burned it half up, took the other half of the water and put the fire out.

—JOE WILEY.

One day I was going through a field and I saw a man tie a butt-head cow's horns to a tree.

—CHARLEY BRADLEY.

I went down tuh de river wid my suit-case an' I couldn't get cross, an' I wuz in uh hurry, too. There wuzn't no bridge or nothin'. So I pulled out my forty-four forty an' fired it off an' jumped on de bullet an' went cross; but I had done lef' my suit-case. So I come back cross on de echo an' got it an' went back cross on de smoke.
　　—EUGENE OLIVER.

Once I wuz out batching, so I come in one evening, wuz kinda tired and made my fire. I forgot just how to put in mah seasoning, so I put in two boxes baking powder, one box soda, sack of salt, and made 'em up and put 'em in de oven and put mah lid on top mah oven. I went out to pick up some more splinters to put on top, and when I come back they wuz rising out through de top of de chimbley. So I went and got me a ladder to go on top de house to hold 'em down, and they riz so high wid me, took me twelve months to come down off de top of 'em, eating my way down.
　　—LONNIE BARNES.

I wuz lost in de woods, and I wuz lost teetotally. I heard uh racket over in de thicket. I looked behind a log. It wuz de moon changin'.
　　—RAYMOND McGILL.

The largest sawmill I ever saw was thirteen stories high at a place by the name of Diddie War Diddie* owned by Jack. It had one band saw that extended through the thirteen

---

*In her "Glossary of Harlem Slang," Hurston defines "Diddy-wah-diddy" as "a far place, a measure of distance" and "another suburb of Hell, built since way before Hell wasn't no bigger than Baltimore."

stories. The fly was so large that every time it made a revolution it was pay-day, paying off by the month.

So being in this town I visited the plant. Jack weighed two thousand pounds and his wife nineteen hundred. While there, they had a son born to them weighing only four hundred pounds at birth. So Jack ordered him killed—said he didn't want no runts in the family.

So I goes up in the mill to the twelfth story and his daughter was setting head blocks on the carriage.

So one of the workmen taken me in the mess hall, and there was a molasses river running through the kitchen and a carriage hauling flapjacks and turning them with a steam nigger.

So it was payday and Jack had forty train loads of money switched in to pay off. Just after paying off, they started to playing the game they call skin*. So on that night John D. Rockefeller and J. P. Morgan came in and stopped the cards and said: "Put up a box car of money, two and one."

The boys that worked for Jack said, "You can go in the kitchen. The cook and chauffeur are back there spudding (playing for small change)."

—Joe Wiley.

One time my uncle he belongst to de church. He wuz an ole member of it. So dey thought dey's put him to doing something, him belongst to it so long. So dey put him to overseeing de young folks. So one night he says, "Son, less me and you go to church." So I tole him I didn't keer if we would.

So we went out and got in de ole Ford and he tole me to jump out and twist de tail. So I jumped out and twisted it—we

---

*Hurston includes a lengthy explanation of a "Georgia Skin Game" in the glossary for *Mules and Men*. The game involves "two 'principals' who do the dealing" and a group of players or "pikers."

drove on. So we got to church about ten o'clock, so wese comin' on back, it wuz two boys stayed in de house mighty rowdy. So he drove on by and stopped and he says, "Son, spose we go in here and see whuta all dis noise in here." I told him I didn't keer if we did.

So he went in and opened de door. First thing I looked at wuz uh forty-five pointed directly. So I curved round and in de old Ford. When I looked in de back, mah uncle wuz in dere, too. Course we didn't makin' but forty-five. I told my uncle I think we kin beat dis heah. So we runned de Ford outside and jumped out. Course we didn't run none but we passed some people whut wuz running. And so a Chrysler got in de way and hit stayed in de way 'bout fifteen minutes. So we got home and went on and went to bed. So I woke up 'bout four hours and fifteen minutes after I got dere and I saw something dartin' by de window. So I hunched my uncle. I tole him to wake up. He says, "Whut's de matter?"

I says, "Look to me lak we havin' trouble here."

He says, "Whut?"

I says, "Don't you see dem people dartin' by de window out dere?"

He said to me, "Git up and see whut 'tis." I looked at him and he looked at me. I tole him to make de thing more better less both of us git up and go see. So he looked up over de door and got his Winchester, cause he hadn't had it but 'bout seventy years, and I grabbed de do' and opened it wide and he thowed de Winchester right in de middle uh de do'. So we looked out and it wuz jes' our shadders four hours and fifteen minutes late getting home.

—WILL THOMAS.

Man went tuh huntin' wid one uh dese muzzle-loaders. He didn't have but one load uh ammunition an' he saw two wild turkeys settin' up in uh tree, an' right over in uh pond he saw some wild ducks, an' over by de pond he saw uh deer an' he heard some noise back of him an' he looked round an' seen some partiges (quail). He wanted all of 'em an' he didn't know whut tuh do. So he stood an' thought an' thought. He took aim, but he didn't shoot at de turkeys, he shot at de limb they wuz settin' on an' de ball split dat limb an' let dem turkeys' feet drop right down thew de crack an' de limb shet up on 'em an' helt 'em right dere. De ball went on over an' fell intuh de pond an' kilt all dem ducks; de gun bust an' de barrel flew over an' kilt dat deer an' de stock kicked de man so hard till he fell backwards an' smothered all dem partiges.

He seen he couldn't tote all dat game home so he went home tuh git his team. He tole his wife tuh put on de pot cause plenty rations wuz comin'. He loaded up de wagon, but he didn't git in, cause he figgered de mule had enough tuh pull thout him. Jus' as he got his game loaded it commenced tuh rain, but he walked on side uh de mule tellin' 'im tuh come up till dey got home—about three miles.

When he got dere his wife ast 'im where wuz de game he wuz talkin' 'bout an' he looked back an' seen his wagon hadn't moved from where he loaded de game. De rain had done made dem traces stretch. So he jus' took de mule out an' wroped dem traces round de gate post an' put de mule up an' went on in de house. De nex' day it was dry an' de sun wuz hot an' it shrunk up dem traces an' about twelve o'clock they brought dat wagon home "cluck-cluck, cluck-cluck" right on up tuh de gate.

—LARKINS WHITE.

DE HONGRY BEAR†

My father wuz out huntin' an' he seen uh hongry bear makin' dead at 'im. He ups wid his gun an' fired, but he missed 'im an' de bear kept right on comin' so fast he didn't have no time tuh load uhgin. When de bear made tuh grab 'im, he run his hand down de bear's throat and clear on thew de bear and out de other end, an' caught hold uh de bear's tail an' give sich uh jerk till he turnt dat bear wrong side out, an' he wuz runnin' de other way (the bear was headed the other way.).

—JAMES PRESLEY.

 Uh man went huntin' one day. He had one load, an' all de shot he had wuz one bullet in de gun.

He saw fifteen wild turkeys on one limb. He wuz afraid he would miss 'em, so he went on.

He saw a bear, and wuz afraid de bullet wouldn't kill de bear—an' he went on.

He saw a cuvey of quails, and he wouldn't shoot at dem— and he went on.

He saw a deer, and wouldn't shoot at him.

He 'cided he'd go back and try de turkeys. So he did.

He took a good aim and split de limb, and caught all de turkeys by de feet. De ball went on and struck de bear, and in his scuffle he killed all de quails. De ball went on and killed de deer. De deer fell in de pond and knocked out fifty bushels of fish. De ball went down de river swamp and cut down uh honey tree. De tree fell cross de river and de honey sweetened de river ten miles up and ten miles down.

—JOE WILEY.

My father wuz a hunter, and whenever he seen a deer he would run along side of him tuh feel him to see if he wuz fat uh-nuff 'fore he'd kill 'im.

Whenever he'd shoot in target practice, he'd shoot and den go put up a target fur de bullet tuh hit after he shot. He uster git round pretty fast.

—FLOYD THOMAS.

I seed de coach whip behind de race runner one day and dey was running so fast de race runner set de broom sage uh fire, and de coach whip wuz sweatin', and de coach whip put it out wid his sweat; and de race runner hopped in de river, and de coach whip hopped in behind him and they had to sprinkle de river, and outen de dust so he could swim. By that time de dust choked me so I had tuh leave.
—John Bird.

My pa had a gun dat shoot so far he had to put salt down de barrel before he shoot it, so de game he kilt wid it would keep till he got dere.
—E. Edwards.

A man went hunting and saw three thousand ducks in a pond. Just as he levelled his gun to fire, the weather turned cool and the water in the lake froze solid, and them ducks flew off wid de lake froze to their feet.
—Peter Noble.

Two mens went out rabbit huntin' an' after they went a lil way, one said tuh de other one: "We needs yo' dawg tuh jump dese rabbits fuh us. We ain't got no gun."

De other one says, "Thass all right. Ah got uh dawg in mah pocket dat'll jump all de rabbits we needs."

"Uh dawg in yo' pocket! Man, you cain't keer no dawg in yo' pocket dat kin ketch no rabbits."

"Thass all right, you jus' wait till we needs uh dawg an' you'll see."

After while dey seed uh rabbit an' de man retched in his pocket an' hauled out de dawg an' set 'im down on de ground.

He wuzn't no biggern yuh fist, but, man, he could cold* stroll behind uh cotton-tail. He got behind uh rabbit an' he wuz runnin' him so fast he run intuh uh tree an' split hisself wide open. De other man said, "Now, whut we goin' do?"

His friend said, "Thass all right, he kin be fixed."

He took an' picked dat dawg up an' stuck dem two sides uh dat dawg tuhgether; but he done it so quick dat he stuck one side upside-down, so dat he had two foots up an' two foots down, an' one-half uh his tail wuz stuck tuh one side uh his head—an' no matter which uh-way de rabbit run he didn't have tuh turn round a-tall—he wuz headed right data way.

—LARKINS WHITE.

---

*In her "Glossary of Harlem Slang," Hurston writes that "cold" means "exceeding, well, etc., as in 'He was cold on that trumpet!' "

[Mosquito and Gnat Tales]

SKEETER AN' DE HOMINY POT[†]

One day down in Texas I went out huntin', but de mos-quitoes wuz so bad till I had tuh run. After while I seen uh ole hominy pot an' I took an' run under it an' turnt it down over me tuh keep off de skeeters. But you know, one uh dem skeeters bored right thew dat pot an' bit me, an' dat made me mad; so I turnt round an' bradded his bill intuh dat pot an' he wuz so big he flew on off cross Galveston Bay wid dat pot bradded on his bill.

—LARKINS WHITE.

Once in my home, too, it wasn't any trees. That was be-tween New York and Chicago, and so it had came a storm and had washed up the railroad track. So the train had to be there in fifteen minutes time and so they didn't know what they wuz gointer do, and up came a skeeter. He wuz so large that they decided to take this musskeeter and make the railroad track outa him. So they taken his feets and made de tires, and taken his bill and made de steel and so that throwed de train to be there in fifteen minutes time.

—LOUIS ROBINSON.

In Louisiana a man was clearing up new ground. The way he would do, he get out where the mosquito could see him, and when the mosquito got after him, he'd run and get behind a tree, and when the mosquito strike at him through the tree, he'd brad the bills and the mosquito would fly off wid de tree.

—Joe Wiley.

Another time we had some tin suits tuh keep de skeeters off us an' they went off an' fetched back can openers an' got us jus' de same.

—William Richardson.

Once there wuz a boiler across de river. They wanted to get the boiler on this side. Mosquitoes were so bad that nobody could stay over there no time. They had a reward of one thousand dollars for de one who brought it across.

So a man got him a sledge hammer and went over there and got into de boiler. Every time a mosquito would pop a bill into de boiler, he would brad it down. So many mosquitoes wuz there they picked up dat boiler and flew across de river.

—Edward Morris.

29 run a hot box between Lakeland and Plant City, and fireman wuz out helping him (the engineer) and de steam died down. He wuz trying to git up steam to make it to the station on time. Mosquito flew long an' blowed de train into Loughman.

—R. T. Williams.

It was a man who lived in the country. One day he was driving some oxen. So he drove the oxen up to the front of my door to get his supper. So he went in and ate his supper, and when he come out the mosquitoes had done ate up his oxen and was sitting on the wagon picking their teeth with the oxen horns.

—WILLIAM RICHARDSON.

I thought I heard an airplane. I looked up and seen it wuz a mosquito. He made at me. I dodged behind a tree. The mosquito broke off his bill in de tree and reached back in his pocket, got another one, screwed it on and went on 'bout his bizness.

—R. T. WILLIAMS.

Me an' my brother went off on uh journey an' when night come we stopped at uh house an' got uh room for de night.

Soon's we turned in de mosquitoes started tuh plagueing us. They was so big they sounded lak a bull lowing. We covered up all over, even our heads, under four blankets an' we could hear 'em flyin' roun' tryin' tuh git tuh us. T'reckly (directly) we heered 'em goin' on off but we was skeered tuh uncover ourselves. Pretty soon we heered 'em comin' back an' we peeped out. Everyone uh dem skeeters had uh little leather bag in his hand flyin' along. When they all got back in de room, they set down de bags an' screwed off them short bills an' took they long bills out them baggs an' screwed 'em on, an' bored right through dem blankets an' got us.

—WILLIAM RICHARDSON.

Me and my buddy went out on a hobo trip and so we come cross a logging camp, 'cided we'd work some, ast de man 'bout a job. So he give us a job loggin', give me uh five yoke ox team, my buddy a six ox team. So we goes into the woods and loads up waggins.

As we wuz coming on back we heard a little something coming through de woods singing. We stopped to see whut it wuz. Whilst we wuz stopped a little black gnat come along. He eat up de six ox team, de five ox team, got one of de horns, got upon de wagon, blowed for eleven more yokes.

—Lonnie Barnes.

I wuz coming from Birmingham going to Montgomery and a car passed me making eighty-five miles a hour. I looked under the steering wheel and I didn't see no man. Got in Montgomery a mosquito had held him up for over speeding. Looked on the steering wheel, it wuz a flea. Put him in jail and it cost him twenty-five dollars for speeding.

—Douglas Shine.

Neatest Trick Tales

A man had three daughters and he was going out huntin' tuh git 'em something tuh eat. So he ast 'em all whut they wanted him tuh bring 'em back. De oldest one tole 'im, "I sho would love a nice rabbit tuh fry."

De nex' one tole 'im, "My mouf is just set tuh smack on a nice, fat cottontail."

De baby tole him, say, "If you don't bring me uh rabbit, I ain't gointer eat uh moufful uh nothin' else."

So he went on out tuh de woods wid his gun, but game wuz scarce. He didn't git but one rabbit and so he had tuh gwan home wid dat. When he got home they all ast him did he bring 'em uh rabbit. He tole 'em, "Well, I ain't got but one so y'all have tuh 'vide it de best way yuh kin."

They wouldn't do dat. Dey all wanted de whole rabbit, so he didn't know whut tuh do.

Way after while he tole de one whut did de sharpest trick could have de rabbit. They said all right.

De first one, she helt up a needle and urinated right through de eye and never touched de sides. De old man says, "Dat's uh sharp trick and I don't see how it kin be beat."

De next one, she urinated in uh thimble and never run it over. He thought dat was swell.

De last one she took uh hick'ry nut and thowed it up in de air and turned up her dress and broke wind and cracked de nut and blowed de goody right slap in de old man's mouf. He smacked his mouf, (gesture of tasting) and says, "You wins de rabbit."

—EUGENE OLIVER.

Once there was three girls went to huntin'. They saw a rabbit and all of them shot at the rabbit, and all of them said they killed it.

So they carried it to the court and the judge said that the one that done the sharpest trick could have the rabbit.

One girl up and poured water through a needle's eye and never touched the sides.

The next one poured a bucket of water in a thimble without running it over.

The last one picked up a hickory nut and threwed it up in the air and took aim and shot it and bust it open and spattered the goody in the judge mouth. He tasted it and says: "You win the rabbit."

—HENRY EDWARDS.

Once there was a man had a daughter and three fellows wuz courtin' her. All of 'em asked for her at de same time and they were all good clean boys. He didn't know what to do, so he said: "I'll give her to the one dat does the quickest trick."

De first one went out and cleaned up a forty acre new ground, broke it up and planted it and had roasting ears for breakfast.

The other one said, "I can beat that." He went one mile

down de road to a spring after water in a cedar bucket and came back and caught de water before it hit the ground.

The other one said, "See what kin I do." He went into the house and got a Winchester. He went out and shot de gun, laid it down and run, overtaken de bullet and brought it back and give it to de girl's pa. So he got de girl.

—LONNIE BARNES.

I wuz courtin' uh man's daughter once, me an' another feller, an' her daddy caught us arguin' 'bout her one day, an' so he said de one dat told de biggest lie could have her. So I said, "Stick uh needle up in de ground an' put uh dime behind it edgeways, an' I kin drive uh Ford right thew de eye uh dat needle an' turn roun' on dat dime an' still have uh nickel change."

—EUGENE OLIVER.

Me and my girl was sitting under a tree fishing one day. A big rabbit jumped in front of us. My girl said, "Oh, how I would like to have a ham off that rabbit."

I gave her my coat, I gave her my shoes, I shot my pistol, I caught up with the bullet and told it to go back and get into the pistol because I had the rabbit.

—PETER NOBLE.

"Mr. Hill doing it."

It wuz once an old man had three sons and they all was off. One wuz naked, one wuz blind, one wuz armless. So de one whut wuz blind he jumps a rabbit; one didn't have no arms kotch 'im; one wuz naked grabbed 'im and put 'im in his pocket.

So they wanted to know from the father which one the rabbit belong to. So he says, "Well, I don't know. The one that can do the sharpest trick."

One shot a rifle and beat the ball to the tree and cut a spot where it could hit. The other two says, "Father, we can do better than that."

So one of 'em says, "I see a red bug in England."

The other one says, "I see his eyes."

—LARKINS WHITE.

A man had seven sons and he sont 'em all off to school, and he had one girl.

An' he had called his boys up an' sont dem to school. One wuz schooled to be a machinist; one a blacksmith; one a mechanic; one a spier; one a crack-shot; and de other wuz a rogue; and one a gluer.

After dey returned back home, father axed dem did dey all have dere learnin'. Tole 'em dat since dey had been gone, de eagle had stole they sister.

Spier axed 'im which way did dey go. He tole 'im dat wuzn't no use to ast 'im cause he couldn't see dat fur.

He got up on top uh de house, put on his spy glasses and tole 'im, "Papa, I see 'im. Eagle has a place in uh fork of a limb cross de deep blue sea."

Tole his carpenter, "Great God, make me a boat!"

Tole his moulder, "Mould me uh motor."

Tole his gluer, "Glue it together."

"All right, boys, let's go cross."

Tole his spier to look see what de eagle wuz doin'. "Papa, she's watching de boat." Rogue axed 'im to stop de boat an' let him out.

Tole de spier look back see whut de eagle is doin'. "Papa, she's comin'."

Tole de crack-shot, "Gun in order."

Said, "Papa, I see 'im."

Tole de spier, "See how fur she is from us now."

"Papa, she's right over dere."

Crack-shot reformed his gun, shot de eagle, but he bust de boat and the gluer jumped down, glued it back together before air drop uv water got in it. That's all that is.

—R. T. WILLIAMS.

Mistaken
Identity Tales

In slavery time there was a man by the name of Tom and he always had prayer before going to bed, and his prayers was always for God to take him to heben away from his hard taskmaster. And his master gone down through the quarters various times and listened to Tom's prayer.

So one night he decided to have some fun offa Tom. So when he was in this prayer, his master knocked on the door, representing himself as the Lord.

In a flat way Tom said to his wife, "Ast who dat."

His master said, "This is God Almighty come to keer Tom to heben."

Tom told his wife, "Tell God I'm not here."

His master, peeping through de hole in de door saw Tom run under de bed naked. He said, "I'm God Amighty and Tom don't come out from under dat bed I'm going to come in there and get him and carry him to heben anyhow."

Tom whispered to his wife to open de door wide. Tom run out from under de bed and out de door and right through the quarters naked as a rooster, wid his master right after him, who he thought was the Lord.

Tom's chile rose up and ast his mother a question, says, "Mama," says, "God's gointer ketch papa and carry him to heben?"

She set dere wid a head rag on her head patching. She clashed at de chile—tole him: "Shet up yo' mouf tellin' dem lies. Don't you know God ain't got no time wid yo' pa and he's barefooted, too."

—GEORGE MILLS.

THE RUNNING DEATH†

Massa had a slave once named Ike. Ike wuz always praying tuh be took into heaven alive. Every night he'd git down on his knees an' pray tuh be took jes like Enoch. One day Ole Massa heard him and made up his mind tuh try 'im out.

So one night he put on uh sheet, all white an' everything, an' went on down tuh Ike's house. Ike wuz down prayen and whoopin 'bout he wanted tuh gwan tuh heaven.

Massa knocked at de do'. (Gesture of knocking on door.)

Ike: "Who dat?"

Massa: "It's me, Ike, it's de Lord come tuh take you away frum dis hard working world."

Ike: (In whisper tuh his wife) "Tell 'im I ain't here."

Wife: "He ain't here, Lord."

Massa: "Then, Dinah, you'll do."

Dinah: (In whisper) "Ike, you come on out frum under dat bed and go on wid de Lord."

Ike: (Whispering) "Oh, go on wid de Lawd. Didn't you hear him say you will do?"

Dinah: "I ain't gwinter do nuthin uv de kind. Youse de one dat always whoopin' and hollerin' fur him tuh come git yuh. An' ef you don't come on out, I'm gwinter tell God you hiding under dat bed."

Massa: "Come on, Dinah."

Dinah: "Ike in here, Lawd, hidin' under de bed from you tuh keep from going on wid you tuh immortal glory."

Massa: "Come on, Ike an' go wid me." (Ike comes very slowly from under the bed.)

Massa: "Come on, Ike."

Ike: (Goes tuh do' and peeps out. He got so skeered when he seed whut he thought wuz death dat he didn't know whut tuh do. So he says tuh ole Massa): "Stand back a little way, Jesus, lemme come out by you." (Massa moved back uh little. He knowed whut Ike wuz up tuh, but he didn't let on. Ike done dat de third time. By den he figgered he had enough room, so he lit out dat door (gesture of swift running flight, passing one hand past the other quickly). He hollered back to Ole Massa: "Ef thou be uh running death, *ketch me!*"

—JAMES MOSELEY.

Once durin' slavery time Ole Marsa had uh nigger an' he uster go up under uh simmon tree tuh pray fuh God tuh come git him way from dis hardworkin' world. Young Marsa heard 'im an' clammed up de tree wid uh rope. When Jack got down under de tree an' begin tuh ast de Lawd tuh come git 'im, de white man said: "If you wanta go tuh heben wid me, Jack, stick you head in de loop."

He let down de rope so Jack could git his head in. Jack prayed on some more an' Marsa said: "Stick yuh head in de loop."

Jack heard 'im dat time an' stuck his head in de loop, an' de white man begin tuh pull. Dat rope got tighter an' tighter round Jack's goozle, an' Jack hollered up de tree: "Lawd, do you know everything?"

De man said, "Yes."

"Well," he said, "if thou be God an' know everything, you oughter know youse choking me tuh death."

—EUGENE OLIVER.

PRAYIN' WOMAN AN' DE BANJO MAN†

There uster be a woman dat went to de prayin' groun' every evenin' jestez soonez she come from de fiel'. You know in dem days niggers didn't have no churches, cause de white folks didn't 'low 'em. Dey uster slip off down in de woods tuh whut dey'd call de prayin' groun' an' have they little doings.

Dis woman, she uster go every day—she wuz so full uh religion. Her husban' uster stay home an' play de banjo, cause he said all dat prayin' wuzn't doin' no good—de white folks wuz still in de lead. De ole woman thought dat wuz weeked an' sinful an' uster beg him tuh put down his music an' come wid her—but he wouldn't.

He made up his mind tuh break her uh all dat prayin' an carryin' on, so he cut cross de woods an' beat her to de tree one day an' listened. She come on an' got down on her knees an' ast de Lord tuh send down His power tuh free de niggers an' tuh take her home wid Him. De husban' kept quiet and after she lef' he cut cross de woods an' beat her back home.

De nex' day he waited till she lef' home an' cut her off agin an' got some rocks an' hid 'em up de tree. When his wife got down an' ast de Lord tuh take her home wid Him, she said, "An' now, Lord, tuh show dat you got de powers tuh keer me home whole soul an' body, send down yo' power."

De man dropped a little rock down an' tapped her on de shoulder. She lak-ted dat, (liked). She raised her voice higher an' said: "Don't be sendin' down no little scraps uh yo' power. Send it so dese white folks'll know dey got tuh set us free—send it down in plenty."

De man dropped a great big rock dat time dat hit her on de head an' knocked her over. She got out from under dat tree an' tole Him, she said: "I didn't ast you for *all* yo' power at one time. I didn't ast you to crack my head wid it." She lit out for home.

De man took de short cut an' beat her home agin, but he didn't hardly have time to git uh seat an' git his banjo in his hands befo' she come in. Soon as she got in de house, she says, "Hurry an' chune up dat thing, ole man, an' less have some music. Ah done got enough power from de prayin' ground tuh las' me de rest uh my days."

—LARKINS WHITE.

GOD AN' DE DEVIL IN DE CEMETERY [†]

Two mens dat didn't know how tuh count good had been haulin' up cawn an' they stopped at de cemetery wid de las' load cause it wuz gittin' kinda dark. They thought they'd git through instead uh goin' way tuh one of 'ems barn. When they wuz goin' in de gate, two ears uh cawn dropped off de waggin, but they didn't stop tuh bother wid 'em jus' then. They wuz in uh big hurry tuh git home. They wuz justa 'vidin' it up, "You take dis'n, an' I'll take dat'un; you take dat'un an I'll take dis'n."

An' ole nigger heard 'em while he wuz passin' de cemetery an' run home tuh tell ole massa 'bout it.

"Massa, de Lawd an' de devil is down in de cemetery 'vidin' up souls. Ah heard 'em. One say, 'You take that'un an' I'll take this'un.'"

Ole Massa wuz sick in de easy cheer, he couldn't git about by hisself, but he said: "Jack, Ah don't know whut dis folishness is, but Ah know you lyin'."

"Naw, Ah ain't neither. Ah swear it's so."

"Can't be, Jack, youse crazy."

"Naw, Ah ain't neither. If you don't b'lieve me, come see for yo'self."

"Guess Ah better go see whut you talkin' 'bout; but if you fool me Ah'm gointer have a hunded lashes put on yo' back in de mawnin', suh."

They went on down tuh de cemetery an' it wuz sho dark down dere, too. They stole up in de gate an' heard 'em jus' lak Jack said, but they couldn't see de two ears uh cawn layin' in de gate.

Sho nuff Ole Massa heard 'em sayin', "Ah'll take dis'n" an' de other one say, "An' Ah'll take dis'n." Ole Massa got skeered hisself, but he wuzn't lettin on, an' Jack whispered tuh 'im, "Unh hunh, didn't Ah tell you de Lawd an' de devil wuz down here 'vidin' up souls?"

They waited awhile there in de gate listenin' den they heard 'em say, "Now, we'll go git dem two at de gate."

Jack says, "Ah knows de Lawd goin' take you, an' Ah ain't gwine let de devil git me—Ah'm gwine home." An' he did, an' lef' Ole Massa settin' dere at de cemetery gate in his rollin' cheer; but when he got home, Ole Massa had done beat 'im home an' wuz settin' by de fire smokin' uh seegar.

—LARKINS WHITE.

Once there was a Negro. Every day he went under the hill to pray. So one day a white man went to see what he was doing. He was praying for God to kill all the white people; so the white man threw a brick on his head. The Negro said, "Lord, can't you tell a white man from a Negro?"

—ARTHUR HOPKINS.

Once there was a man, he had a son and he died. Every night the man would go to the graveyard and pray to the Lord to let him see his son. One night a man decided to satisfy his wishes, so he hid in the graveyard. So that night the man went to pray. The other man rose up with a sheet over his head. The father said, "Go back, son, I have seen." The ghost came a little closer. "Go back, son, I have seen." The ghost came a little closer.

"Go back, son, go back, I tell you! That's the reason you are in the graveyard now—your head is so damn hard!"

—Joe Wiley.

A woman had a little boy who was always cussin'. She did everything to break him, but couldn't. So one time when he wuz sleep she got somebody to help her put him in a coffin to skeer him. Thought maybe that would break him. So they put him in de coffin and set de coffin in de cemetery and hid theyselves behind de tombstones to lissen. After while de lil boy woke up and set up in de coffin and looked all round and says, "Well, I'll be damned if this ain't judgment day and I'm de first son of a gun up."

—L. O. Taylor.

Once there was an old man, he had a son and two good dogs. They didn't have any guns, so every night they would go hunting. They would cut sticks. The man told the boy that a coon hollered like a man. The boy was afraid of the old man. One night the dogs chased a coon up a tree. The old man went up the tree and told the boy that when the coon fell down, to kill him with the stick. The old man fell out of the tree, and the boy began to beat him with the stick. The old man said, "Oh, Lordy, son, this is me."

The boy said, "Oh, hell, pa said a coon hollered like a man. I have you now."

So he beat the old man half to death before he knew it was his father.

—Edward Morris.

Once there were two men who was stealing old Master's hogs. They had a hole in the floor, and when the hogs come under, they would hit the hogs in the head with a stick. One day the man said, "Now, when a hog comes out, you hit him and kill him."

The hogs came out so fast that the man couldn't get a chance to kill a single one of them. The other fellow came crawling from under the house and said, "Did you get them?"

This man thought he was a hog, so he hit at him and hurt him so bad until he could not talk; but somehow he said: "I told you to notice *hogs* and you noticed *me*."

—WILL HOWARD.

PIG IN DE POKE[†]

One time way back a white man sent his Negro hand to another plantation to get a pig for him. He went and got it, but on the way back it was hot and he was tired, so he sat down to rest and dozed off to sleep. Some white men came along and saw him. They knew who he was and everything, so they thought it would be fun to take out the pig and put in a possum—so they did.

When he got home his boss asked him, "Well, Sam, did you get the pig?" "Yas suh, an' he sho is uh fine one, too. He kin crack corn already." "Well, let's see him." Sam poured the possum out of the bag, thinking it was the pig. He looked, the white man looked, neither one didn't want to believe his eyes. "Look here, Sam, is you dat big a fool to let 'em put a possum off on you for a pig?" "Boss, I 'clare dat wuz uhh pig when I put 'im in dere." "Well, you just turn round and go right back over the creek and get me a pig. Furthermore, you tell Hiram Bickerstaff he better not try any tricks on me, else I'll sink him wid lead."

The Negro went on back and he was awful tired by this

time, so he sat down at the same place and went to sleep again. The men saw him and knew what he was going back for, so they slipped the pig back into the bag and went away. When he woke up he heard the pig grunting in the bag and peeped in to see if it really was a pig again. He looked at the pig and scratched his head and said: "Pig, be somebody. Don't be switching back and forth. Either be a pig or a possum, but be whut you is."

—Louise Noble.

Fool Tales

THE SIX FOOLS[†]

A fellow went to court a girl. After he had courted her a long time, he began to talk of marriage. Her parents were very glad to hear him speak of it, for he was rich and strong. So they told the girl to go down in the cellar and draw some beer. They wanted to be merry, you know.

The girl took the pitcher and went down in the cellar to draw the beer. She turned the thing, you know, and let the beer run into the pitcher. While it was running, she got to thinking that if the young man *did* (should) propose to her in earnest, and she should accept him, and they get married and have a child—what would she name it?

She sat and thought and thought and the beer ran and ran. After a long time her mother wondered, what can be keeping our daughter? So she went down to see what was the matter. "What is the matter, daughter, you don't come on back with the beer?" "Mama, I just got to thinking, that if the young man should ask me to marry him, and if I should accept him, and if we should marry and have a child—what would we call it?" "Daughter, that *is* something to think about." So she sat down beside the girl and began to think, too. The beer was still running.

They thought and thought, and after a long time, the father came down to see what was the matter. "Wife! What are you doing letting all my good beer waste like this? I will be ruined! Our daughter hasn't married the young man yet, remember." "Well, we just been wondering what to name the baby if the young man does propose marriage to our daughter, and she should accept, and they should marry and have a child." "Now, that *is* something to study about. I never thought of that." So he sat down and began to think, too.

After a while, the young man got worried and came to see about them all. "What are all of you doing sitting here in a flood of beer?" The father said, "We are just studying what to name the baby in case you and daughter get married and have one." "Well," said the young man, "you are the three biggest fools that I ever heard talk of. I am going traveling for a year, and if I find three fools as big as you, I'll come back and marry the girl."

He traveled and traveled, and after a while he saw a man leaping up in the air before a bush with some clothes on it. The man just kept on jumping up in the air and falling back. "What are you doing?" the young man asked. "Those are my trousers on the bush and I am trying to get into them." "Well, why don't you take them in your hand and draw them on?" "I never thought of that," said the man and he did so. "That's *one* fool," said the young man, and went on.

Way after while he saw a man trying to pull a cow up on the roof of a barn by a rope around her neck. He pulled and pulled, but he could not pull the cow up on the barn. "What are you trying to do?" asked the young man. "See all that grass growing on top of the barn? I am trying to take the cow up there so that she can eat it." "Why don't you go up there and toss it down to her?" the young man asked the farmer. "Oh, I never thought of that." "That is two fools," the young man said and traveled on.

One day he saw a woman rushing in and out of her house,

pushing a wheelbarrow. She had a wide board placed in the door like a gangplank and was dashing in and out, in and out with the wheelbarrow. "What are you moving in that wheelbarrow? I can't see anything in it." "Oh, I have scoured my kitchen and I am trying to haul in some sunshine to dry it." "Why don't you open the doors and windows and let it dry?" "Oh, I never thought of that." "Well," said the young man, "I have found three fools as big as those I left, so I will go back and marry the girl."

By that time I left.

—HATTIE REEVES.

There was a ole man told his wife to make slop for the hogs. While he was out on the plantation working, she made the slop in de well. Caught all de hogs in de well and said, "Drink your food!"

When the husband come he wanted to know if de hogs had been fed. She said, "Yes, dem is de biggest fools me ever did see. Me put the hogs in de ole well, but dey wouldn't eat."

Ole man say, "You de biggest fool I ever did see." Dat de way wid geechies*.

—HATTIE GILES.

SAVING FOR MR. HARD TIME†

One time there was a man and he had a wife and she was sorta silly. He would save his earnings and his food and store it back, and tell her that he was saving it for Mr. Hard Time. So one day a man came along begging and told her he

---

*Or Gullah; a mix of West African and the coastal areas of Georgia and the Carolinas. May also be used as a derogatory term for an inarticulate Southerner.

was Mr. Hard Time. So she went and got all the money and all the food he had been saving and gave it to this man. When the husband came, he found so many things gone he asked her, "Where is my things I told you to put up for hard times?"

She said, "Lordy massa, Mr. Hard Time came by and I gin him dem things."

—HATTIE GILES.

Women Tales

Once there was a lady sitting by the fire. She and her little boy was making rolls out of cotton. So her sweetheart came, and later her husband.

So she placed her sweetheart in the basket and covered him with cotton. She and her old man started talking; but the little boy says, "Papa, I could raise hell here tonight."

The lady talked louder to drown the boy's voice, but the boy kept on saying, "Papa, I could raise hell here tonight."

After he had kept saying this a long time, the old man said, "Well, raise it then."

So the little boy reached into the fire and got out a red hot coal and throwed it into the basket, and the man caught on fire, and the man jumped out and took out down the road, and as far as you could see him you saw fire.

—CHARLEY BRADLEY.

Once there was a man who wanted to catch up with his wife. So he pretended he was going to work, and sent a little boy to his house to spend the night. His wife baked a cake of corn bread and fried some meat and gave it to the little boy and sent him upstairs to bed. Then she baked a pig with an apple in his mouth, a sweet potato pone. By this time her sweetheart came, so she said: "You better eat, as we have plenty to eat this afternoon."

But he said, "Let us talk, we have plenty of time to eat."

So her husband knocked on the door and she told her sweetheart to get up the pot racks.

The old man asked her if a little boy had come to spend the night, and she said, "Yes, he is upstairs sleep."

The old man said, "Come down, little boy." The boy came down stretching as if he had been asleep. So the old man asked him what did he know.

The little boy said, "Well, I don't know much, but what I do know I'll tell that!"

"Once my father had a potato patch. Sow kept coming in there until it made my father mad, and father picked up a brick as big as that potato pone in that oven and knocked a pig out of that sow as big as that pig in the stove with that apple in his mouth. Every since then that sow has been afraid of my father as that man is of you up that pot rack."

—Arthur Hopkins.

There was another woman that had a sweetheart. So one night they retired and her husband come. So she put her sweetheart under the bed where she had a basket where a hen was setting on some eggs. The husband laid down in the bed and the hen pecked the sweetheart under the bed and he said, "Good God! I am snake bit!"

The woman said, "Hush! My husband will hear you."

The hen pecked him again and he said, "I am snake bit!"

The woman repeated "Hush, my husband will hear you."

But the man hollered "I don't care who in hell hears me, I say I'm snake bit."

—Charley Bradley.

A lady once married and her husband never would stay home, so she said she'd go to de hoodoo. So she went to the hoodoo and she ast de lady. So de lady said, "Here you come, and I know whut you come for. You havin' trouble with your husband."

"Yes, m'am, I certainly is." Says, "All right, whut kin ' do?"

Says, "All right, come take me to yo' house."

She goes and she walks in, says, "Tell you whut you do—" say, "get you some constrated lye, scrub yo' house, wash all yo' clothes, comb yo' head, powder yo' face, make up your bed, light and neat, and don't have a thing to say to him when he come in."

So de husband come in dat night. He walks in de house and looks all round. He looks at her and she was clean, head was combed, bed was turned back, and his water was fixed. They sits out on de porch a little while, then he walks in and says: "Dear, let's go to bed."

So they went to bed. She got up de next morning and went back to de hoodoo lady and paid what she charged and de hoodoo lady told her to jest keep dat up twice per week and her husband would always go to bed and go to sleep.

—J. W. WADE.

CRUEL WIFE†

This woman was so cruel till he couldn't please her no way he done. Las' one night he come in from makin' support for her, an' he said: "Oh baby doll, is you tired uh me?"

And she said, "Yes, I don't want you on no terms no matter whut you do."

"Well, I'll tell you how tuh get rid uh me."

Says, "All right, tell me."

He said to her, "Well, I got a brand new rope dere behind de head uh de bed. You take it and cair me soon in de mornin' tuh de river bank, tie my hands behind my back, and get on de hillside and run and shove me overboard."

She says, "I really will."

So dat morning dey went on down and she tied his arms, roped 'em behind his back. So she got on de hillside and ran wid great speed, and jes' fo' getting' tuh him tuh make her shove, he made one step aside, an' overboard she went.

Hollered, "Save me, ole man, save me."

"How can I save you wid my arms tied behind my back?"

—ROBERT BAILEY.

There wuz uh woman once an' she didn't have no wash-pot; so she wuz always sending round tuh first one house an' another tuh borry they pot. But one day she got lucky an' bought herself uh pot; so she sent round tuh everybody: "Now, I got uh wash-pot uh my own an' I don't lend an' I don't borry."

Dat went on all right fuh uh spell till one day some devilish boys wuz chunkin'* an' dey struck her pot an' broke it. Den she sent round tuh everybody: "I lends an' borries, too."

—NIGGER BYRD.

There was a widow woman didn't have no husband. She been trying to get one for years. Every Sunday she uster dress up and put Cologne water on herself and primp her mouf up little to go to church.

After while a new preacher come to pastor there that didn't have no wife, and so dat Sunday she primped her mouf just so. So she was late for preaching, so she cut cross de field for de nigh cut, so she seen de mule was out and in de corn. So she

---

*Throwing or throwing rocks.

tried to drive him out without unfixing her mouf. So she says, "You mule, git out dat corn; oh, you mule, go on out de corn!"

De mule didn't pay her no mind, so she unprimped her mouf and says, "You damned ole crazy mule! git out dat corn 'fore I lam you wid lightning!"

And de mule went out. "Now look whut you done done! Done made me open my mouf wide. Now I got to go all de way back to de house and primp it agin befo' I kin go tuh meeting.

—L. O. TAYLOR.

The reason there ain't no women in de army is cause they squats to pea (urinate) and de minute one does it, they all wants to. De enemy would slip up and kill 'em all while they was squattin' down.

—E. EDWARDS.

Reason women folks always poke de fire if they set down by one is one time uh man wuz burnt up in uh fire, an' de women been searchin' fur his privates ever since.

—DAUGHTER SEWELL.

School Tales

There wuz a woman who sent her boy to school to learn everything.

She had a young cow and went out to milk her, and the cow kicked all the milk out the bucket. She called her husband to assist her in milking the cow. He come out and felt responsible to help his wife, so he said: "I'll put a rope on her head."

He helt the cow while she milked her. She kicked the milk over again that she had given.

He said, "I know what! We sent our boy to school to learn everything—he'll know how to milk this cow."

So he calls the boy out and he comes out and ties the rope to a tree. He felt more responsible than his pa, so his mother began to milk again. The cow kicked that over and the boy said: "Father, she needs a weight on her back."

He looked all around but didn't see anything heavy to put on her back. So he had a long-legged father, and so he tole him to get up there on the cow's back. So he got up there and he tied his legs together under the cow's belly.

The cow begin to jump one side to the other, and he

wanted to get down. He hollered, "Cut the rope, son, cut the rope!"

And instead of cutting the rope from his father's legs so he could get down, he cut the rope to the tree. His father remained tied to the cow. She went running through the bushes.

There was a sister coming up through the woods. She saw him and said, "Wait a minute, brother, where you going?"

He said, "I don't know, sister. God and this cow knows."

—GEORGE MILLS.

Man sent his daughter off tuh school fur seven years. Den she come home all finished up. So he said tuh her: "Daughter, git you things an' write me uh letter tuh mah brother." So she did.

He says: "Head it up," an' she done so. "Dear brother, our chile is done come home from school all finished up, an' we is very proud of her." (To daughter): "You got dat?"

She tole 'im, "Yeah."

"Our dog is dead an' our mule is dead, but I got anuther mule, and when I say (the clucking tongue and teeth sound used to urge mules), he moves from de word . . . Is you got dat?" She told him, "Naw." He waited a while and he ast her again, "Is you got dat down yit?"

"Naw sir, I ain't got it yit."

"How come you ain't got it?"

"Cause I can't spell (clucking sound)."

"You mean tuh tell me you been off tuh school seven years and can't spell (clucking sound)? Well, I could almost spell dat myself. Well, jest say (sound) and go on."

—ROBERT WILLIAMS.

Man sent his son off to school for seven years. When he come home that morning they had breakfast. His pa said, "Son, pass me det taters."

De boy said, "Don't say taters, say po-tatoes."

After while de ma says, "Son, pass me de 'lasses."

Say, "Don't say 'lasses, say mo-lasses."

His pa says, "Our boy done gone off and lost his senses. He done come back here puttin' 'po' on taters and 'mo' on 'lasses."

—PETER NOBLE.

Miscellaneous Tales

GOOD-TIME WILLIE[†]

Once upon a time there wuz a man named Good-Time Willie. He wuz working in de army for seventy-five cents and so he quit de army and went on down de road. He met a man settin' on a stump and he had uh heap uh strops uh round him. Good-Time Willie said, "Ain't you all crippled up?" He say, "I got seventy-five cents you kin git half of dis."

The man told him to keep the money and Good-Time Willie asted him whut his name wuz. He say it wuz, "Disap-pear-And-Run-Out-Of-Sight." Good-Time Willie tole him there wuz a fortune at de end of de road for him and they both went on down de road and they soon met another man.

He wuz settin' upon a stump and Good-Time Willie asted him what he wuz doing settin' dere, and he tole him his name wuz "Change-De-Weather." He tole him to let him see some of his work and he set his hat on one side and started it to raining, and then he set his hat on top his head and it faired up.

Then Good-Time Willie tole him, "Come and go with us. There is a fortune at de end of de road for you."

They went on down de road and they saw another man in de ditch and Good-Time Willie asted him: "What wuz he doing dere," and he said, "I blow water down de stream to grind de government corn."

So Good-Time Willie tole him to come and go with them, there was a fortune at de end of de road for him. All of 'em went on down the road. They met another man breaking down pine tree tops, throwing 'em over de mountain in his back yard. So Good-Time Willie asted him what he wuz doing and he said: "I'm breaking off pine tree tops throwing 'em over in my back yard."

So Good-Time Willie tole 'im: "Come and go wid us; there is uh fortune at de end of de road for you." All of 'em went on down de road till they got to de king's house, and so de king tole 'em: "If they had a man out dere could outrun his daughter to de well he could marry his daughter."

So Good-Time Willie tole Disappear to go and de king give both of 'em a bucket and he loosed one of his strops and disappeared and went out of sight.

So he got his bucket of water and laid down and went to sleep. De girl had done got her water and she wuz fixing to go up de step at home and Shoot-Well shot at Disappear and shaved his moustache off. He jumped up and got his bucket and beat de girl in de house.

De king said: "You have won my daughter—tell you what I'll do." He got some moonshine and he made 'em all half-drunk, and he tole 'em he'd give 'em a place to stay. That night he went and got seven firemen and started to burn 'em up.

Good-Time Willie woke up and shook Disappear, and Disappear shook Change-the-Weather and he tole 'em not to worry. So he started to making it hailing and storming, killed all de firemen and dat next day de king said: "Boys, I tried to harm you but I couldn't do you no harm. Tell you what I'll do—I'll give you three car load of gold."

So Stormy man got him a sack and sacked up all de gold he could and sent back down to king for three more carloads, and so de king come down dere to kill 'em. Blow-Stormy tole 'em

to git behind him and blowed 'em all up in de air and de king
said: "Let me down easy, kind Willie."

I stepped on a pin, de pin bent, and dat's de way de story went.
—A. C. WILLIAMS.

SCISSORS[†]

There was a man that [had] a contrary wife. I don't keer
what he suggested, she'd go jus' the other way.

One day he looked up at the sky and said it was time to mow
the hay, but she said it wasn't. They got into a fuss, but he jus' finally told her he was gointer mow it no matter what she said.

Then he looked around and said, "Where is my mower?"

She said, "There it is, but you don't need no mower to cut
no hay. It oughter be done with the scissors."

"Who did you ever see cut hay with scissors?"

"Everybody with any sense. Jus' because these fools round
here ain't got no better sense than to cut it with a mower is no
reason why YOU should be a bigger fool than you have to.
Cut it with scissors."

"Woman, do you want to make a fool outa me with your
scissors? No, I'm not going out to no hayfield with no scissors!
I'll take the mowing-machine and nothing else."

"And I'll take the scissors, you hammer-heel fool."

"No, you won't either. You won't go atall to worry me whill[e]
I work. You stay right home and use those scissors patching."

"Oh, yes, I will go too. You can't stop me, and I'm going to
cut hay, too, the way it should be cut—with scissors."

Sure 'nough, she went on with him hollering "scissors" in his
ear every step. He couldn't make her hush and he couldn't make
her go back, and she stayed on his heels no matter where he
walked. They got into a tussle on a little bridge they had to cross
and she fell overboard. She went down the first time and hollered
"scissors" when she come up. She hollered "scissors" the next

time she come up. The third time, she was so weak she couldn't say nothing—but she stuck up her hand with her fingers crossed.

She drowned, and when they found her body it was way upstream—she was too contrary to float downstream like other folks.

—ARMETTA JONES.

(European derivative)

De man wuz name Sam. He had been gone from home ten years an' he come up to this white man's place an' he hired him. He worked for twelve months for this white man for one hundred dollars. An' the end of the year he paid 'im de one hundred an' he tole him, say, "If yo' give me this one hundred dollars, I'll tell you something that will be worth two thousand dollars to you."

He give it to 'im. Says, "Well, now, I have worked twelve months an' I wanted tuh go home and I have nuthin' to go home with."

"Well, Sam, work another twelve months for another hundred dollars." So he worked another twelve months and so when the end uh de year he paid 'im this one hundred dollars.

He said, "Well, Sam, ef you give me this one hundred dollars, I'll tell you something that will be worth three thousand dollars tuh you." So he give it tuh 'im.

Says, "Well, now I want tuh go home, boss, and I haven't anything tuh go with. I know my wife is lookin' for me."

"Well, Sam," says, "work another twelve months fur another one hundred dollars." So he went tuh work and worked de twelve months.

At de end he says, "Give me dat one hundred dollars an' I'll tell you something dat will be worth ten thousand dollars tuh you." So he give it tuh 'im.

Says, "Well, boss, I must go home, money or no money."

"Well," he says, "ef you go, I haven't anything tuh give you but uh loaf uh bread to take home wid you. Now, don't cut it. Break it. Now, on your way home, don't take a nigh cut. Keep de road home."

An' in travelin', when he come tuh the nigh path through de hammock, he started tuh take it, but he thought of what this man tole 'im, tuh keep de road. Jes' as he turnt back into the road, a peddler turned into this path an' in a short time heard de peddler screamin' and hollerin'. Somebody had done robbed 'im and put 'im to death. So he traveled on till that night. He come tuh somebody's residence and he thought of what de white man tole 'im—not to stop over night with uh ole man with uh young wife, so he got up and went out. Shortly after, he heard a noise in de room joining his, an' de ole man an' his wife wuz puttin' another traveler tuh death.

De next night he retched home and he went in de house and saw quite a young lad lying in de bed wid his wife. He went out doors and picked up de ax and went back in de house; but he thought of whut de white man said: "Don't do nuthin' in de night whut you might be sorry of next day." So he threw de ax down and went in and woke his wife and found out it wuz his son in de bed.

"Well, ole woman, I've been gone ten years or more and I come wid nuthin'. I worked three years for one man and all he give me wuz one loaf uh bread and he tole me not tuh cut de bread, but to ast de blessing and break it."

He ast de blessing and broke de bread, and he found three years' work in de bread. Den he tole her all de white man told 'im.

—DELLA LEWIS.

A man courted a woman once and married her. She was powerful pretty and he was proud. So that night after they had done got married it come time for them to go to bed.

So he went outside to give her time to git in de bed first. That's de way men always does wid a new wife.

Way after while he come in to git in hisself. De wife had done took off her wig and hung it on de bed-post. Her false teeth was layin' on de dresser, her cork leg was standin' over against de wall, and her cork arm was layin' cross a chair. One of her eyes was soakin' in a glass of water on de dresser.

He was so put out he didn't know whut to do. He looked at all her parts strowed around and he looked at de woman in de bed. He tole her, "I don't know whether to git in de bed wid dat half of yuh or to sit up wid de rest."

—ELIZA AUSTIN.

VARIANT ON A STORY TOLD
BY HATTIE REEVES[†]

One day de ole man decided to go git him uh load uh wood, and he got uh pail uh water and sat it in de yard and tole de old lady, "If dis pail uh water turn tuh blood, you turn dese dogs aloose, cause you most know I'm in trouble."

So de ole man, he got down in de woods and started tuh cut on uh tree. And uh bear got after 'im and he dropped his ax and run up de tree. De ole bear, he picked up de ax and looked at it. (The bear reads the name on the handle.) The bear says: "Dis name is Whimmer G. Martin." So he begin to chop on dat tree where de ole man was to de tune of de man's name: "De Whimmer G. Martin! de Whimmer G. Martin! de whim! De Whimmer G. Martin, de Whim!"

Ole man says, "Wait, Mr. Bear, lemme pray uh prayer befo' you kill me."

Ole bear says tuh 'im, "Pray it fast."

Man said (calling his dogs): "Come August, come Sparrow, come Bon Bon Pree!"

Bear says (chopping): "De Whimmer G. Martin, de Whimmer G. Martin, de Whim!"

Man says agin, "Wait, Mr. Bear, lemme pray one more prayer befo' you kill me."

"Pray it fast! Whimmer G. Martin, de Whim!"

Man said, "Come August, come Sparrow, come Bon Bon Pree!"

De tree wuz beginnin' to fall and de dogs wuz at de edge of de woods.

Bear says, "Whimmer G. Martin, de Whim!"

'Bout dat time de dogs jumped on de ole bear and kilt 'im. De ole man jumped down outa de tree and took de dogs, and de bear, home and tole his wife, "See how good my dogs is? Saved my life. If you hadn't turnt my dogs loose I'd be uh gone man, dat's all."

—John Smith.

MAN WITH THREE COUGHS[†]

Once uh man had de consumption real bad, an' he went tuh uh doctor tuh see whut he could do fur him, an' de doctor tole him, say: "Youse got it too bad tuh help. Fack is, you ain't got but three mo' coughs left an' you'll be dead. So you better be mighty keerful."

He went on home walkin' jes as keerful as he could, but he stumped his toe and it made 'im cough. He say, "Umph, dat's one of my coughs gone already."

Dat night he got in uh sorter draft and he coughed again. "Umph, umph, another cough gone!"

Next day he went tuh look over his field and he coughed de third time—so he says, "Well, I reckon I'm dead." So he laid down by uh log an' folded his hands. He laid dere a long time, when uh ole sow wid some pigs come long and begin tuh root him. He wanted tuh make uh gwan off, but he figgered he couldn't. He kept on talkin' out de side uh his mouth: "Gwan! gwan! gwan! I say." But de ole sow kept on rootin' and rootin' till finally he hollered out loud, "Gwan way from here, you damned ole hawg! I'd git up from here and half kill you if I wuzn't dead."

—MARY DASH.

Uh nigger wuz cuttin' wood (cord wood). He got tired an' set down under a shade tree and went tuh sleep. When he woke up he saw a rattlesnake had rolled cross him. He looked up and saw de snake lickin' out his tongue. He wrote uh note and pinned it on his breast: "Found dead in de woods—bit by a rattlesnake." He folded his arms and died.

—GEORGE MILLS.

The boy courted the girl for a long time and then he married her. First night of married life, 'bout twelve o' clock, he ast her to tell him all the boys she had ever had and he would tell her all the girls he had had.

After she tole him, she called so many names he stopped her. He said, "That's enough. I don't want to hear no more, you ain't nothin' but a whore. I'm going to Alabama."

Early de nex' morning she went back home. Her pa met her at de gate. Ast her whut the matter wuz. She said, "Father, I can't tell you."

Father said, "I know dat trifling nigger ain't done beat you de first night. Wife, take our daughter upstairs and find out whut's de trouble.

While he staid downstairs and eve-dropped, she tole her mother, "My husband ast me to tell him how many boys I ever had and he would tell me how many girls he had courted, and when I tole him, he said I wuzn't nothin' but a whore and he wuz goin' to Alabama."

Mother said, "You sho wuz a fool. I been with your father over forty years, always have had twelve or fifteen men on him and he ain't never knowed nothin' about it."

De father says, "You kin bring me down my hat. Here's another damn fool Alabama bound."

—"SKINNY" FLOYD THOMAS.

Once there was an old woman who went off once on a train with her little grandson and she didn't have the fare for the little boy. So she put him under her skirt. So the grandmother keep on fizzling on the little boy's head, so he got out from under her skirt. The conductor came around asked the boy where had he come from. The little boy told him, "I was up under grandma's skirt and you wouldn't have seen me if grandmother hadn't fizzled on my head."

—CLIFFERT ULMER.

There was once an old man and a old woman who lived in the country with their little girl. So a man came from the city to visit them. They did not have but two beds, so the man had to sleep with the girl. The old woman put a pillow between the man and the girl. The next morning they got up and hitched the team up to go to town and took the old man's daughter. Riding along the wind blew the girl's hat off her head over the fence. The man got out to get the hat. She said, "Never mind, brother, I don't see how you can climb over a fence when you couldn't climb over the pillow last night."

—N. A. JAMES.

G–r–a–s–s grass
H–o–p–p–e–r hopper
Never specks tuh stop
Till I git on top.
—Nora Lee White.

Uh man tole uh tale on de boll weevil agin. Uh man wuz up on de hill an' he heered uh turrible racket down de hill, an' he went an' run down de hill tuh see whut it wuz—an' whut you reckon he found? Mister bool weevil wuz whuppin' lil boll weevil cause he couldn't keer two rows at a time.
—Larkins White.

BOLL WEEVIL†

White man wuz drivin' past uh cotton patch an' uh boll weevil flew onto his steerin' wheel an' said: "Lemme drive yo' car."

White man said, "Why, you can't drive it."

"Don't tell me Ah can't drive it! I drove in uh thousand last year an' Ah'm goin' tuh drive in two thousan' dis year."
—Larkins White.

JORDAN CAR†

De Jordan car is de only car not named after uh man. Know how come it tuh be lak dat? You know when dey make a car dey take it out on de road and try it out tuh see whut it will do. So de man got his car all made, and he had a nigger workin' for 'im. So he took 'im along tuh watch de speedometer.

He floored de accelerator an' she shot un tuh seventy. De nigger's eyes begin tuh pop out. De man ast him, "How am I doing, John?"

"You doing seventy, boss."

He floored de gas again and she shot up tuh eighty. By dat time John wuz shaking lak he had uh chill. He seen death comin' straight at him. So he hollered, "Git back, Jordan! Git away, death!" So de man named de car "Jordan".

—WILLIE ROBERTS.

Once there was an old man, woman and boy. They were eating, and the old man got through first and he got his pipe and went on the porch and sit on the bannister. He fell off and broke his neck. The boy was de next one got through eating and he went on the porch. He saw his grand-father had fell and broke his neck, so he went and told his grandmother about it and she said: "Wait till I git through eating and I will bellow for him."

—HENRY EDWARDS.

One ole couple wuz livin in uh house wid de kitchen built uh little off from de house, an' dey had dey lil granson livin' wid 'em.

De ole woman, she lakked her pipe. One night she wuz set-tin' dere smokin' when uh big blow uh wind come up, so she layed way her pipe an' went on intuh de house an' went tuh bed.

Pretty soon uh turrible wind come long an' blowed de kitchen down, an' kilt de ole man; but de lil boy got out an' run intuh de house an' tole his grandmaw: "Grandmaw! Grandmaw! De kitchen done blowed down an' kilt grandpaw!"

De ole lady says, "Umph, umph! An' Ah bet it broke mah pipe, too!!"

—HANDY PITTS.

"Say, boy, when you die, what you be thinking about?"

"Oh, man, I want to be buried in the center of the white folks' graveyard."

"Yes, what's that good for?"

"That's the last place the devil goes to look for a nigger."

"Yes, but when I die I want to be buried in a rubber coffin."

"What's that good for?"

"So I can go bouncing through hell."

—JERRY BENNETT.

FISHING ON SUNDAY †

There was a man that always went fishing on Sunday. The people told him not to go, but he went anyhow.

He baited his line and threw it overboard and tied the lines to his arm. The fish was so long in biting that he fell to sleep.

A catfish bit the line and he was so big till he jerked the man overboard and he was hollering. So the people came. He went down and came up. The last time he hollered, "Tell my wife—tell my wife to fear catfish and God."

—GEORGE HARRIS.

"Tomorrow is Sunday morning, if we should all live to see it. Tell Aunt Jane to tell Uncle Tom to tell de cow to tell de sweet milk, to tell de clabber to tell de buttermilk, to tell de butter to meet de biscuits in de morning on de breakfast table. Tell Aunt Jane to see to it."

—EUGENE OLIVER.

Once upon a time there was a poor ole lady and she didn't have no husband, but she had five children. One day she said: "Well, Lord, I ain't got no bread for my children to eat."

So she went out to find some bread for her children to eat.
So de children were saying: "My belly ake, my belly shake, I
wish I had some cornbread cake."
—LOUVENIA ENGLISH.

There was a man didn't know what corn was. So one
day he was out walking and one of his friends asted him
to dinner. He went in and sat to the table. He had corn for
dinner. The man ate all of the corn off the cob and said: "Lady
put some more beans on my stick."
—JOE WILEY.

Me and pa went to church. We started to church one
Sunday and pa was late for church and he had a Ford
car. He was driving pretty fast at the rate of eight miles a week.
So pa went in church and went to sleep. A fat lady got to
shouting and jumped in pa's lap and pa grabbed her around the
waist and hollered, "Son, step on the zillerater (accelerator)! I
got the steering wheel."
—ARTHUR HOPKINS.

Do you know how come the Amercans are not in war?
No.
Because my father was a farmer. He raised most everything,
but only one thing Uncle Sam could use. It was only sweet po-
tatoes sent to France by the train load. But he raised one so big
they couldn't get it in a box car. Had to load it on the flat.
So they sent it on to France and the Kiza (Kaiser) saw it, and
he got hongry right then and ast for a piece; and the lutant
(lieutenant) heard him and run and told his soldiers: "Hang up
the sword and hang up the flag, for the Kiza done ask for peace."
—WILL HOWARD.

Once there were two men. One was larger than the other. They were traveling one day and they came to a pond of water which was too deep for the small man to cross. So the big man said, "Get on my back an' I will take you across."

So the little man did so. While they were in the middle of the stream the little man says, "Gee, yo' breath stinks like karn (carrion)."

The big man ast him, "Whut you say up dere?"

The little man says, "I says yo' breath smells like violets."

As soon as they got across, the little man jumped down and said: "Yo' breath stinks like a dead horse and I speck yo' body smells worse."

—F. Bradley.

One time uh man wuz drunk an' he had uh five gallon demijohn full uh whiskey totin' it home, an' he had tuh cross uh fence. De moon wuz shinin' bright an' he could see de fence, but he wuz too drunk tuh utilize hisself. When he got on top de fence he fell an' dropped his jug; but he fell on one side an' de jug on de other side. He wuz too fur under de weather tuh git up, an' heard de likker runnin' out de jug sayin', "goody, goody, goody."

He said, "I know yuh good, but I jus' can't git tuh you."

—Cliffert Ulmer.

Five men want six orders. One order pig ears, one pig foot, one pig tail, one chittlings, two hawg snouts. Tell dat to de cook. Hey cook, git your grease hot, fixing to throw one at you, one walking, one flooping, one switching, snatch one from the rear, two rooting and let her roll.

I want a chocolate cake with icing and jelly roll smeared over the top. Tell dat to the cook. Say, cook, send me a brown-skin lady wid a thin dress on, doing the shinny-she-wobble serving sweet jelly roll.*

—ARTHUR HOPKINS.

Once there were two men that would steal. They were rogues. They had done stole everything they could think of. So one day they went to a church. One of the men went up to the pulpit. All he could find was a Bible and the leaves turned and the reading said: "Thou shalt not steal."

The man called his buddy and said, "Read this."

So he read it and said, "Oh hell, I'll steal Thou."

—CHARLIE BRADLEY.

Once there was a man stole some sheep and they put him in jail. His lawyer told him he could clear him for fifty dollars. Say everything the judge ask him to say "ba-a."

And the judge asked him was he guilty of stealing sheep and he said, "Baa-aa."

So the judge said, "He is crazy; take him out of here."

As he was going out the lawyer asked him for his fifty dollars, and he told him "baa" and went on down the street saying, "Baa, baa."

—ARTHUR HOPKINS.

De police thinks so much of buzzards in Charleston dat one took uh ham sandwich outa my hand, and de police hit me up wid uh blackjack cause I looked lak I didn't lak it. De street cars turned wrong-side outers to keep from running over one.

—TARRYSON PARLOR.

---

*"vagina" or "sex."

THE NIGGER AND THE GOAT[†]

Once they tried a colored man in Mobile for stealing a hog. So he was very poorly dressed and somewhat dirty. So the judge told him, "Six months on the county road, you stink so bad."

A white man was standing there and he said, "Judge, he don't stink. I've got a nigger who smells worse than a billy goat." The judge told the man to bring the nigger over so he could smell him.

The next day the man took the billy goat and the nigger to the court house and sent the judge word that he had the nigger and the goat out there and which one did he want first. The judge told him to bring the goat. When he carried the goat in, the goat smelled so bad that the judge fainted. They got ice water and bathed the judge's face until he revived. Then he told them to bring in the nigger. So when they brought in the nigger, the goat fainted.

—JOE WILEY.

My father had a red silk shirt. He washed it and hung it out to dry so he could have it tuh wear tuh Sunday-school. De billy goat et up de shirt. My daddy got mad and tied de goat on de railroad track so de train could kill him. When he seen dat locomotive bearin' down on him, de goat coughed up de shirt and waved de train down.

—FLOYD THOMAS.

In de old days when folks was seeking religion they went to a mourning-ground. There was a big ole nigger name Ike used to lead all de mourners to de praying ground.

One right pretty gal wid big legs, she fell under conviction. So Ike didn't lead her, he thowed her crost his shoulder and toted her on down thew de swamp to ground. It was getting on towards night and he wagged on thew de woods singing:

> It'll take us all night long, baby,
> It'll take us all night long—
> Drinking de wine.

He laid her down when he got there and got down on his knees. He was looking from side to side as hard as he could to see who saw 'im whilst he was easing up her dress.

Another man was out there seeking and he spied old Ike. He hollered at 'im, say: "Whut're you doin there, Ike?"

Ike says: "I ain't doin a damn thing, but you fixin to go off and tell a damn lie."

—MACK C. FORD.

DE LYING MULE†

A nigger name Sam useter work for a white man dat had a she mule. So he useter clam up on de edge of de crib and go wid de mule. He kept it up, every day, every day.

So one day another man dat could throw his voice caught him at it and he throwed his voice and made out like de mule said "Sam, git down off me and leave me alone, o' I'm gointer tell de boss on you."

Sam jumped down off de mule and fastened up his britches and went on up to de house. De white man was sittin on his porch smokin a seegar.

"Now, whut do you want, Sam?"

"Boss, I done heered 'em say dat mule uh yourn kin talk. If she come up here tellin her lies on me, dontcher b'lieve her."

A man said, "Hey, Sam, did you go tuh de campmeetin' like you said?"

"Yeah, man, I went."

"Did you see a pretty girl over dere wid a big pink hat on?"

"Yeah, I seen her."

"Well, I give her dat hat. Did you see dat swell dress she had on?"

"Yeah, I seen it. Sho was pretty."

"I give dat tuh her. Did you notice them swell slippers she had on her feet?"

"Yeah, I seen them, too."

"Well, I give 'em to her. And look, Sam did she have a fine fat baby in her arms?"

"Sho did."

"Well, I give dat tuh her, too."

—DAD BOYKIN.

One time after Jack Johnson and Jeffries fought, my pa said to me: "You hitch my mule to the buggy. I am going down and fight Jack Johnson."

I said, "Pa, don't do that. That's the champion of the world."

"You hitch my mule to the buggy."

So down the road we went and we met Jack Johnson. I said: "There he goes now."

Pa said, "I want to see you, Jack." So Jack got out of his car and pa got out of his buggy, and there was a fourteen feet wire fence on each side of the road. So pa said, "Jack, I'm going to whip you this morning." And he begin to motion at Jack Johnson. Jack hit pa a uppercut and knocked him over the fourteen feet fence. So pa got up and come to the fence and said, "Mr. Johnson?"

Jack said, "What is it?"

"Knock my mule and buggy and boy over the fence, please."

—JOE WILEY.

White Man: Hello, nigger, have you ever called a train?

Nigger: Yep, Cap, dass all I ever done. I mean nuthin but call trains.

(The train is coming and the nigger goes to the waiting room door.) Says he, "Hey, you fellows in dar, you better gitcher ticket if you gwine anywhar, cause dat train out dar gwine each an' everywhere. That's all."

—MARY DASH.

Geechies sho do love gold teeth. One time uh geechy married uh girl an' went off tuh work, an' she had uh baby whilst he wuz gone. When she wrote 'im de baby wuz born he come home right away tuh see if de youngun wuz his. He come in de house an' went straight tuh de bed an' looked at de baby. First thing he did wuz tuh open de baby's mouf an' look, den he says: "Dat ain't my baby. Naw, sir! Dat ain't no child uh mine."

Jus' like all de geechs he had uh mouf full uh gold teeth an' he looked at de baby agin. His wife said yes dat wuz his baby, too, an' wuz jus' like 'im. Everybody who wuz sittin' there said so, too; but he wouldn't have it dat way. "Well," he says, "if dat is my child, where is his gold teeth?"

—CLIFFORD ULMER.

THE MOBILE DISASTER[†]

Have you heard about the wreck? Dolphin run into Royal Street, skint up St. Francis Street, Conti layin' at de point of death.

—GEORGE HARRIS.

One day I was going down the road; I was real hungry. I heard something call me, "Hey, Mister, take me," so I looked around, couldn't see anything. It called again. I told it to come on. It was a ham of meat. I walked on down the road a piece further after I got the ham. I heard another call. I told it to come—it was a big pan of biscuits. So I walked on down further; I heard something call again, "Hey, take me." I told it to come on. It was a big can of syrup.

I decided to take lunch.

After I took lunch I got up and started on off. I heard something say, "Hey, Mister, are you a tooth dentist?" I told him no and asked him why. He said, "Oh, I wanted you to work on my wife's teeth. She wore them off eating grass."

—Arthur Hopkins.

Two niggers went out stealing and they promised when they got thew stealing to meet each other at de forks of the road; and stid of meetin' his partner, he met de sheriff dere. He hollered, "Hey, Oh partner," fust and he says, "I beat you stealin' tonight."

Sheriff ast him whut did he steal. "I stole uh cow and sold her and I stole a mule an' sold him, and come by old lady Lan's and got dat big ole Shanghai rooster."

De sheriff helt him up and said, "You don't know who you talkin' to, do yuh? I am the sheriff."

Nigger says, "Well, do you know who I am, Mr. Sheriff?" and the sheriff said no. He says "I'm de lyingest nigger you ever met. I ain't stole nothin."

—Baby-face Turl.

Once it wuz hard times and two men wuz sworn buddies went out tuh hunt. Dey didn't ketch nothin, but when dey wuz most home dey seen uh deer layin' down sleep in uh cane patch.

One uh de men said: "Look here, de Lawd done blessed us. Look at dat big fine deer. Less shoot 'im."

De other said, "All right, but first less we 'vide 'im up."

"All right, I'll take one uh de hindquarters an' you take de other."

"Dat's all right wid me. Now I'm gointer give my wife's folks one front quarter."

"It's all right wid me; an I'm gointer give my uncle on my ole man's side uh front quarter."

"Dat's good, an' we kin sell de head tuh ole man Tody an' make uh stew outa de heart an' lights. Now who gointer git de liver?"

"I'll tell you whut! Less give it tuh my sister's husband."

"Naw indeed, he done me outa uh fat shoat one time an' I ain't had no use fur 'im since. Less we give it tuh de preacher."

"Naw, I wouldn't give 'im air if he wuz stopped up in uh jug. I caught 'im kissin' my side gal. Less give it tuh my nevvy (nephew)."

"Naw, I won't 'gree tuh dat neither. Whut's de matter wid you—always tryin' tuh git de big end uh things fuh yo' folks? Naw! naw! I mean NAW!! I'll fight yuh first."

Jus' den de deer heard 'im an' jumped up an' run off faster than de word uh God an' nobody didn't git de liver.

—JAMES PRESLEY.

Once there was an old man and an old woman who lived out in the woods. One day the old woman said to the old man. "Old man, what would you do if a bear would come?"

"I would take my gun and shoot his head off."

So after while a big grizzle bear came up in the yard. The old man jumped up and ran up in the lauf (loft), the old woman took the gun and killed the bear—then she called up to the old man: "Old man, old man, come on down. I done killed the bear."

The old man said: "The doggone bear done made me so mad that I messed all over myself. Bring me some more rags up here."

—ED MORRIS.

MAN & DE LION†

One day a man was riding uh horse down de road. He had him a shotgun an' uh pistol an' uh razor. He met uh bear an' de bear says tuh 'im, "Wait uh minute. They tell me dat you goin' round tellin' folks dat youse de king uh de world."

Man said, "Thass right. Don't you b'lieve it?"

"Naw, I don't b'lieve it. Git down and fight."

They went tuh fightin' an' de bear begin tuh squeeze an' squeeze, an' so de man knowed he couldn't stand dat long; so he out wid his razor and cut de bear in de side—cut 'im deep, too. De bear turnt loose and drug off in de bushes tuh try tuh git well. De man went on down de road.

De lion smelt de blood and come found de bear where he was layin' in de bushes and started tuh eat 'im. De bear hollered, "A-aw, Brother Lion, don't tetch me, please. Ah'm *so* sore I don't know whut to do. I met de king uh de world and he done cut me all up so Ah'm 'bout tuh die."

De lion roared at 'im. "Don't you lay dere an' tell me you done met de king uh de world when you ain't met *me*! Ah'm de king uh de world an' ever'body knows it! Arr-rr-rrr I got a good mind tuh tear yuh tuh pieces."

"Aw, Brother Lion, don't tetch me, please. If you hadda seen 'im you would of said he was de king, too."

"Where is he at? Jus' lemme see 'im an' Ah'll show him who is king uh de world."

"Well, you jus' set down here and wait awhile and he'll come long and you kin meet 'im."

So de lion set dere. After while he saw a old man comin' down de road. He jumped up and got ready. "Is dat him, Brother Bear?"

"Naw, dat's uh uster-be. Jus' wait uh lil while mo'."

After while a lil boy come down de road. De lion jumped up again and got ready tuh fight. "Is dat him?"

"Naw, dat's uh gointer-be. He'll be long here tureckly."

After while here come de man ridin' down de road. "Thass him! Thass him, Lion! Here he come!"

De lion jumped up and give his tail uh coupla cracks and run out in de middle of de road and got right in front de man. He hollered, "Hold on dere! They tell me you goin' round strowin' it youse de king uh de world?"

"I am, don't you b'lieve it?"

"Naw, come on let's fight."

De man didn't git down off his horse dis time—he jus' up wid his shotgun and let de lion have one barrel right in de face. That was too much for de lion. He wheeled tuh run. De man let him have de other barrel under his tail. De lion made it into de woods to where de bear was and tole 'im, say, "Move over dere an' give me uh place tuh lay down dere. I done met de king uh de world, I know it."

Bear ast 'im, "How did you know it, Lion?"

"Cause he made de lightning in my face and thunder in my hind parts . . . So I know I done met de king."

—LOUIS CROOMS.

DE ANIMAL CONGRESS[†]

De elephant an' de monkey an' de wolf an' several other beasts had uh convention to find out which wuz de ugliest animal, and they said de one dat wuz voted de ugliest had tuh go tuh de well an' bring uh pail uh water. De monkey got up an' got de water bucket an' said: "I'll go git de water dis time, but I don't crack." (He means to say he doesn't joke about personal appearances.)

—JAMES PRESLEY.

Every Friday all the mocking birds go to hell to carry a grain of sand to put out the fire; that is why no one ever hears a mocking bird sing on Friday.

—BERTHA ALLEN.

We wuz upon uh terbaccer truck goin' after terbaccer plants. When we wuz goin' we seen uh goat justa chewin'; when we come on back he wuz still chewin' an he ast us: "Whose truck is dat?"

We tole 'im, "Harly Moss, why?"

He say, "Oh, nothin'."

—NORA LEE WHITE.

Hurricane met de tornado in Fort Lauderdale. So they went and had breakfast together.

Hurricane ast de tornado, says: "Where you been and whut you been doing?"

Tornado says: "Oh, I been down in Cuba messin around. Where you been?"

"I been to Palm Beach kinda bumpin de bump. Tell you whut let's doo. Soon as we git thew breakfast, let's go down to Miami and let's shake dat thing."

—M. C. FORD, MIAMI.

WHY THE WAVES HAVE WHITE CAPS*

The Sea and the Wind was both women. They both had children. The Wind tole the Water, "My children is better than yours. Some flies in the air, some walks on the ground, and some swims the water. They got all kinds of pretty feathers. They kin sing. Yours can't do nothin' but swim."

The Water got mad at the Wind for talkin' like that, because she was mother of all the birds. So next time a lot of birds come down to drink, the Water caught 'em and drownded 'em. The Wind know she left her children down by the Water, so she keep passin' over callin' her children. Every time she calls 'em, they show they white feathers to let her know where they is, but de Water won't let 'em go. When it storms, the Sea and the Wind is fighting about the children.

—LILY MAY BEALE.

---

*This tale is repeated in a slightly different version, later.

Talking Animal Tales

De brother in black is lak de monkey. He wanter do everything he see somebody do. They was an engineer on de I. C. had a pet monkey and he use to let him ride wid him sometime. One day he stepped off to git his orders and de fireman to ketch air, and de monkey jumps up in de engineer's seat and opens de throttle and pulls her out. Down dat road him and dat wheeler. They sent wires ahead, "Look out ahead! Monkey on de rails." Well, he run her till his steam died down.

Another time he had his monkey on de ship and de monkey could talk, so he bet a million dollars his monkey could talk, and de man bet him a million different. So he tried to make dat monkey talk. Monkey wouldn't say a word. "Bet I'll make you talk." He tied dat monkey to de anchor chain. De chain wuz just running overboard. Way after while it jerked dat monkey up. When he got up to de rail he hollered, "Snub her, boss, snub her."

—JERRY BENNETT.

Man wuz goin' tuh give uh purleau supper, but he didn't have nothin'; so he went an' stole uh chicken an' brought it home. Well, he put on de water tuh clean it an' his cat come up an' says: "Unhunh, I see you got uh chicken. Gimme de liver an' gizzard, please, m'am."

Thass de way cat got uh talkin'—they says "m'am" tuh ever'body, even uh man.

He never paid no 'tention tuh de cat. He took an' cooked dat hen wid uh plenty rice an' set it back till his friends come.

Being de man uh de house he wuz first one tuh dip in de pot an' he took de gizzard an' et it, an' it made 'im sick right off cause dat chicken wuz poisoned.

They called de doctor an' put 'im tuh bed an' uh rockin' cheer wuz standin' close up facin' de bed an' de cat got up in dat cheer an' set dere an' rocked, an' she tole de man: "I sho is glad I didn't eat none uh dat chicken. Goody, goody, goody! sho is glad I didn't eat none uh dat chicken. Thass whut you git fuh eatin' dat gizzard 'stead uh givin' me some." (The gizzard is believed to be the only dangerous part of a chicken fed on nux vomica.)

—"Nigger" Bird.

Old feller one time had a mule. His name was Bill. Every morning he go to ketch 'im say, "Come round, Bill."

So one morning he slept late, so he decided while he wuz drinkin some coffee he'd send his son to ketch old Bill.

Told him, say, "Go down dere, boy, and bring me dat mule up here."

Boy, he such a fast aleck, he grabbed de bridle and went on down to de lot to ketch old Bill.

He say, "Come round, Bill." De mule looked round at him. He told de mule. " 'Tin't no use you rollin yo' eyes at me—pa want yuh dis mawnin. Come on round and stick yo' head in dis bridle."

Mule kept on lookin at him and said: "Every mawnin, it's come round, Bill—come round Bill. Don't hardly git no night rest before it's come round, Bill."

De boy thowed down dat bridle and flew back to de house and tole his pa, "Dat mule's talkin."

"Aw gwan, boy, tellin yo' lies. Gwan ketch dat mule."

"Naw, pa, dat mule's done gone to talkin. You hatta (have to) ketch dat mule. I ain't gwine."

Old man looked at old lady, say: "See whut uh lie dat boy's tellin."

So he gits out and goes down after de mule himself. When he got down dere he hollered: "Come round, Bill."

Old mule looked around and says: "Every mawnin it's 'come round Bill'."

De old man had a lil fice dog useter foller 'im everywhere he go, so he lit out wid de lil fice right behind 'im. So he told de lady: "De boy ain't tole much of a lie—dat mule sho is talkin. I never heered uh mule talk before."

Lil fice say: "Me neither. I got skeered." Right through de woods he went wid de fice right behind 'im. He nearly run hisself to death. He stopped and commenced blowin and he says: "I'm so tired I don't know whut to do." Lil dog run and set down in front of him and went to hasslin and he says, "me, too."

Dat man is runnin yit.

—A. D. FRAZIER.

Once the hounds wuz chasin' a fox and had run him all night long. And soon the next mornin' he wuz runnin' crost a mountain and looked back and seen the sun rising all red. He said to hisself: "Doggone my running soul! I done set de world on fire."*

—ARTHUR HOPKINS.

---

*Hurston repeats this tale later, attributing it to Eugene Oliver.

A cross-eyed gnat and a one-eyed fly had a collision, and they's suing each other yet.
—N. A. James.

Once a lady had a polly* and he was awful bad. A man came along selling coal. The polly told him to drive around to the back and drive back this evening and get your pay. So the man came back that evening after his pay. The polly didn't answer, so the lady answered and the man said: "I came after the pay for the coal."

She said, "I haven't ordered any coal."

The man said, "I know you have!"

She thought about her polly and said, "I bet that old polly ordered that coal. She caught the polly and choked him and threw him back under the house. She had killed a rooster for dinner. The polly began to come to, so he raised up his head, looked at the rooster's head and said, "Hello friend, what are you doing under here—are you ordering coal, too."
—Arthur Hopkins.

Man had a cat. Every evening he come home from work he bring a piece of meat for his supper. De cat meet him and ast: "Is dat ham?"

Man say: "Yeah, I'll give you a piece."

After while, times got tight. He got a lil piece of meat. Cat met him. "Is dat Ham?"

Man say: "Naw, God damn yuh, dis is bacon and you ain't gointer git a smell, neither."
—Clarence Beale.

---

*A Gullah term, variant of "pollydo," or "polydore": a male friend or boyfriend; Apollo.

Animal Tales

ROOSTER AND FOX

A bunch of chickens and a rooster wasn't roosting very high. Fox would go there every morning and catch a hen till he caught all the hens. Rooster says: "I'm going to change my roosting place and roost higher."

So next morning Fox got dere before sunrise and rooster setting way up in de tree.

"Good morning, Brer Rooster."

"Good morning, Brer Fox."

Brer Fox says: "Brer Rooster, I got good news for you. Come down."

"No, I don't want to come down. It's too early. Whut is the news?"

"Come on down so I kin tell it to you."

"No, go ahead and tell it. I can hear you. Whut is the news?"

Fox says: "Law is now, fox eat no mo' roosters, hounds run no mo' foxes. Ain't dat good news?"

While they was talking they heard the hounds ow-ooo . . .

Fox says: "Hush, Brer Rooster, whut's dat I hear?"

Rooster say: "Dat ain't nothing but dem hounds."

Fox says: "Well, believe I'll go."

Rooster say: "Whut you skeered of? Didn't you say de new law say hounds run no more foxes?"

Fox says: "Yeah, but them hounds liable to run all over dat law and break it. Good-bye, Brer Rooster."

—M. C. FORD.

THE FROG AND THE MOLE

Frog used to have a long big tail and no eyes. Mole had eyes and no tail. So when one day de mole come up out de ground wid his eyes full of dirt he was just wiping his eyes and gittin de sand out. Soon's he looked round he seen de frog sittin up wid his big tail and no eyes. So he said: "Say, Brer Frog, whut you want wid dat big ole tail for? Tain't no good to you?"

Frog said: "Whut you want wid dem eyes and live in de dark all de time? Besides you roots yo' way and gits 'em full of dirt."

Mole says: "Les' swap, Brer Frog."

So they did. Now de frog got eyes and no tail and de mole got tail and no eyes.

—M. C. YARD.

WHY THE DOG HATES THE CAT

Cat and de dog wuz good friends one time. Both of 'em loved ham. So they put in together an' went to town an' bought 'em one. It wuz a great big ham. So de dog he toted it first. He said: "Our ham, our ham, ours, ours, ours."

Come time for de cat to tote it awhile. She says: "My ham, my ham, my ham."

Dog toted it agin. He says: "Ours, ours, ours."

Cat took agin. She says: "My ham, my ham."

Dog says: "Sis Cat, how come you always say 'my ham' when you totes de ham? I always say 'our ham'."

Cat didn't say nothin but when they got almost home de cat

sprung up de tree wid de ham and set up dere eatin it up.

Dog says: "Our friendship is broke up forever. I can't climb no tree, but you got to come down sometime and when you *do* . . ." (a significant shaking of the head).

—MACK C. FORD.

WHY DE DONKEY'S EARS IS LONG

Once upon a time there wuz a man he named all de animals. He named de lion, lion; he named de bear, bear; he named de tager, tager; he named de wolf, wolf; he named de fox, fox; de mule, mule; and all de other animals, so when he got to the donkey, donkey act stubborn. He caught de donkey by his ears and he pulled donkey's ears and dat's whut make de donkey's ears so long now.

—NATHANIEL BURNEY.

DE REASON DE WOODPECKER
GOT UH RED HEAD

When all de animals wuz in de ark de woodpecker started tuh peckin' on de wood. Ole Nora tole 'im tuh stop cause he had done pecked uh hole nearly thew de wall, an' Ole Nora saw he wuz goin' tuh drown everybody; so he tole 'im tuh stop uhgin an' when he caught 'im peckin' de nex' time, he hauled off wid uh hammer an' hit de woodpecker on de head an' made it bleed. And that's how come de woodpecker got uh red top-knot t'day.

—CLIFFORD ULMER.

WHY DE BUZZARD AIN'T GOT NO HOME

Every time it rains the buzzard says: "Lawd, I wish I had a place to stay." But as soon as it fair off, he say: "Who want to be bothered wid any home? It's too nice flyin' 'round." But soon's it starts tuh rainin' again he says: "Lawd, I sho' wish I had a home. If it ever stops rainin' I'm sho' goin' build me a home." But he never do. So that's the reason the buzzard never have no home.

—ARMETTA JONES.

THE FOX AND THE HOUNDS

Once the hounds wuz chasin' a fox and had run him all night long. And soon the next mornin' he wuz runnin' crost a mountain and looked back and seen the sun rising all red. He said to hisself: "Doggone my running soul: I done set de world on fire."*

—EUGENE OLIVER.

WHY DE ALLIGATOR IS BLACK

De alligator was laying in the marsh sunning hisself and catching flies when Brother Rabbit dashed in and run right cross him and wake him up. That made Brother Alligator mad. He said: "Brother Rabbit, what you doing running over me that way and waking me up outa my rest?

Brother Rabbit say: "You'd run over somebody, too, if you'd been troubled like me. The hounds is behind me and I am in plenty of trouble."

---

*Hurston includes this tale earlier, attributing it to Arthur Hopkins.

Brother Alligator say: "Trouble? What's trouble?"

Brother Rabbit say: "Brother 'Gator, don't you know what trouble is?"

Brother 'Gator say: "No, I don't know nothing 'bout no trouble. I ain't never heard tell of it. What is it?"

Brother Rabbit say: "I'll show you." So he went off and took a lightwood torch and set that marsh afire all the way around. Then he went off and waited.

When the alligator felt that heat he made a break for de water, but no matter which way he run there was fire there. You know, before that, the 'gator was all pretty and white, but time that fire got thru scorching him he was black as a coal. Way after a while he burst thru the flame and heat and hit the water wham! An' where he had done got burnt black all over he's been black ever since.

And that is how the 'gator found out how trouble was.

—EUGENE OLIVER AND MARY DASH.

THE FLIES AND GOD

The flies was so small till everything trod on 'em you know and keep 'em back. And the flies held a conference—they wanted to know what to do. So they says: "We'll go up to heben and tell God about it." So they got one right after the other—one right after the other.

"Say, Lord, we ain't got no weapons to fight with and no way to protect ourselves, and we can't get nothing to eat."

So God said: "Go on back and when you get back I'll fix it so you'll git the first taste of everything."

So they did and they never fail.

—M. C. FORD.

WHY DE CAT HAS NINE LIVES

One time it was very hard times and de man had a wife an' five chillun an' dey didn't have nothin' to eat. Dey looked, but dere wasn't a dust of meal nor flour in de barrel, so he fixed him up a pole and dey all went down to de water. So he fished an' he fished till he caught seven fish; one for himself an' one for his wife an' one for everyone of his five chillun. Den he said: "I b'lieve I'll keep on fishin' till I catch one for de cat an' one for de dog." So he did. But jus' as he pulled out de las' fish, he broke his hook. So he said: "It's good I got a fish for everybody, 'cause I done broke my hook an' I ain't got no mo'."

So he went on up to the house an' dey cleaned dem fish and fixed dem. Then he seen he needed a bucket of water so him an' de ole lady went after de water, an' dey tole de chillun, "Don't let de cat touch de fish. He sho' will bother it if you don't watch 'im."

So while dey was gone, the children got to playin' an' forgot all 'bout de cat an' de cat took an' got up on de table an' et up seven of de fish. Dat was all he could hold.

When de man come back an' found out de cat had eat up de fish he said: "Dese two lil fish can't save us." He looked at the cat an' his stomach was so full it was 'bout to bust so de man knowed them other two fish would kill 'im. So he said to the cat: "Since you de cause of all de rest of us starvin' to death, I goin' make you eat dese two fish an' kill you."

So he made de cat eat de fish an' it bust him open and he died. So de man an' his wife an' his chillun an' de dog starved to death.

So dey all went up to heaven an' when dey got dere God put de man on de scales to weigh his soul an' de cat come up an' looked at 'im so funny till God knowed there was somethin' between the man and the cat. So he asked de man: "What's between you an' dis cat?" So de man tole him whut de cat had done. So God tole Gabriel says: "Grab dat cat an' throw him outa here." So because de cat had nine lives in his belly, he was fallin' for nine days befo' he landed in hell.

So dat's why de people say de cat has nine lives.

Goat fell down an' skinned his chin
Great God-amighty, how de goat did grin.

WHY DE PORPOISE'S TAIL IS ON CROSSWISE

Now, I want to tell you 'bout de porpoise. God had done made de world and everything. He set de moon and de stars in de sky. He got de fishes of de sea and the fowls of de air completed.

He made de sun and hung it up. Then he made a nice gold track for it to run on. Then He said: "Now, Sun, I got everything made but Time. That's up to you. I want you to start out and go round de world on dis track just as fast as you kin make it. And de time it takes you to go and come, I'm going to call day and night."

De Sun went zoonin' on cross de elements. Now, de porpoise was hanging round there and heard God what He tole de Sun, so he decided he'd take dat trip around de world hisself. He looked up and saw de Sun kytin' along, so he lit out too, (Gesture of swift flight), him and dat Sun!

So de porpoise beat de Sun round de world by one hour and three minutes. So God said: "Aw naw, this ain't gointer do! I didn't mean for nothin to be faster than de Sun!" So He run dat porpoise for 3 days before He caught dat porpoise and took his tail off and put it on crossways—still he's de fastest thing in de water.

—M. C. FORD.

THE LION AND THE RABBIT

De lion he lived in a rock cliff. He fooled de other varmints. Dasa way he had to git his livin' to keep him from gwine 'bout.

One day de rabbit he passed thata way and de lion said to him to come by and give him some water.

Rabbit he staid way out at de openin' and looked all round at de ground and everything. He told de lion, "I wouldn't mind comin' but I see dese tracks all gwine in and none comin' out. I'm kinda in a hurry anyhow, so I guess I betta go 'long."

De lion sorta had a taste for rabbit dat day, so he tried to hold him dere till he could git upon him. But de rabbit wuz jist ez slick ez he wuz sly. De lion den see he couldn't git de rabbit dat time, but he figgered he'd tole him on and lay for him; so he says: "Brer Rabbit, you mus' come set wid me some time. I laks to talk wid yuh. You comin' back dis way, aintcher?"

"If I have any business back dis way, I'm sho comin' back, but if I don't have no business, I sho' ain't comin' back. You down here 'stroyin' all de other varmints."

De rabbit went booky-ty-boo, booky-ty-book on down de road all day. 'Bout sundown he come to a clearin' where folks wuz workin'. It war a man and his ole lady and a passle of younguns. De man had a big ole shotgun. De rabbit laid low and watched him for a spell, keepin' outa wind of de dawgs. Dey passed on from de field to de house, and de rabbit wheeled and loped back to where de lion wuz laid up.

"Hello, Brer Rabbit, I see you come back. You come to set wid me dis time, I reckon. You know, I'm sorta po'ly. Don't look lak I'm goin' to mend a-tall."

"Naw, Brer Lion, ain't got time to set down. I got so much business. I jist come back by to let you know I seen a place yistiddy where's so many varmints, you'll be glad to let some of 'em live."

"Where dat at, Brer Rabbit?"

"Oh, 'bout a day's journey from here."

"Will you keer me dere?"

"Yeah, if you wanta go."

"All right, I'll be proud to go. Youse mah best friend, Brer Rabbit. Dese here other varmints see me lay dere 'bout to starve to death and dey won't come nigh me."

So he got hisself ready and followed de rabbit on off down de road, de rabbit keepin' his eye on him all de time and keepin' a safe distance ahead—never would let de lion git upon him close 'nough tuh harm him. Dey traveled and traveled till finally dey got to de fiel' de rabbit seed de day before. De rabbit stopped de lion and put him in de aidge of de woods.

"Lay down heah, now, right heah. Man be long after while."

"Whut *is* Man?" ast de lion, cause up tuh dat time he hadn't never seed no man.

"You'll see," de rabbit tole 'im.

"I ain't never heered tell nuh talk uh him befo'," de lion said.

De rabbit kept him low and dey waited till de man would knock off and start home. De sun wuz still high. Dey seen somebody comin' down de road.

"Whuss dat yonder comin'—dat Man?"

"No, no, lay down, Brer Lion."

"But whut is it?"

"Dass a lil boy—thass a will-be. Lay down."

By and by de horn blow for supper at de quarters and de man and his folks left de fiel' and start comin' cross a foot-log t'wards where de lion wuz hid.

"Rabbit, whuss dat yonder?"

"Shh-hh, dass Man."

A horn was hanging from his shoulder. De lion saw it and ast, "Whuss dat hangin' down on his shoulder?"

"Dat's his voice."

"Whut's dem all round him?"

"Dat's de imps dat his voice calls."

"Whuss dat long thing on his shoulder?"

"Dat's de stick he spits fire on de world wid."

De lion got his bristles all up and ast, "Do you know how I kin git in contack wid him?"

"Yas," de rabbit tole 'im, "go right down de hill and git on dat foot-log. He's bound to cross dere."

De lion romps down on de foot-log soon's he seen de man git on it. De dawgs tackled 'im, but he wuz too severe for de dawgs. De man ups wid his shotgun and cracks 'im off and blinded de lion. He wheeled and run. Man wuz too severe for him.

Dat rabbit lit out soon's he sont dat lion on to de foot-log. He done some fas' traveling back up de country.

Two or three days later de lion wundered on back to his old vicinity. De rabbit was dere all along, eatin' up whut wuz dere. He heered de lion groanin' on top of de hill and come out dere an' seen 'im. De rabbit had done took de lion's house.

"Who dat?" ast de rabbit.

"It's me, Rabbit. Go way f'om me, Rabbit. I don't want no mo' to do wid you. You got me in all dis trouble wid Man."

Ev'vy since den, Man been takin' de lions, but only de cubs; cause de ole lions is too severe to be took alive.

—WILLIAM JONES.*

---

*In her original manuscript, Hurston had prefaced this tale with the following statement about William Jones: "William Jones is an ex-slave. He tells many anecdotes of his share in the Civil War. By the gospel according to Jones, it would have availed the North little had they twenty U. S. Grants and had they not one William Jones on their side."

Biddy, biddy, ben
My story is end
Turn loose the rooster
And hold the hen.

De crane wuz hongry, so he caught uh eel and et him. But you know de crane ain't got no gizzard. He got a craw and dat's all. Soon's he swaller de eel he run right on through him out de other end and headed for de water. De crane seen him and caught him and swallowed him again. Right on through. De next time de crane swallowed him he backed up against a big ole tree and says, "Hot damn you! You won't git away dis time. I got dead wood on you now."

—JERRY BENNETT.

WHY THE WAVES HAVE WHITE CAPS*

The sea and the air was both women. They both had children. The air tole the water: "My children is better than yours. Some flies in the air, some walks on the ground, and some swims the water. Yours can't do nothin' but swim."

The water got mad at the air for talkin' like that because she was mother of all the birds. So next time a lot of birds come down to drink, the water caught 'em and drownded 'em. The wind knowed she left her children down by the water, so she keep passin' over callin' her children. Every time she call 'em, they show they white feathers to let her know where they is, but de water won't let 'em go. When it storms, the sea and the wind is fighting about the children.

—LILY MAY BEALE.

---

*Hurston includes this tale earlier, in a slightly different version.

*[Hurston's manuscript includes here a second—identical—version
of the tale "Why De Donkey's Ears Is Long."]*

HOW COME DE 'GATOR HATE DE DOG

God made both of 'em without a mouth, an' de 'gator and de dog made up a plot to get each of 'em a mouth. An' so de dog had de 'gator tuh cut his mouth first. So de dog tole de 'gator tuh stop and de 'gator stopped.

And den de 'gator tole de dog tuh cut him uh mouth, and de dog tuk de knife and went to cuttin' de 'gator mouth; and de 'gator says, "Hold, Brer Dog," and de dog kept cutting right on and cut de 'gator a great big mouth.

An' every since den, de 'gator been mad wid de dog.
—CHRISTOPHER JENKINS.

WHY DE 'GATOR GOT NO TONGUE

One time all de varmints wuz going tuh have uh big frolic, but they didn't have no band; so de committee went round seeing who would help out wid de music. De dawg said he'd lend his horn—dat's whut he plays; an' de frog said he'd lend his accordion; an' den Brer Dawg went tuh de 'gator tuh see if he would lend his tongue fur uh bass drum. De 'gator lent it tuh 'em an' de dawg—he wuz de head uh de committee—took it on down intuh de piney woods, an' they frolicked all night long and played de drum an' danced till they wore out Brer 'Gator's tongue; den de dawg wuz shame tuh face de 'gator.

That's how come de 'gator been mad wid de dawg ever since an' he eats all de dawgs he kin ketch, tryin' tuh find his tongue.
—WILLIE MAY MCCLARY.

[Hurston's manuscript includes here a nearly identical version of "Why the Gator is Black," attributed to Willie May McClary.]

DE RABBIT WANTS UH TAIL

De rabbit saw de long bushy tail de squirrel got and he wanted one, too; so one day he says, "Squirrel, how did you git yo' long tail? Ah sho would be proud tuh own one lak dat."

"Well, Ah tell yuh, Rabbit. Ah did some tricks fuh Ole Master, an' He gimme dis tail."

"Well, Ah'm willin' tuh do some, too. B'lieve Ah'll go see 'im."

So he went tuh see Ole Master (God). He tole 'im, say, "Yes, you kin git uh long tail if you do some tricks for me."

Rabbit wuz so anxious he said, "Jus' tell me whut you want done an' Ah'll go do it—don't keer whut it is."

"Well," said Ole Master, "first thing Ah wants you tuh do is tuh go git me some rattlesnake teeth."

De rabbit didn't know where he wuz gointuh git dem rattlesnake teeth, so he cruised round awhile schemin'. But one day he saw de rattlesnake all quirreled up an' he said, "Brer rattler, Ah b'lieve de blacksnake is uh whole heap bigger an' longer dan you is, sho do."

"Naw, he ain't neither. You *know* he ain't bigger, an' Ah know Ah'm longer dan he is, even thout mah rattles."

"Ah hates tuh doubt yuh, Brer rattler, but Ah'm bound tuh think he's de longest. You better stretch out an' lemme measure yuh."

While de rattler wuz stretched out, de rabbit whammed 'im in de mouf wid uh club an' knocked out all his teeth and grabbed 'em up an' run back tuh Ole Master wid 'em.

"Thass pretty good, now go git me two bottles of deer eye-water."

Rabbit went on off to de woods an' set round tryin' tuh study up uh way tuh git deer-eye-water. At las' one day he seen de deer trottin' long, an' he stopped 'im.

"Say, brer deer, know whut Ah seen de other day?"

"Naw, whut did you see, brer rabbit?"

"Ah seen brer wolf leap right through dem two trees you see growin' over dere. Ah don't speck tuh see dat done no mo' whilst Ah lives. Fack is, nobody kin do dat but brer wolf."

De deer looked at de trees. They wuz two trees growin' right close together.

"Gwan, rabbit, you know Ah kin beat brer wolf an' anybody else jumpin'. Jes' you watch me."

He leaped through de trees and got stuck, so he couldn't git loose, so he looked round at brer rabbit an' said, "You better go git uh ax an' chop down one uh dese trees so Ah kin git loose."

"All right, brer deer, but lemme hang dese two bottles on yo' horns tuh keep from settin' 'em on de groun'."

He hung de two bottles on his horns jes' so they would hang at de corners of de deer's eyes. Den he went on round behind de deer wid uh big stick an' went tuh work on his hindquarters. He tole 'im, he said, "You gotta cry me some eye-water fo' Ah git you loose. Now you CRY!"

He worked on dat deer till he cried him up two bottles uh water. Den he took dem to de Ole Maker an' he said, "Thass jes' all right! Now take dis box an' keer (carry) it twelve mile out in de country befo' you open it an' you'll find yo' tail inside."

It wuz uh great big box an' de rabbit put it on uh wagon an' drove out in de country wid it. He counted de miles an' he wuz so anxious tuh git his tail dat he almost stopped two or three times, but he thought he better not cause de Ole Maker might take his tail back, so he drove thirteen miles for fear he had done missed countin' one. Den he took de box off de wagon an' set it down.

Soon as he done dat, he heard somethin' inside say "Urrrr!" He said, "Thass mah tail turnin' roun'." He jekked (jerked) off one uh de boards an' he heard dat noise agin. When he pulled off de las' board, out jumped two hounds an' took right after 'im. He beat 'em tuh uh dead holler log by uh inch, but hounds is been uh rabbit's tail ever since.

—JAMES PRESLEY.

[Hurston's manuscript includes here a second version, nearly identical, of "Why De Buzzard Has No Home."]

DIRT-DAUBER AND BEE

De dirt-dauber come to de bee one day to get him to teach him how to make honey. De bee went to work right away an' he tole de dirt-dauber to get some dust from de flowers an' he would show him whut to do with it. De dirt-dauber said, "I know, I know," (imitation of his song) and flew on off an' come right back wid a load uh dirt.

"Aw naw," de bee tole him, "you don't need dat to make honey! Go git some sweet dust from de roses an' flowers."

Dirt-dauber said, "I know, I know," and flew on off again an' back he come wid some more dirt. Bee sent him off agin an' he did it agin. After awhile de bee got tired uh foolin' wid dat dirt-dauber, an' he tole him, "Looka here, if you knowed how near you was in two*, you'd learn how to make honey instead of totin' dirt."

—ARMETTA JONES.

---

*The dirt-dauber has a very small waist.

The alligator and de rabbits was having a squabble. De rabbits said there was more rabbits than alligators, and the 'gators said there was more 'gators than rabbits. So they all lined up cross de creek like de rabbit told them (the 'gators). De rabbit said he was going to count de 'gators as he hopped across de creek on they noses. And so just as he got to de last 'gator, he said he didn't care nothin' 'bout countin' 'gators, he just wanted to git to de cabbage patch over on dat side. And just as he said dat, de 'gator said, "You ain't gone yet," and bit off his tail. And that's whut makes de rabbit's tail so short.

—CATHERINE WILLIAMS.

The snake went to God and said, "Please do something 'bout me. You put me on my belly in the dust and everything steps on me and tromps me down. They stomps on my chillen and 'stroys my generations."

God thought about it and tole de snake, "I don't want y'all tromped out so I am goin' to give you poison in your mouth so you'll be de most dangerous animal in de world." So He did.

The other animals come to God and said, "Do something about dat snake. He got poison in his mouth and he is 'stroying us every time we step in de bushes. He is 'stroying our generations. We all is skeered to walk."

God thought about that, so he sent for the snake and said, "I give you poison to protect yo'self from your enemies; but youse killin' everything dat moves."

Snake says, "Well, you knows I'm in de dust. All I kin see is feets comin' to tromp me and my generations. How kin I tell who is my enemy?"

God scratched His head and thought about that, so He says, "Put dis bell on de end of you tail and ring it every time you see feets comin'. Yo' friends will be keerful after dey sees you. If it's yo' enemy, you and you."

Ever since then, snakes been had rattles.

—ARTHUR HOPKINS.

Once it wuz de rabbit an' de elephant an' de fox, an' dey were givin' uh frolic dat night, yuh know. It wuz uh girl dey all wanted tuh marry an' dey said de one dat danced de dust outa uh rock could have her.

Brother Rabbit had been workin' an' he wuz tired. So he cooked his supper, washed his feet, filled his shoes full uh ashes an' put 'em on an' den shined 'em an' went on tuh de dance.

Dey made de 'nouncement agin after he got dere dat de one whut danced de dust out de rock's gointer git de girl.

De fox danced fust. He cut an' he capered an' flung hisself head over heels, but he didn't raise uh speck uh dust.

De elephant he got up an' danced, but he didn't raise no dust. Den dey ast de rabbit tuh try. He helt back an' when dey kept on at 'im, he said: "Brother Elephant didn't dance it out big as he is, so Ah know Ah can't. Ah'm little an' he's big."

But after while he got up an' danced an' de house got so full uh dust dat dey couldn't see—so he got de girl.

—NORA LEE WHITE.

HOW THE GOPHER WAS CREATED

Cliffert Ulmer is doin' dis!

God was setting down by de ocean makin' all de fish and things and throwin' 'em in. De devil wuz settin' dere watchin' Him. He made de whale and He th'owed dat in. He made mullets and th'owed dem in. He th'owed in sharks and trouts stingaree (stinging ray) and after while He made uh turtle and th'owed dat in, and it swimmed off like all de other things He had done th'owed in. De devil looked at de turtle and says, "Shux, I kin make one uh dem things."

God tole 'im, "Naw, you cain't neither."

"Aw, yes I kin, too. Who cain't make one uh dem things? They sho ain't nothin' to make. Anybody could make one, they jus' cain't blow de breath uh life in 'im."

"I know you cain't make none, but if you think you kin— go head and make it and I'll blow de breath uh life in it fuh you."

So de devil went on off and made it and brought it back and de Lawd blowed de breath uh life intuh it and th'owed it intuh de sea. It swum back out. You see, God wuz gittin' His dirt from by de water, but de devil had done got some high land dirt. Devil th'owed 'im back and he swum right back out agin. He th'owed him in *agin* and he swum back out de third time. God says, "Unh hunh, I tole you dat wuzn't no turtle."

"Yes, it is uh turtle, too."

"Naw, it ain't no turtle, neither."

"Yes, it is so uh turtle."

"Naw, it 'tain't neither. Dontcher see it won't stay in de water? All turtles likes de water. Dat ain't no turtle."

Devil say, "Yes, dat is uh turtle, too—anyhow it'll go for one." And dat's how come we got de go fors (gophers).

—CLIFFORD ULMER.

Once there was a rabbit and he had a good friend named Brother Fox. One day Brother Rabbit met Brother Fox and said to him, "Brother Fox, I know where there is a big piece of ham laying out there in the old field and all you got to do is to tie a string on him and carry him home for your wife and children."

So they went on down there and Brother Rabbit said, "There it is, Brother Fox." So they tied a rope on the big piece of ham. Brother Rabbit broke him a little switch and hit the ham. Up jumped the horse and the way he did run. He ran as fast as the wind. Brother Rabbit said, "Hold him, Brother Fox, hold him."

"How can I hold him when my feet can't touch the ground?"

Brother Fox decided to get even with Brother Rabbit. He called all of his friends together and told them what had happened. He said that he was going to play like he was dead and he knew if Brother Rabbit knew he was dead they could catch him. He sent one of them after Brother Rabbit. He came up and looked at Brother Fox and shook his head and said the latest style was, if a man is dead, he would turn over and Brother Fox turned over. Brother Rabbit said that that was a lie as no dead man could turn over, and he left.

—L. O. TAYLOR.

The snail wuz crossin' de road for seben years. Jus' as he got crost, a tree fell and jus' missed him. He said, "Gee! it's good to be fast."

Know why possum ain't got no hair on his tail? Ham cut it off for banjo strings.

Once a rabbit and a fox wanted to go with the same girl. The rabbit had told the girl already that Brother Fox was his riding horse. So one day Brother Fox went to Brother Rabbit's house and said, "Brother Rabbit, you going to see the girl today?"

"No," says Brother Rabbit, "I am sick, I can't go I tell you."

"Well, I'll tell you what I'll do, I will ride you half way down there."

"Then all right," says Brother Rabbit, "but you will have to let me put a saddle on your back."

"No, I can't do that."

"Well, I can't go."

"All right, you can put it on." So he put it on.

"I will have to have a bridle in your mouth."

"All right." He put it on.

"I need some spurs on me." He put those on. "Now I need a switch."

So they started to the girl's house—they ran and ran and ran. When Brother Fox saw the house about fifty feet away, he said: "Get off now," but Brother Rabbit put the spurs to him and away he ran right up to the house. Brother Rabbit jumped down and ran into the house and said: "I told you Brother Fox was my riding horse, I told you Brother Fox was my riding horse, I told you. Ha! Ha!"

—JERRY BENNETT.

DE GOPHER IN COURT

De gopher wuz called intuh court. De judge an' all de jury wuz all turtles. An' de gopher got up and looked around, an' ast de court could he be excused. De judge ast him why, an' he told de judge: "Blood is thicker dan water."

—MARTIN WHITE.

HAWG UNDER DE HOUSE

Ole man and woman was in de bed trying to sleep an' uh ole sow was under de house wid her pigs uh gruntin' an' scratchin' an' makin' so much noise till he said:

"Le's git up an pour some hot water through de hole an' run dat sow out from under dis house."

So they did an' when de hot water hit de sow, she said: "Whoosh! Shoosh! Who scald?"

De little pigs, they say, "Us, us, us, us, us, us."

—MARY DASH.

Once a ole goose uster live down in a holler log. She wuz settin' an' uh fox grabbed her. She tole him, "You don't wanta eat no ole po' settin' goose. Wait till I git fat, then I'll let you eat me and you kin git some meat off me. You kin eat de lil geeses, too."

De fox said all right. He kept on coming back every day or two to see if she wuz ready. De goose took her lil geeses and hid 'em, and went and got some dogs and hid 'em in de log. De fox come long pretty soon and says, "Ready or no ready I'm going to eat you today."

She says, "Don't eat me, eat dem tender lil geeses in de log."

So de fox went to de log and dashed in and turnt right round and tore out wid dem hounds right after him. De dogs says (chant): "Ah, ah, Ooo-ah . . . If you don't come go with me you won't get to town today."

De goose hollered, "Ketch him, ketch him," and geese been hollering dat ever since.

—JERRY BENNETT.

Tarrypin an' de fox run uh race for uh girl. It wuz uh five mile race. De tarrypin took an' fooled de fox. He got some uh his friends an' put one at each one uh de posts an' one at de startin' place; den he went on over tuh de girl's house an' set on de porch an' crossed his legs.

When dey set out on de race de fox sprung way ahead. He figgered he had done left de tarrypin way behind. He jus' knowed he wuz gwine win dat race; but when he got tuh de fust mile post dere wuz de tarrypin scufflin' long uhead uh him. He hopped on past de tarrypin tuh de next mile post; but when he got dere, he seed de tarrypin uhgin. He strained on down de road cause he wuz sayin' tuh hisself: "Ah knows Ah kin beat dat ole tarrypin runnin'."

He lit out an' run lak lightnin' tuh de next post an' dere wuz de tarrypin waitin' agin. De fox laid out he wuz runnin' so fas' tuh beat de tarrypin tuh de house an' he took an' run up de steps an' fell down he wuz so tired, an' dere wuz de tarrypin settin' crossed legged on de porch laffin' an' talkin' wid de girl. De fox ast de tarrypin, he says: "Brer Tarrypin, Ah knows Ah kin beat you runnin'. How come you beat me tuh de house?"

De tarrypin lit uh seegar an' said: "Ah, Lawd! Uh heap sees, but uh few knows."

—LARKINS WHITE.

Once there was a rabbit and uh bear. The rabbit would go round to Brother Lamb and steal a lamb every evening for supper. So one evening he went round; they wuz eating and they begin to tell 'bout somebody been stealing they lambs.

So de rabbit told 'em every time he go to the bear's house he have roast lamb. So he told 'em that he wuz gointer make Brer Bear tell them the truth about it.

So he went and got his fiddle and went over to Brother Bear and told him that Brother Lamb wanted them to play for him tonight.

So they begin to practise and de rabbit says, "Did you, did you, did you?"

The bear says, "Yes, I, yes, I, yes, I."

They said dat twice, last verse was: "Didn't you steal Brother Lambkin's sheep?"

"Yes, by God, I did it."

So that night they both dressed and went over to Brother

Lamb's house. Brer Rabbit, he took a seat by the door and de bear over by de chimbley. So they begin to play. Rabbit said, "Did you, etc." Bear said, "Yes I, etc." Said dat twice. So last time Brer Rabbit said, "Did you steal Brother Lambkin's sheep?"

"Yes, by God, I did it."

So all de lambs jumped on Brother Bear and beat him, and the rabbit grabbed him uh lamb and run.

—EDWARD MORRIS.

When we lived in the country one day I went out in the field and I heard a noise, and I look around and saw a tick calling a red bug to get some trash out of his eyes. And the red bug got the rail off of my fence and got the trash out of the tick's eyes.*

—JERRY BENNETT.

THE SNAIL AND HIS WIFE

De snail's wife got sick. She was rollin' from side to side in her bed. So she tole her husban': "Oh Lawdy, I'm so sick. Please go get de doctor for me an' hurry up. I don't speck I'm goin' be here long."

So he said, "All right."

So she laid there seven years rollin' an tumblin' wid misery. So after seven years she heard a scufflin' at de door. So she said: "Oh, I'm so glad. Dat's my husban' done come back wid de doctor." So she hollered an' tole him: "Is dat you, baby, wid de doctor?"

He say: "Don't try to rush me. I ain't gone yet."

—PETER NOBLE.

---

*Hurston had written "Tall Tale" in the margin next to this tale.

THE SNAIL CROSSES THE ROAD

The snail was crossin' de road for seven years an' jus' as he got across a tree fell an' it would uh hit him if he'd a been where he was six months befo'. So he tole everybody: "See, dat tree jes' missed me. So that jes' goes to show you it's good to be fast."

—PETER NOBLE.

Appendix 1

Negro Folk-tales from the Gulf States*

SOURCES:

I. Alabama (Mobile & Suburbs, i.e. Plateau, Magazine Point, Prichard)

    Collected   Dec. 16, 1927–Jan. 12, 1928

               June 4, 1928–Sept. 3, 1928

A locale of sawmills, lumber camps and fishermen. Illiterate and barely literate, except some school boys who told me tales.

II. Florida (Loughman Sawmill, Eatonville a purely Negro village, Lakeland, Mulberry, Pierce in the Phosphate Mines Country, Eau Gallie, a Truck-farm and fishing village; and Miami, a tourist town with more than half of the Negro population being Bahamians.)

    Collected: Loughman Sawmill:

               Jan. 15, 1928–March 20, 1928

---

*This second partial title page was originally page three of the Hurston manuscript.

Eatonville: March 20–April 18, 1928
Phosphate Country: April 19–June 2, 1928
Eau Gallie: April–Aug. 1929
Miami: Aug.–Nov. 1929

III. Louisiana—(New Orleans and Bogaloosa)

New Orleans is a huge and cosmopolitan city with many and marked characteristics. Very European, very American. Bogaloosa is a huge industrial center, sawmills, paper mills, chicken hatcheries and reforestation nurseries.

Collected: New Orleans: Sept. 1928–March 1929
                          Nov. 1929–March 1930
              Bogaloosa: Nov. 1929

Appendix 2*

1. Della Lewis: An illiterate woman around 70 years old. Born in West Florida. Mother of 11 children by 9 different fathers. Has always lived in Florida. Occupation: Midwife.
2. Eugene Oliver: About 3rd grade education. About 20 in 1928. Occupation: Sawmill hand.
3. Mary Dash: About 35. Married, from Georgia. Domestic.
4. Tarryson Parlor: About middle age. Sawmill worker, from Miss.
5. Mae Oliver: Sister to Eugene Oliver, of about the same educational level. About 22 in 1928.
6. R. T. Williams: About 40. Works in an orange grove. Born in Georgia.
7. Julius Henry: Illiterate. About 14 in 1928. Born in the neighborhood.

*Hurston's list of 122 sources originally appeared at the front of her manuscript. Joe L. Wiley is not included on this list but is credited with many tales published here (and elsewhere) by Hurston.

8. Belle Williams: About 13 in 1928. Sister to Julius Henry. Married.

9. Robert Bailey: Middle age. From Georgia. Worker in orange grove, barely literate.

10. Fred Cooper: About 20 in 1928. Grove worker, barely literate. Born in South Florida. Grandson of Della Lewis.

11. Willie Roberts: Bootlegger. About 33. Born in Eatonville, Florida.

12. John Smith: About 33. Born in Georgia. Sawmill hand.

13. Christopher Jenkins: About 21. Born in Florida. Worker in phosphate mines.

14. Cliffert Ulmer: About 23. Born in Florida. Sawmill hand.

15. James Moseley: About 45. Born at Eatonville, Fla. Chauffeur and yard man.

16. Sarah Sewell: Born in Eatonville, Fla. Age 41. Housewife.

17. Matthew Brazzle: Born in Fla. About 70. Gardener and mayor of town.

18. Soddy Sewell: Born in Florida. About 21. School boy.

19. Isiah Hurston: Born in Alabama. Age 31. Preacher.

20. "Nigger" Bird: Born South Carolina. About 25. Grove worker.

21. George Brown: Florida. Truck gardener. Age 28.

22. Louvenia English: Born in Georgia. About 30. Domestic.

23. Jonathan Hines: Florida. About 29. Waiter.

24. Louis Black: Born in Pierce, Fla. (a phosphate mining camp). About 11, in 1928. In 4th grade.

25. Hattie Reeves: Born island of Grand Command, West Indies. About 50. Domestic.

26. Lillian Green: Born Florida. About 12. School girl.

27. Catherine Hardy: Born Fla. About 10. A school girl.

28. Geneva Woods: Born in Georgia. About 20. A house-wife.

29. Eliza Austin: Born in South Carolina. About 50. A laundress.

30. Charlie Jones: About 30. Born Florida. Laborer.

31. Dad Boykin: Born Georgia. About 80. Bum and roustabout.

32. L. O. Taylor: Tenn. About 30. Preacher.

33. Nora Lee White: South Carolina. About 23. House-wife.

34. Larkins White: Georgia. About 40. Sawmill hand.

35. James Presley: Musician, sawmill hand. About 40. Born in Georgia.

36. W. M. Richardson: Born in Florida. About 35. Or-ange picker and packer.

37. Handy Pitts: Middle Georgia. About 38. Sawmill hand.

38. Bertha Allen: Born in Georgia. About 55. Boarding-house keeper.

39. Ed Morris: Born Mobile, Ala. Age 15. 8th grade.

40. N. A. James: Born in Louisiana. About 40. YMCA sec-retary.

41. Peter Noble: North Alabama. About 22. Garage worker.

42. Jerry Bennett: Born in Louisiana. About 39. Sawmill hand.

43. J. Williams: Born in Mississippi. Sawmill hand. About 50.

44. Ed Edwards: Born in Alabama. About 17. About 6th grade.

45. Mrs. Louise Noble: About 48. Former country school-teacher. Born in Florida.

46. Baby Face Turl: About 65. Drives garbage wagon. Born in South Carolina.

47. Raymond McGill: About 35. Born in Florida. Works in phosphate mines.

48. Martin White: Born in Georgia. Age 50. Phosphate worker.

49. Floyd Thomas: Born in Florida. Age 23. Phosphate miner.

50. John Bird: Age 33. Born in Florida. Bootlegger and jail bird.

51. Carrie McCray: Prostitute. Born in South Carolina. Age 30.

52. Rebecca Corbett: Cook. Age 35. Born in Georgia.

53. Nathaniel Burney: Age 9. School. Born in Florida.

54. A. R. Cole: Laborer. Age 40. Born in Texas.

55. Louis Robinson: Age 11. School. Born in Florida.

56. Arthur Hopkins: Age 18. Born in Florida (reared in Alabama). School boy, but loads lumber at sawmill in summer.

57. George Mills: Born in South Carolina. Age 62. Deputy sheriff in Mobile, Ala.

58. David Leverett: Born in Alabama. Age 19. Sawmill.

59. Charley Bradley: Age 22. Sawmill hand. Born in Alabama.

60. Henry Edwards: Alabama. Age 19. Laborer.

61. George Harris: Farmer. Age 38. Alabama.

62. Douglash Shine: Age 26. Sawmill hand. Alabama.

63. Will Thomas: Boom-man. Age 28. Alabama.

64. Mannie Barnes: Born in Mississippi. Age 28. Sawmill hand.

65. Will House: Boom-man. Age 30. Georgia.

66. Hattie Giles: Age 39. Alabama. Housewife.

67. David Leverett: Age 19. Sawmill hand. Alabama.

68. Lorenzo Morris: Age 18. High School. Born in Alabama.

69. Richard Edwards: School boy. Age 15. Alabama born.

70. Armetta Jones: Domestic. Age 42. Georgia born.

71. Mack C. Ford: Age 55. Gardener. Florida.

72. Sarah Lou Potts. Born in Alabama. About 40. Tuskegee grad.
73. William Jones: Mobile, Ala. Ex-slave. Born near here.
74. Mrs. Sally Smith: Born in Tarkwa, Gold Coast. Brought to America in 1859.
75. Jessie Smith: Her son. About 60. Farmer of Bogue Chitts, Ala.
76. Russel Singer: About 17. Lumber mill. Alabama.
77. Clifton Green: About 20. Laborer. Alabama.
78. Uless Carter: About 20. Laborer.
79. Sam Hopkins: Born in Florida, reared in Alabama. About 14.
80. Gennie (Jenny) Murray: Born, Georgia. Moved to Ala. Age 40. Housewife.
81. Will Howard: Alabama. About 30. Lumber-mill hand.
82. Willie May McClary: Born Ga. Lives at Eatonville, Fla. Age 17 yrs.
83. Ed Langston: About 55. Born in W. Florida, now in Eau Gallie. R.R. section hand.
84. Clarence Beal: Eau Gallie. About 30. Garden hand.
85. Mrs. Annie King: Born in Florida. About 70. Cook.
86. Maybelle Frazier: Housewife, when out of jail. About 38. Born in Florida.
87. A. D. Frazier: Georgia. About 53. Barber when free.
88. Willie Fullwood: Turpentine worker. About 25.
89. Buster Williams: Age 20. Born in Georgia but reared in Mulberry, Florida.
90. Virginia Williams: Age 19. From Ga., but visited Mulberry, Fla.
91. Etta Lee Leonard: Pierce, Fla. School girl. 11 years old.
92. Jeannette Moore: Pierce, Fla. School girl. 10 years old.
93. Pearline Black: Pierce, Fla. School girl. 13 years old.
94. Catherine Williams: "   "   "   10 years old.
95. Pete Bryant: "   "   School boy. 11 years old.

96. Lulu Anderson: School boy. About 9.

97. Edward Frazier: Born, South Carolina, reared in Fla. Miner.

98. Tom Saunders: Age 42. Born, Va., keeps restaurant.

99. Rachael Moore: Age 60. Born Georgia. Laundress.

100. Marguerite Campbell: Age 22. Born in Florida. Domestic.

101. Lillian Green: Born Florida. Age 13. School girl.

102. Jessie Lee Hudson: Born Georgia. Age 28. Housewife.

103. Viola Ballon: Born in South Carolina. Age 33. Domestic.

104. C. S. McClendon: Florida. Age 40. Phosphate miner.

105. Louis Robinson: Born in Florida. Age 21. Laborer.

106. James Graham: Born in Miss. Age 42. Laborer.

107. Jesse Long: Age 56. Carpenter. Native of Tennessee.

108. Ed Davis: Bogaloosa, La. School boy, 17 years old.

109. Mrs. Fields: 1928 found her an invalid in New Orleans, Louisiana Hospital. She is about 70 years old.

110. Edith Knowles: School girl of Pierce, Fla. 11 years. old.

111. Gus Ramsey: Bahamian. Age 35. Laborer.

112. Ned Isaacs: Bahamian. Age 32. Sings.

113. Merle Wood: Bahamian girl. About 12 years old.

114. Dorothy Wood: Bahamian girl. About 14 years old.

115. Reuben Roker: Bahamian of Miami. Age 20.

116. Harold Tinker: Bahamian. Age 22.

117. William Weeks: Bahamian. Plantation owner.

118. Richard Barrett: Jamaica, B.W.I. Age 40. Chauffeur.

119. Mrs. Vera Taylor: Bahamian from Cat Island. Age 40.

120. Mrs. Sally Boles: Age 50. Born in Florida. Housewife.

121. Bunkie Rolls: Age 50. Truck gardener.

122. Horace Sharp: Age 55. Small shop-keeper.

Appendix 3

Stories Kossula Told Me*

1. Free men ain't got [illegible]
2. Four men who betrayed dey friend
3. The Monkey and the Camel
4. The Lion and the Rabbit
5. The Orphan Boy and Girl and the Witches
6. The Six Fools
7. The Man, the Woman and the Ready-to-Tame
8. The Devil and the Rabbit
9. Why the Bear Has No Tail
   Long Poem
10. Have you heard about the wreck?
11. I seen a man so black
12. I seen a man so ugly
13. I seen a man so ugly he didn't die

---

*Kossula, or Cudjo Lewis, one of the last surviving slaves of the ship *Chlotilde*, about whom Hurston wrote in "Cudjo's Own Story of the Last African Slaves," *Journal of Negro History,* 12 (Oct. 1927) and in her unpublished biography, *Barracoon*. Some of these tales seem to be included here, but Hurston's listing may be to establish cross-reference and, through Kossula, something of the age of the tales.

14. I saw a man so ugly till at night
15. I seen a railroad so crooked
16. I saw a country so hilly
17. I saw a country so hilly till they shoot the corn
18. I saw a man shoot another with a gun
19. I saw a man so ugly
20. Once there was a rabbit and uh bear
21. A man and his wife had a colt
22. A man had a wife and she was so small
23. A man went hunting
24. The First Man
25. In slavery time there was a man by the name of Tom
26. There wuz a man in slavery time always meddling
27. Once there was an old man, woman and boy
28. Once there was a man and the preacher came to his house
29. Man who stole hogs
30. The mule had sprouted little jackasses
31. Man who didn't know what corn was
32. "Son step on the zillerator!"
33. Saving for Mr. Hard Time
34. Old man, wife and hogs
35. Burning creek and trout
36. Man who bradded mosquito bills
37. I seen a man so ugly
38. "   "   "
39. I seen a horse so poor
40. I seen a horse so poor
41. I seen a mule so poor
42. I saw a horse so poor
43. Once I was an engineer on train
44. Rockefeller and Ford was woofing
45. There was a man so stingy
46. I knowed a man and he was formen and he was so stingy

47. Man so smart he had the 7 year itch
48. Once there was a man had a daughter
49. Sellin' roasting ears in heaven
50. Barrel swell up and burst wid rain
51. Once there wuz a boiler across de river
52. De Lawd is Comin' By
53. Mississippi River and de punkin tree
54. On hobo trip in Texas
55. Hard Wind
56. Juice of watermelon caused de rain flood
57. Moon toting a light for de sun
58. Fish came swimming up the road
59. Once I wuz out batching
60. De little black gnat
61. Paul and de ½ pint shinny
62. Ole colored man and de gold watch
63. Ant Dinah on de Coolin Board
64. De man who heard Gabriel and cussed
65. De men who beat dere shadders
66. Catfish who drowned in sweat
67. John, Bill, and de ole Master
68. Snail crossing the road
69. Story of de Jonah
70. How Disa Abraham, Fadda de Faithful
71. "Got 1000 tongues"
72. Rev. Full Bosom and the mourners
73. It taken 9 partridges to holler Bob White
74. 2 revival preachers and "the doleful sound"
75. Man who wanted to catchup with his wife
76. Little boy who raised hell in basket
77. "I am snake bit"
78. The butt head cow's horns
79. I have seen it so cold
80. "I tole you to notice hogs—"
81. "Your breath smells mighty dam bad"

82. In Miss. a black horse run away with white lady
83. Steam from locomotive wuz milkin' cows"—
84. Train in N. Orleans
85. Ala. River running so fast
86. "I done set de world on fire" (fox)
87. Five men want six orders
88. Car, mosquito, and flea
89. "Can't you tell a white man from a Negro"
90. "Shoot the gas to her son, I got the steering gear"
91. Ole Master and John and God dam
92. Colored man and billy goat
93. John and Ole Massa and lightnin
94. The boy and the cow
95. 3 girls, judge, and rabbit
96. The meanest man
97. Fishing on Sunday
98. Why Negroes are black
99. "God ain't worth a dam when a bear"—
100. Man who stole oil from heaven's lamps
101. Preacher and de lamp eel
102. Why Americans are not in war
103. Hen who gave rooster the blues
104. "Oh hell, I'll steal Thou"
105. Dady so small, bedbug pitcher
106. "Baa, ba"
107. Why all lady people got devil in them
108. "Boots or no boots"
109. Once there was a man so lazy
110. Took 1 match sit the river on fire
111. "I wanted you to work on my wife's teeth"
112. Lady and bad polly
113. The Tall Man
114. When he want it to rain
115. "God grant it"—"God dam it"
116. De witch who stole boy's money

117. John and Massa and whut's under de wash pot
118. John, Massa and swimming bluff
119. Rabbit, elephant, fox frolic
120. "Stay on board lil childen"
121. The Shortest Man
122. The Biggest Cabbage
123. The Hanted House
124. An dey all got different daddies
125. Ole Massa and nigger deer-hunting
126. Niggers is so skeered uh white folks
127. Uncle and heavenly blackboard
128. The seed-tick
129. Why Negroes Have Nothing
130. Mosquito bills
131. Tin suits tuh keep de skeeters off
132. De White Man's Prayer
133. What is the biggest chickens you ever saw
134. Uh sweet potato so big
135. "If Thou be God . . . Youse cholkin me tuh death"
136. Boll Weevil
137. 5 gallon demijohn—uh goody, goody, goody
138. The little boy and his grandma
139. Why de Gator Got No Tongue
140. Why de Gator is Black
141. Two men out huntin de little dog an de rabbit
142. Man and girl and picked chickens
143. Ole massa and nigger visitin' girl
144. Tarrypin an' fox run race for girl
145. The Boy from Hell
146. Why God Made Adam Last
147. Ole Massa and John an' de bear
148. Goat an' tobacco truck
149. If dat my child, where . . . gold teeth
150. Man went huntin' wid one uh dese muzzle-loaders
151. Cat an' de liver an' de gizzard

152. "I lends an' borries, too"
153. De Reason de Woodpecker Got Uh Red Head
154. De sworn hunter buddies an' de deer liver
155. "Yuh got tuh gum it lak hell"
156. De men dat melted in Miami
157. De devil don't do everything they say
158. De Hongry Bear
159. De Preacher an de Sheep's Tails
160. De bullet from de 44-40 an' de echo
161. Skeeter an' de Hominy Pot
162. De tallest man
163. "Stick uh needle up in de ground"—
164. There wuz uh man so ugly
165. [not legible in the original manuscript]
166. De Flyin' Negro
167. Why a parrot drops dead
168. Big Talk
169. The man who forgot God's name
170. "If you take up time . . . you won't be nothin.'"
171. I'd go some here and keep books for somebody
172. 4 niggers and de blacksmith shop
173. "Papa's head so lousy"
174. 3 bluebirds
175. Why they use raw hide on mules
176. Monkey and dog
177. [not legible in the original manuscript]
178. "Raccoon"
179. Jesus Christ and de $98
180. "Don't send dat boy Jesus"
181. [not legible in the original manuscript]
182. Free slave and de panter
183. So dey had de picnic and not de wimming match
184. The Bull and God
185. Everytime ma cook eggs, pa cuts de Damn fool
186. "You kin have it I don't need it"

187. "Hold 'im Ned"
188. "6 months for yo' skillet"
189. "Squealin' Jenny"
190. 2 boys and de biggest lie
191. Cryin' for stale biscuit
192. Two mens and de bear
193. Why we Squinch (Screech) Owls
194. Ole Marster, corn field, and bear
195. John an' Massa's ridin' horse
196. Brer Rabbit and Brer Dog and Convention
197.   "   "   "   "   "
198. Ole woman (Scat you rascal!)
199. Monkey: My people, my people"
200. "Tongue brought me here"—
201. From Pine to Pine
202. De brothers an' de persimmons
203. "Long as dere's limb, dere's ropes"
204. It wuz so hot once a cake of ice..."
205. It wuz de moon changin'
206. De Gopher in Court
207. When de weather gits hot de gopher—
208. Poor Land
209. Rich Land
210. De peas grunting trying to git out de ground—
211. A Hunter
212. A lady so cross-eyed
213. A woman so black
214. He'd shoot and den put up a target—
215. De honey sweetened de river
216. "Found dead in de woods—bit by a r. Snake"
217. Hog in de Cradle
218. I seen a man so black
219. I seen a man so tough
220. How come de gator hate de dog
221. Cat and dog race

222. Why we have Thanksgiving
223. The long horse and pig that died from old age
224. Lady with donkey, cat, rooster
225. Grandmother with large family
226. Beans and the Girl
227. [not legible in the original manuscript]
228. Cheap groceries in hell
229. Girl and mother and man who stole food
230. Little country boy and blessing
231. Why the ole man liked the camel best
232. Ole man and snake: "Oh, it is so hot"
233. Blind man, naked man, armless man on rock
234. Red bug had lost his eye and wrecked train
235. Lazy boy, smart boy, and bear
236. He saw sadness and joy
237. I've seen the wind blow so hard
238. Why we have kings and queens
239. Man and devil's daughter
240. Hairy man, little boy and little girl
241. Runaway slave and snake
242. Poor varmints don't rest on Monday
243. Devil, lil girl, lil boy, and her mother
244. Alligator and rabbit's squabble
245. Mosquito and monkey wrench
246. Lazy husband and woman and cake
247. Bear, woman and her baby
248. Woman and daughter and Devil
249. I seen it rain so hard
250. "My belly ake," etc.
251. Two preacher brothers
252. I seed de coachwhip behind de race runner, etc.
253. 2 blocks of ice gatherin' li'dard knots—
254. "I don't lak dat red-eyed 'gator"
255. Why the Donkey has long ears
256. "Lordy, make my bottom wider"

257. Baptist and Methodist deacons in sinking boat
258. Methodist and Baptist preacher
259. Good Time Willie
260. Long, long boy
261. 3 dogs, Thunder, Lightning, and Jack
262. Wolf at rabbit's funeral.
263. Difference in de climate—cucumber 4 ft. long
264. Fine Foot, Big Head, Big Gut, and apple tree
265. Sweet Papa Black
266. Wedding night
267. I'm the biggest liar you ever met
268. Buzzard and Hawk
269. "Job ain't never had a pair of britches"—
270. Preacher and woman making date
271. Brer Rabbit and Brer Frog
272. Johnny and the 7-headed lady
273. Brer Rabbit and de pea patch
274. Cleanest white woman in U.S.A.
275. Massa and Jack and fortune telling (variant)
276. Isaac and Daphne and grocery order for Lord
277. Dat dog dat eat out dat pan up in Canada
278. Negro, devil, bet of $1,000
279. De longest bullet and de deer
280. 3 sons: naked, blind, armless
281. Muskeeter and railroad track
282. Massa Martin and Ike and watermelon patch
283. Stingy man in heaven
284. White man and nigger shooting crap in heaven
285. Christopher spreading his mess
286. [not legible in the original manuscript]
287. Nigger and son and 200 lashes
288. 'Tater house
289. Bale of hay and a jack
290. "You mustn't say hide you must say skin"
291. Ole John and Massa's hogs

292. John in the Smoke-House
293. Jack and Massa's wife
294. Jack and de devil
295. John and de Horse
296. Ole Massa and John and groceries in sycamore tree
297. Bear in de cane-patch
298. Sheep in de cradle
299. Man with three coughs
300. 2 Boys, a Sweet Potato and God
301. Sam
302. Ole Massa's Gun
303. Sambo
304. "Didn't dat nigger fly"
305. The Running Death
306. Too many folks is preachin' dese days
307. Why women folks always poke in de fire
308. The Blacksmith
309. The Carpenter
310. My father made a boiler so big
311. I seen uh man so stingy
312. "He ain't worth uh damn in uh bear fight"
313. Spell: (clucking tongue & teeth sound used to urge mules)
314. Brother wuz de head fireman
315. Nigger and Pres. Harding at Heaven
316. "God, don't stand no jokin' dese days"
317. Dis punkin wuz raised offa mosquito dust
318. Buzzard in Charleston
319. Tell Aunt Jane to tell Uncle Tom to tell de cow
320. I seed uh man running so fast
321. I seen a man so stingy
322. I seen a man so stingy
323. I know a man who wouldn't walk—
324. I know a man so stingy
325. I know a man so big

326. Man and 7 sons and daughter and eagle
327. Mosquito and engineer
328. De poorest horse
329. Hosses: Three Color and Changeable
330. I seen a man so low
331. De train ran so fass
332. I'm uh walkin on de water, oh be baptized
333. Cruel Wife
334. I seen it so cold
335. Have you ever called a train
336. De workinest pill
337. The poorest ground I ever did see
338. De darkest night
339. Run so hard we lost our feets in de mud wash
340. Jordan Car
341. Whammer G. Martin's dogs, sparro, bon bon Pree
342. I seen ground so rich
343. Once it wuz so cold
344. "Chris'mus gift"
345. Father, John, Frank, and $5,000
346. Who had de right to meet de girl?
347. "A gander can pick it just close as a goose"
348. What is the hardest wind you ever seen
349. Best trained mule
350. Man so dangerous
351. Lady, husband, and hoodoo
352. "Clunk . . . think I'm goin' pay you"
353. Massa and John and ketchin' de devil
354. "Dat's too d. much pepper"
355. De crane, eel
356. Lil cussin' boy and de coffin
357. Let the Holy Ghost ride—walk
358. Cross-eyed gnat
359. "Done make me open my mouf wide"
360. One day the wind blowed so hard

361. Another time it blowed so hard
362. Another time it blowed so hard
363. A punkin so big
364. School boy and "Mo" on 'lasses
365. De biggest apple
366. Platform under de calf
367. Gun shoot so far
368. Fastest colt
369. Why there ain't no women in the army
370. De brother in black is lak de monkey
371. Why geese holler "Ketch him"
372. Red bug, rail, trash in tick's eyes
373. John and de Devil and de Girl
374. Why possum ain't got no hair on his tail
375. Rabbit and Fox and same girl
376. Ole man, ole woman, and bear in loft
377. I know man so hungry
378. Down in Ga. ain't no brooms
379. Man with gold penis
380. Jack and Mary and father in tree
381. Preacher and boys and dirty under hat
382. Brother Rabbit and Brother Fox and piece of ham
383. "The fun is all over now"
384. I was a flying fool
385. Lil boy travelling, old man and woman and lil girl and Peas
386. Want to be buried in rubber coffin
387. I saw a man so ugly
388. Man falling on white woman
389. Country man and oxen
390. Man who fished alligator and took him home
391. My brother was so swift
392. Sugar cane so large
393. Bow-legged biscuits (I saw a man so hongry)
394. De biggest cabbage
395. Huntin' rabbit (fast bullet)

396. Man and hardheaded son ghost
397. Man, son, 2 dogs on coon hunt
398. Newlyweds and corn and rooster
399. Grandmother, lil boy on train
400. Old man and woman and girl and pillow
401. How cold have you known it
402. 3 boys going with same girl and dynamite
403. Lil boy and preacher and bear
404. Sawing down the big tree
405. "What angel need with ladder?"
406. Preacher had his congregation
407. "Naw, I ain't whistlin'—I'm pizen—"
408. Woman describing the fiddle
409. Woman and ginny-blue calico dress
410. Devil, man and gun
411. Why wimmen ain't had no whiskers
412. Why woman's vagina was moved
413. "Whut did he die wid Elder,"—
414. White man, son and nigger
415. How the gopher was created
416. Why churches are split today
417. Uh hard wind
418. Two hoboes and pigeons
419. Hawg Under de House
420. Uncle Ike in de Judgement
421. Uncle Jeff and the Church
422. Pig in de Poke
423. Gabriel's trumpet
424. The Monticello Legend
425. Moufy Emma
426. De Animal Congress
427. Every Friday . . . mocking birds
428. De Rabbit Wants Uh Tail
429. Why de buzzard has no home
430. Dirt dauber and bee

431. Massa and Jack and rooster
432. Prayin' woman an de banjo man
433. God an de devil in de cemetery
434. Scissors
435. Why de nigger been working hard
436. The devil and the daughter
437. Why mules have no colts
438. Why all animals look down
439. The Snake and the Gum Mallimie Tree
440. Why the dog has a small waist
441. "After all it was only a mouse"
442. Adam and Eve
443. The Solomon Cycle
444. Queen of Sheba, Solomon, and thirst
445.   "   "   "   and theft of water
446. How Man got his moustache
447. Devil in Cat Island; God in Bahamas
448. The Old Woman and Her Child
449. The Cane Field
450. The Farmyard
451. Brer Bookie and Brer Rabbit
452. The Devil And a Horse And Goat
453. The Sperrit House
454. Dog and Brer Goat
455. [number skipped in the original manuscript]
456. Why Women Talk So Much
457. The Three Sons
458. Why de Porpoise's Tail is on Crosswise
459. Why the Cat Has Nine Lives
460. How we got tobacco
461. Rooster and Fox
462. The Flies and God
463. Man and de Boy
464. Woman Smarter Than Devil
465. Cat, man, and ham (bacon)

466. How the storm came to Miami
467. "It'll take us all night long, baby"
468. Why we say "Unh Hunh"
469. De Lying Mule
470. The Four Story Lost Lot
471. Ole fortune-teller woman and Brer Ishum
472. High Walker and Bloody Bones
473. High Walker and Bloody Bones
474. De Witch Woman
475. "I could drink uh quart uh dat—"
476. "I bet I go Higher than you" (Bapt and Meth.)
477. Baptizing preacher and deck of cards
478. The Frog and the Mole
479. Farmer Courtin' a Girl
480. Why the Dog Hates the Cat
481. "Come round, Bill"
482. Why the Waves have White Caps

Perennial

Books by Zora Neale Hurston:

EVERY TONGUE GOT TO CONFESS
Negro Folk-tales from the Gulf States
Foreword by John Edgar Wideman
Edited and with an Introduction by Carla Kaplan
ISBN 0-06-093454-9 (paperback) • ISBN 0-694-52645-2 (unabridged audio)

A collection of African American folklore compiled from Hurston's anthropological travels through the American South in the 1920s. These 500 tales reflect the sorrows and joys of African American heritage with wit, wisdom, compassion, and style.

THEIR EYES WERE WATCHING GOD
ISBN 0-06-019949-0 (hardcover, with a foreword by Edwidge Danticat)
ISBN 0-06-093141-8 (Perennial Classics paperback)
ISBN 1-559-94500-1 (abridged audio) • ISBN 0-694-52402-6 (unabridged audio)

In this American classic, Hurston tells with haunting sympathy and piercing immediacy the story of one black woman's evolving selfhood through three marriages.

"There is no book more important to me than this one." —Alice Walker

JONAH'S GOURD VINE
Foreword by Rita Dove
ISBN 0-06-091651-6 (paperback)

Hurston's first novel tells the story of John Buddy Pearson, "a living exultation" of a young man who loves too many women for his—and their—own good.

"A bold and beautiful book . . . priceless and unforgettable."—Carl Sandburg

MOSES, MAN OF THE MOUNTAIN
Foreword by Deborah McDowell
ISBN 0-06-091994-9 (paperback)

Taking off from the familiar story of the Exodus, Hurston blends the Moses of the Old Testament with the Moses of black folklore to create a powerful novel of the persecution of slavery and the dream of freedom.

"A narrative of great power." —*New York Times*

SERAPH ON THE SUWANEE
Foreword by Hazel V. Carby
ISBN 0-06-097359-5 (paperback)

A departure for Hurston, *Seraph on the Suwanee* is the story of two turn-of-the-century white "Florida Crackers" at once deeply in love, and deeply at odds.

"A simple, colorfully written, and moving novel." —*Saturday Review of Literature*

♨ Perennial

Books by Zora Neale Hurston:

MULES AND MEN
A Treasure of Black American Folklore
Foreword by Arnold Rampersad
ISBN 0-06-091648-6 (paperback)

"A classic in style and form. . . . Introduces the reader to the whole world of jook joints, lying contests, and tall-tale sessions that make up the drama of the folk life of black people in the rural South." —Mary Helen Washington

TELL MY HORSE
Voodoo and Life in Haiti and Jamaica
Foreword by Ishmael Reed
ISBN 0-06-091649-4 (paperback)

Based on Hurston's visits to Haiti and Jamaica in the 1930s, this travelogue paints an authentic picture of ceremonies and customs of great cultural interest.

"Strikingly dramatic, yet simple and unrestrained . . . unusual and intensely interesting." —*New York Times Book Review*

DUST TRACKS ON A ROAD: REVISED
An Autobiography
Foreword by Maya Angelou
ISBN 0-06-092168-4 (paperback)

First published in 1942, this is Zora Neale Hurston's exuberant account of her rise from childhood poverty in the rural South to a prominent place among the leading artists and intellectuals of the Harlem Renaissance.

"Warm, witty, imaginative, and down-to-earth by turns, this is a rich and winning book by one of our genuine, Grade A folk writers." —*The New Yorker*

THE COMPLETE STORIES
Introduction by Henry Louis Gates, Jr., and Sieglinde Lemke
ISBN 0-06-092171-4 (paperback)

This gathering of Hurston's short fiction—most of which appeared only in literary magazines during her lifetime—spans the years 1921-1955 and includes such works as "John Redding Goes to Sea," "Cock Robin Beale Street," "Hurricane," and "Book of Harlem."

Available wherever books are sold, or call 1-800-331-3761 to order.